THE WINTRINGHAM MYSTERY

THE WINTRINGHAM

MYSTERY:

CICELY DISAPPEARS

A. MONMOUTH PLATTS

ISBN: 978-1-957990-19-4

Contents

I THE PHOTOGRAPH   7
II CICELY IN DIFFICULTIES   13
III STEPHEN MEETS A FRIEND   19
IV STARCROSS IS UNEASY   25
V THE LIGHT THAT FAILED   33
VI THE SÉANCE   37
VIII OUT OF THE DARK   51
IX THE TELEPHONE CALL   59
X A PAWN IN THE GAME   65
XI THE COLONEL'S THEORY   73
XII THE WATCHERS   83
XIII TRAGIC NEWS   91
XIV MR MAINWARING'S AFFAIRS   99
XV WHAT ANNETTE CONFESSED   109
XVI AN UNEXPECTED EXPLANATION   115
XVII MILLICENT'S STORY   121
XVIII KEEPING WATCH   127
XIX COLLECTING EVIDENCE   133
XX STEPHEN'S INSPIRATION   139
XXI A FRONTAL ATTACK   147
XXII THE NEXT MOVE   157
XXIII CICELY APPEARS   163
XXIV THE TRUTH AT LAST   167

I THE PHOTOGRAPH

BRIDGER, confidential valet to Stephen Munro, Esq., of 196B Half Moon Street, was a man of singularly equable temperament. Even the fact that he laboured under the first name of Ebenezer, which is enough to upset anyone, did not appear to cause Mr Bridger any sleepless nights; he bore the burden with the same calm stoicism with which he had carried out his duties for the last eight years as servitor to Mr Stephen Munro, both as batman in France and as general valet-housemaid-private-secretary in the more strenuous times of peace. Bridger was forty-two to his master's twenty-seven, and life held no further disillusions for him.

This was fortunate, because Stephen Munro, eating the admirable kidneys and imbibing the faultless coffee which Bridger had prepared, was meditating the disclosure of a piece of news which to anybody not so fortuitously equipped would have been less of a disillusionment than a plain cataclysm.

He drew his purple dressing-gown a little more closely round his tall, lithe, athletic frame and leaned back in his chair. 'There's one thing I will say for you, Bridger,' he remarked with the contented sigh of the delectably fed, 'you can cook kidneys.'

'Yes, sir,' Bridger agreed stolidly, preferring his employer a heavy silver box. 'Cigarette, sir?'

'Thanks.' Stephen extracted one from the box and applied it to the match which Bridger was now holding out to him. He inhaled a couple of deep mouthfuls of smoke, and began to stroke the hair on the left side of his head with a gesture that was habitual to him. Stephen's hair was inclined to be distinctly curly, and though this had delighted the heart of his mother, Stephen himself regarded it in the light of an affliction; as a small child he had thought that assiduous stroking movements must succeed eventually in smoothing it out, and though, like Bridger, life held few more illusions for him, the habit persisted.

'Bridger,' observed Stephen with the utmost cheerfulness, still mechanically smoothing the unsmoothable. 'Bridger, I'm afraid I've got a bit of a shock for you.'

'Yes, sir,' replied Bridger politely, beginning to clear away the breakfast things.

Stephen inhaled again and blew out a thin cloud towards the ceiling. 'I suppose,' he meditated, 'that if anybody had come along during the last half-dozen years and asked you what I was, the answer adjudged correct would have been that I was a gent of independent means, wouldn't it?'

'Yes, sir.'

'Exactly. And that would have been the truth, Bridger. For the fact of the matter is that my means have been a jolly sight too independent. They've taken unto themselves wings, Bridger, and flown away.'

'Yes, sir, said Bridger, apparently unmoved.

'That's right,' Stephen approved. 'Don't be sympathetic; I know perfectly well I don't deserve it. But one must live up to one's principles, mustn't one? And my guiding principle has always been Safety Last.'

'Yes, sir, Bridger assented with a shade more emphasis, his thought perhaps on certain incidents connected with the late European fuss—incidents which had gained for Captain Munro both a D.S.O. and a Military Cross.

'So when I stepped conveniently into possession of Uncle Alfred's small wad just when I needed it at the end of the war,' Stephen went on, as if constrained to defend himself against imputations which had never been spoken, 'I quite rightly decided to have half a dozen years of life and let the future go to pot. You agree with that, I do hope, Bridger?'

'Yes, sir,' said Bridger, rattling plates and cups together.

'Well, it's gone. Oh, do stop that row, man! How can I tell you the story of my young life while you're playing at thunderstorms with that crockery?' Perhaps Stephen's nerves were not quite so non-existent as he would have liked to suppose.

Bridger stopped rattling and stood respectfully to attention.

'Anyhow,' Stephen continued, 'the long and the short of it is that I've come to the end, Bridger. Exit Stephen Munro, Esq., gentleman of leisure, through trap-door L.; enter Steve Munro, world's worker. In other words, I've got to start on a job of hard labour.'

'Yes, sir,' Bridger agreed laconically.

'You're a difficult person to move, Bridger,' Stephen complained, gazing at his servitor not without admiration. 'Would you say anything except "Yes, sir" if an angel came and called you one night and told you the last trump was blowing the réveillé and you were wanted on parade? I suppose you realize that what this mass of verbiage really amounts to as far as you're concerned is the sack?'

'Yes, sir.'

Stephen sighed. 'One day I shall give you a dictionary, Bridger. I think you'll find it interesting reading. Some of the simpler bits you might even learn by heart—words like "and" and "the", and even "no", you know. No, don't begin eyeing the crocks; you can wash them up later, if it's worth the trouble. For the moment you've got to listen to me. I must talk to somebody, and you're the only person available. I've been looking for a job now for thirteen weeks, Bridger!'

'Yes, sir.'

'A relapse,' Stephen commented aside. 'Well, never mind. Yes, for thirteen weeks! And could I find one? No, I could not. There seems to be a distinct slump in the market for promising young men. However, I did land one in the end, and what's more, I start work this very day. Which is lucky, for I've only just got enough money to pay you a month's wages in lieu of notice, or whatever the phrase is, and buy a ticket to take me down there.'

'Yes, sir.'

'All the furniture and everything portable in here was sold weeks ago, and the proceeds, I regret to say, spent. You can pack a couple of suitcases with what clothes I've got left, and hang on to anything you particularly fancy. Got that?'

'Yes, sir.'

Stephen jumped up suddenly and hurled the stub of his cigarette into the fireplace. 'Bridger, do you think an earthquake would surprise you? Really, you are a most exasperating man. Still, I've not finished yet. I wasn't going to tell you this last bit, but you've goaded me into it. Prepare, for the first and last time in your life, to be genuinely startled, Bridger! This post I told you I've got. Down, false pride, and up, Steve, the world's toiler! I've taken on a job as a footman, Bridger!'

Stephen eyed his servitor closely; not a blench was visible.

'Yes, sir,' he replied calmly.

'Oh, Lord!' Stephen groaned. 'You're not human, Bridger. Really, you're not. You ought to see a doctor about it.'

And then at last Bridger spoke. 'You see, sir,' said Bridger quite chattily, 'I knew all this before.'

'The deuce you did! How on earth?'

'These things get about, sir,' replied Bridger vaguely, his stolid face completely without expression. 'You've got a job with Lady Susan Carey, at Wintringham Hall, Sussex. They haven't had a footman there lately, only a butler,' he continued amazingly, 'but Lady Susan's going to do a bit more entertaining now, so they think they'd like a footman as well. You're expected to assoom your duties after lunch this afternoon, as a house-party is arriving today.'

If master could not startle man, certainly man succeeded very thoroughly in startling master. Stephen gazed at him as if he could hardly believe his ears.

'How in the name of all that's holy do you know all this?' he managed to articulate.

Bridger lifted the tray and turned towards the door. 'Because I took the liberty of applying for the post of under-gardener myself, sir, seeing that you wouldn't be wanting me any longer. I start work there this afternoon. I shall be able to see your luggage safely to the Hall for you, sir.' He walked serenely across the room.

As he reached the door, Stephen found his voice again. 'Bridger!' he gasped. 'Is there anything you've missed, by any chance? What—what's

Lady Susan's age?'

Bridger paused. 'Sixty-seven, sir,' he replied, unmoved. 'And Miss Carey, her niece—Miss Millicent Carey, who lives with her, is thirty-four. Miss Rivers, Lady Susan's companion, is—'

'Go away!' Stephen moaned, waving feebly, 'Go away, Bridger. You're—you're indecent.'

'Very good, sir,' said Bridger courteously, and went.

Stephen recovered himself with an effort, strolled over to the table and lit another cigarette. Bridger was always springing these surprises on him. Stephen knew that under that wooden face lurked a singularly acute intelligence.

The connection between the two was a strong one. During the two years they had spent as officer and man in France they had saved each other's lives with monotonous regularity, and the Military Cross which Stephen had won for rescuing his batman from a bullet-swept no-man's-land was matched by the D.C.M. which the neat extrication of his officer from a trench teeming with Huns had gained for Bridger. That they should have joined forces again when peace came was as natural as it was inevitable, and Bridger had made an excellent manservant. His pleasures were harmless, his vices non-existent, and his chief delight the cultivation of a pose of wooden imbecility. They appreciated each other excellently.

Stephen smiled a little ruefully as he recalled the conversation which had just taken place. Right up to the very end he had been meticulously careful to preserve intact the small sum, insignificant in itself but of paramount importance during these last few harassing weeks, that represented Bridger's wages for a month; and in all his own troubles he had never lost sight of the fact that his was the responsibility not only for himself but for Bridger as well. And in the latter respect he really had succeeded rather well. After diligently canvassing, he had discovered a club acquaintance who was in need of a valet. Singing Bridger's praises in the loudest possible key, he had secured the job for him, at a very comfortable salary indeed. Now that had all gone by the board. That Bridger would not hear for one second of any such arrangement was only too patent. Although, because they were Englishmen and tongue-tied, no words would ever pass between them on the subject, Stephen was inexpressibly touched by this culminating proof of the man's devotion. When the ship sinks, it is not only the rats who leave it; the first mate usually ranges himself rather with the rats than with the captain.

For himself, Stephen really cared very little. He was one of those fortunate people who are able to take life lightly, who never worry over the future and who have a sense of humour sufficiently developed to enable them to look the present in the face and laugh at it. If he had troubled to analyse his feelings, he would have found them compounded of a small modicum of regret that his pleasant time had really come to an end at last, and an overwhelming curiosity as to what life was going to be like under the conditions now laid down for it. For Stephen was no snob. That a public school and Varsity man should be reduced to accepting a post as a footman in the sort of house he had been visiting all his life as a guest did strike him, it is true, as a trifle quaint; but it struck him far more forcibly as a really tremendous rag. Somehow Stephen couldn't quite see himself as a footman, and the things he couldn't see always interested him much more than those he could.

As he thrust his hands into the pockets of the purple dressing-gown and strolled into his bedroom to make his final preparations, Stephen felt absurdly as if he stood on the threshold of some great and exciting adventure—which, as a matter of fact, is exactly what he did!

His particular household gods were few, for Stephen was not acquisitive by nature. Two or three football groups, a few photographs, and other similar possessions were soon retrieved from wall and drawer and thrown on to the bed for Bridger to pack later, and Stephen glanced round the room for anything that he might have overlooked.

His eye came to rest on a large framed photograph which stood on the mantelpiece.

It was a portrait, head and shoulder, of a girl. He picked it up and, leaning an elbow on the mantelpiece, gazed at it for a full minute. The face was a striking one. Under level brows two large dark eyes, quick with intelligence and humour, looked out into space, and it seemed as if a little smile hovered round the full, perfect cupid's bow of a mouth; the nose was beautifully straight, the nostrils sensitive and the hair dark but full of unexpected lights. Across the bottom right-hand corner was written in a firm hand, as full of character as the face itself, 'Yours, Pauline.'

Stephen had not overlooked this photograph. He had been only too well aware of it. The truth was that he had been shirking the issue. Now he began slowly to take it out of its frame.

With an unconscious straightening of his shoulders as if to brace himself for some peculiarly difficult task, he tore the photograph across and across with quick nervous movements and threw the pieces on to the loose paper in the grate.

'Footmen can't keep photographs like that, I'm afraid,' he murmured to himself with a valiant attempt as a whimsical smile, as he fumbled in his pockets for a match. 'They might lead to awkward complications.'

He stood for a moment, watching the flames lick and twist the thin cardboard with their hot tongues; then with an almost imperceptible shrug of his shoulders, turned to the door.

'Bridger!' he shouted in stentorian tones. 'When the blazes are you coming along to pack my things, you wooden-faced son of Belial?'

II CICELY IN DIFFICULTIES

WINTRINGHAM HALL was a fine old Tudor house, spacious, rambling, gabled and mullioned, mellow red brick outside, oak panelling, blackened by the centuries, within. It was everything that an old house should be; it had a secret staircase and a real priest-hole, and it had belonged to the Careys ever since it was built, over four hundred years ago. Its present owner, Lady Susan Carey, was a fitting chatelaine for its ancient glories, a fierce, cynical, overbearing, inexpressibly dignified little old lady, with a body as fragile as her soul was fierce; but after her death, alas, the glories of Wintringham Hall must be allied to some other name, or at any rate after the death of her niece, Millicent, for there were no male Careys in the direct line. Lady Susan bore a perpetual grudge against her niece for not having been born a boy.

Lady Susan, a younger daughter of the Earl of Hayford, had married her late husband, Sir John Carey, at the age of only nineteen. To their lasting disappointment, the couple had had no children of their own, and Lady Susan had therefore virtually adopted Millicent, the daughter of a younger brother of her husband's, when the latter had been made an orphan by her mother's death nearly twenty years ago.

Sir John Carey had been killed by a fall in the hunting field, and at first it was thought that his wife would not survive the shock. On hearing the news Lady Susan had fainted for the first time in her life, and for nearly a week she had lain in her big bed, hovering between life and death. The doctor had diagnosed a weak heart, hitherto quite unsuspected, but Lady Susan's strong constitution and grim determination had pulled her through the crisis. Ever since then, however, she had been warned to avoid like the plague any over-exertion, and the doctor had given it as his confidential opinion to Millicent that a similar shock might be the end of her. He was in fact in the habit of coming up to the Hall at least twice a week in order to assure himself that no such contretemps had occurred, and was in consequence able to afford a very much better make of car than would otherwise have been the case.

The house-party now expected was the first to be given in Wintringham Hall since Sir John's death, and was to consist almost entirely of the friends of Millicent and of a nephew of Lady Susan's, Freddie Venables, a son of Lady Susan's only sister, on whose joint behalf it had been arranged. With the exception of a certain Colonel Uffculme, an old friend of Lady Susan's, to represent the older generation, the gathering, with a couple of unimportant exceptions, would be composed of young people.

On the afternoon of the day upon which Stephen was to arrive, a warm, sunny day in September, Lady Susan and her niece were sitting together after lunch in the drawing-room, the rigid use of which for half an hour each day at this time, and for an hour after dinner, Lady Susan strictly enjoined. Her mother-in-law had sat in that drawing-room for half an hour after the midday meal and at least an hour after dinner every single day of her married life, and her grandmother-in-law before that; and what was correct for them was correct for Lady Susan. She was seated in a big armchair on one side of the huge old-fashioned open fireplace, in which the customary log fire of winter had not yet been lit, and Millicent sat in a smaller chair opposite, trying hard to pretend that she was perfectly at her ease.

Millicent never had been at ease in the presence of her aunt ever since she could remember. As a small girl the old lady had terrified her, and she did so still; in her presence Millicent never felt more than six years old. But she knew that Lady Susan despised weakness more than anything else in this world, and therefore she was constrained to spend her whole time in trying desperately to simulate the ease she could not feel. Her aunt, she knew only too well, despised her already quite heartily enough without being afforded grounds for any further feelings of the kind.

'Did you tell Martin to bring the young man in here as soon as he arrives?' Lady Susan demanded suddenly after a long silence.

Millicent started slightly. She had been day-dreaming into the fire and, for the moment, forgotten her aunt's presence. She was a mild, inoffensive, well-meaning creature, with a face not unlike that of an amiable horse, and she spent most of her life striving so hard to do the right thing and invariably doing the wrong one. It was not surprising that she looked her full thirty-four years.

'Yes, Aunt Susan,' she replied with nervous haste. 'Yes, I told him.'

'You surprise me, Millicent,' observed Lady Susan, and relapsed into grim silence again.

Millicent sighed. Inaudibly.

'I suppose you didn't remember to tell Parker about the car for Cicely?' Lady Susan returned to the attack a minute or two later. It always irritated her when Millicent actually had done something right; it took the gibe out of her mouth most unfairly.

Millicent looked alarmed. 'Oh!' she said faintly. 'No, I—I'm afraid I didn't, Aunt Susan.'

'Well, one could hardly expect it, could one?' replied the old lady caustically. 'You're like a boy scout, Millicent. One good deed a day is enough for you.'

'I'll ring for Martin and ask him to tell Parker now,' Millicent said, jumping to her feet.

'Don't bother. I told him myself. I thought it would be wiser.'

Millicent resumed her seat. 'He can take Cicely for the four-forty-three and wait at the station to pick up anybody who comes on the five-nine, couldn't he?' she remarked in tones which she hoped were lightly conversational. 'And we can have tea at four.'

'That great thought had already occurred to me,' Lady Susan replied crushingly.

Millicent ventured no reply.

'On the whole, Millicent,' the old lady went on maliciously. 'On the whole I think it's a good thing you weren't born a boy after all. The Carey men, at any rate, have always been—'

A fortunate diversion at that moment cut Lady Susan short and spared her unhappy niece from any further home-truths. The door opened and two girls entered the room. One of them, a fair, pretty girl of medium height, was wearing her hat and coat; she advanced across the room.

'Ah, Cicely!' observed Lady Susan, in a tone far more amicable than that reserved for her niece. 'Got your things on already, my dear?'

'Yes; do you want Miss Rivers for a bit, Lady Susan? I want a little exercise before my train goes, and I know Millicent will be busy half the afternoon. Could you spare her to go for a little walk with me?'

Lady Susan glanced at the other girl, who was hovering deferentially, but not exactly humbly, just inside the door. She had the nondescript air of the born companion, neither well dressed nor precisely dowdy, neither good-looking nor positively ugly, though the big horn spectacles she wore and the way in which her darkish hair was dragged ruthlessly back from her forehead did not tend to improve any claims to good looks that she might have possessed. One always had to look twice round a room before realizing that Miss Rivers was in it; she had brought the born companion's talent for self-effacement to a fine art. In general build she was much the same as the other, but there all resemblance ended.

'I think I can manage to get along without Miss Rivers for an hour or so,' Lady Susan replied. 'Doubtless Millicent will be able to spare me a minute or two from her other duties if I really require it.' It was perhaps the most unfortunate of all Lady Susan's habits where Millicent was concerned, to put an even sharper edge on her gibes when her own competent, unobtrusive little paid companion was also present; poor Millicent had a difficult task to uphold her dignity in face of Miss Rivers.

'But do you think you ought to go for a walk, dear, with that cold of yours?' Lady Susan went on.

'Oh, I think it'll do it good,' Cicely replied, smiling her thanks, and Miss Rivers silently effaced herself in search of her hat and coat.

'Funny thing,' remarked Lady Susan with deliberation, 'that girl never seems to have to slam a door after her. She's only been with us two months, but—well, never mind!'

Millicent, to whom this veiled allusion appeared only too obvious, coloured painfully. She reminded Lady Susan irresistibly at such moments of a pink and rather pathetic rocking-horse, but there were limits to the old lady's cruelty, and she kept this impression to herself.

Cicely ventured a tactful intervention. 'Isn't it a perfectly gorgeous day, Lady Susan?' she remarked with pointed innocence.

Lady Susan smiled appreciatively. As a general rule she made a point of disliking the girl of the times, with her cigarette-case, her knowledge-ability and her insufferable superiority; but, on the other hand, she did like somebody who would stand up to her, which certainly neither her niece nor her companion would ever dream of doing, and Cicely Vernon, the daughter of an old friend, of lineage as old as her own but as impoverished as she herself was wealthy, had always been a special favourite.

In fact, if the truth were told, Lady Susan had a greater affection for Cicely than for any member of the younger generation; she had the girl to stay with her on every possible opportunity, and it was a source of acute disappointment that a previous engagement for a yachting trip had prevented Cicely from being a member of the coming house-party.

'All your arrangements made, my dear?' she asked, in unwontedly gentle tones, as Cicely dropped into a chair.

'Yes, Lady Susan. I get up to town about six, pick up my heavy luggage at my club and catch the seven-ten down to Folkestone and join the yacht there.'

'And you sail tonight?'

'I don't know. I suppose that depends on tides and things. We're all to be on board by midnight, so probably that means we sail in the small hours of tomorrow morning.'

'You don't think you're cutting it rather fine, only allowing yourself an hour in London?'

'Oh, no!' Cicely replied, in a somewhat listless voice.

Lady Susan glanced at her curiously. The girl's face was pale and there were deep shadows under her eyes. Her manner, usually so vivacious and cheerful, was heavy, and she spoke in weary tones.

'Well, let's hope this trip sets you up, my dear,' Lady Susan said briskly. 'I've thought all this last week that you've been very much off-colour, and it seems to have been getting worse instead of better. Nothing the matter, I hope?' she added, almost gently.

Cicely started slightly. 'Oh, no, Lady Susan!' she replied quickly. 'Nothing at all, thank you.'

'You look to me as if you were sickening for something,' Lady Susan said frankly. 'Even Millicent's noticed it.'

'Yes,' Millicent agreed deprecatingly. 'I told Aunt Susan that I thought the change would be good for you.'

'Who are these people you're going with?' Lady Susan demanded. 'The Seymours? Never heard of 'em.'

'Oh, they're—they're some people I got to know in London,' Cicely replied in somewhat nervous tones. 'You wouldn't know them. He's a—a stockbroker. Very rich, of course. And very kind.'

'Humph!' observed Lady Susan without enthusiasm. She rose to her feet. 'Well, I must leave you for a moment. There's somebody waiting to see me. But I'll be back in a minute.'

Cicely waited till the door had closed behind her hostess. Then she turned to Millicent. 'Millicent,' she said abruptly, 'can you lend me fifty pounds?'

'Fifty pounds?' Millicent repeated with shocked surprise. 'But I lent you a hundred only last month.'

'I know.' Cicely twisted her handkerchief in her lap. Her voice held a note of nervous eagerness. 'I know, and you were a brick, Millicent. But I must have fifty more. I've got to get it from somewhere, and—and—Oh, do say you will!'

'It would be very inconvenient.' Millicent hesitated. 'Have you been—gambling again, Cicely?'

'No. I mean—yes! Yes, I have. But I won't any more, I promise you. And I'll let you have it back very soon. Millicent, I must have it before I go. It's terribly urgent.'

'Well, just this once,' Millicent conceded reluctantly. 'But let me have it back as soon as you can, dear, because I'll have to take it out of the housekeeping. And really, Cicely, you must take yourself in hand. No wonder you're looking so poorly. This gambling craze of yours—'

Millicent proceeded to exercise the lender's privilege of reading a severe lecture to the borrower. Cicely received it with fitting humility and grateful promises to mend her ways for the future.

Lady Susan's return brought it to an abrupt end, and a desultory conversation filled up the time till Miss Rivers came down.

As the two girls made their way out of the room they passed the butler sailing into the presence of his mistress.

'The new footman is here, my lady,' he announced in the tones of mingled deep respect and self-conscious dignity which only a butler out of all the race of men can achieve. 'I have him in the hall.' He spoke as if the newcomer were some curious kind of domestic animal, at present tethered to the leg of the hall-table.

'Then bring him in, Martin, and let me have a look at him,' quoth Lady Susan.

'Very good, my lady,' replied Martin with dignified deference, and sailed out again.

III STEPHEN MEETS A FRIEND

STEPHEN'S feelings, as he followed the massive back of Martin into the drawing-room, were something of a surprise to himself. He had expected to feel only a pleasurable amusement combined with a certain amount of mild excitement; instead he found himself unmistakably alarmed. His short interview with Martin had been enough to warn him that his employer was something of a formidable character, and a horrible fear seized on him that he might not prove satisfactory. Visions of an ignominious exit from the back door accompanied him across the thick carpet.

The penetrating gaze which raked him as he came to a halt a few paces away from the old lady's chair did not help to reassure him, and his quick eye detected traces of a distinct nervousness on the face of his younger mistress who had actually engaged him.

'This is the young man, my lady,' Martin announced, a trifle superfluously.

'Hum!' observed Lady Susan, continuing to bore the unhappy Stephen with her piercing eyes. 'So you've never been in service before, eh?'

'No, my lady.'

Well, in that case you'd better understand that you wouldn't be in my service now, if it wasn't for this fantastic shortage of trained manservants,' Lady Susan continued, with devastating candour. 'As it is, I suppose we have to make the best of things. You think you'll be able to make something of him?' she added, turning suddenly to Martin.

'Yes, my lady, I fancy so,' the butler replied smoothly. 'The young man had already expressed to me his anxiety to learn.'

'Well, let's hope that he doesn't make too big a fool of himself and us,' observed Lady Susan, though without very much hope in her voice. 'Very well, William, Martin will explain your duties. As for me, please understand that I forgive most things in this world except one, and that is incompetence. A knave I don't mind, but a fool I won't have in this house—if I can humanly avoid it. I might overlook your stealing my pearls if you did it cleverly enough; but if you upset a plate of soup down the back of any of my guests, you leave the house within five minutes. That will do, Martin.'

Stephen walked delicately out of the presence. As he went he caught sight of a rapid look and a confidential half-smile exchanged in a fleeting second between his younger mistress and her butler; evidently there were understandings in that house which were necessarily secret from its chatelaine.

'A determined old lady, Lady Susan is; oh, very determined, you mark my words, young man,' Martin remarked in a bland undertone as they crossed the huge hall.

'I'm marking them hard,' Stephen agreed with feeling, following the other through the green baize door which separated the servants' quarters from the rest of the house.

The next hour was a busy one for Stephen. First of all he was conducted to the kitchen and ceremoniously introduced to his fellow servants, a bewildering vista of faces of which he could recall later only one—that of the lady's maid, Miss Farrar, not by any means the pert little French lady of fiction, but a middle-aged person of gaunt and attenuated aspect and brisk, uncompromising speech. Stephen felt vaguely disappointed in her.

Having thus made his formal entrance on the scene, Stephen was conducted with due solemnity to the butler's pantry, where, over cigarettes (supplied by Stephen) and a glass of port (supplied unwittingly by Lady Susan), Martin proceeded to instruct him in his duties.

As he listened to the unending flow of words that fell from the butler's mouth Stephen's heart sank. He had somehow the idea in his mind that a footman's job was a pleasantly easy one. It was only a very few minutes before he realized that nothing could be further from the truth.

Besides waiting at meals, seeing that any fires in all the rooms were in full swing, and keeping them supplied constantly with logs, always being on hand to do anything anybody wanted, sleeping in the butler's pantry with the silver, attending to the front-door bell and performing a hundred other odd jobs, he would also be expected to convey the guests' luggage upstairs, if any male guest had not brought his own man, to unpack it for him, and, in the same circumstances, valet him during his stay, lay out his clothes for him, lend him the things he had forgotten to bring, and pack for him when he went away.

'It seems to me,' said Stephen politely, 'that a footman's life is not an idle one.'

A bland smile made its appearance on the butler's round, butter-coloured face. 'You're right, William. Not by a long chalk, it isn't. Indeed, no.'

'Why do you call me William?' Stephen wanted to know. 'Lady Susan called me William, too.'

'We always call the footman here William,' Martin pointed out with soft reproof.

'But I thought I was the first footman here. Didn't they have a parlourmaid before?'

'Since the war we did. Oh, yes. But before the war, when old Sir John was alive, there was always a William. We haven't done much entertaining, not since then, but now we think we ought to do a bit more of it. And that's why you're here, young man.'

'I see,' said Stephen.

Martin looked at him curiously, and his voice took on an even smoother flavour—smooth, Stephen felt, to the point of oiliness. 'Now, what would have brought you into this kind of business, William, if one might ask? You don't look to me like the sort of young fellow to answer an advertisement for a footman. It seems to me in a way strange, William. Very strange, if one might put it so strongly.'

Stephen glanced at the other with distaste. It had not occurred to him before, but he now realized that he had taken an instinctive dislike to Martin almost from the very first moment. He was so bland and oily and smooth. Stephen was reminded irresistibly of Mr Chadband from Bleak House.

However, he had no wish to quarrel with the man, and so answered civilly enough: 'What brings anybody into any line of business? Lack of loose cash, I'm afraid.'

'Ah!' said Martin, nodding ponderously. 'Indeed? Is that so? Well, dear me!'

But it took more than that to choke Martin's curiosity. For the next quarter of an hour Stephen was fully occupied in parrying the ingenious ways in which the other endeavoured to extort further information to satisfy his apparently unbounded inquisitiveness.

'I say, by the way,' he remarked at last, after trying a dozen other means of diverting the embarrassing stream of questions and innuendoes, 'oughtn't I to be getting into my togs?'

Martin blushed a dull yellow-ochre at the directness of this rebuff, but, at any rate, Stephen had found the diversion he wanted. The other produced the garments, for which Stephen had already been measured on his previous visit, and ten minutes later that young man, feeling as if he were in fancy dress and wondering acutely whether his calves really looked as nice as he hoped, had drawn on his flunkey's coat just in time to answer the front-door bell. Hurriedly conning over in his mind the instructions he had already received, he crept out into the hall.

It was very much simpler than he expected. All he had to do was to open the door, stand aside while a fluffy little person rushed past him with a whirl of diaphanous draperies, furs and perfume, and make his way outside to receive her luggage from the chauffeur. Martin, who had followed him into the hall, took complete and competent charge of the fluffy little person as soon as she had passed the threshold.

'If this is all there is to it,' murmured Stephen to himself as he staggered up the back stairs a few minutes later under the weight of a huge trunk, 'I'll pull through swimmingly.' The trunk was far too heavy to leave Stephen any time for worrying about his metaphors.

He returned to the butler's pantry not a little pleased with himself.

'I say, Martin,' he remarked, 'do you think I could go down to the station in the car that's taking Miss Vernon? I left my suitcase there, and the car could bring it up for me with the other luggage; and I'd be back to look after it all right.'

Martin received this suggestion reluctantly, but gave a grudging consent. Having helped to carry in the tea, therefore, Stephen made himself ready to go down to the station. He had taken Cicely's luggage downstairs and was waiting to load it on to the car when Millicent fluttered out with some labels in her hand, and asked him to tie them on. And as he did so Stephen glanced at them idly. They bore the inscription, in what he deduced later to have been Cicely's handwriting, 'Vernon—passenger to Folkestone, via Victoria.'

'Lucky girl!' thought Stephen as he bent over his task.

At the station Cicely intercepted him as he was lifting her boxes off the car preparatory to proceeding on to the platform with them. 'Don't bother about that, please,' she said. 'The porter will see to it. I shan't want you any more.' She held out her hand towards him.

As far as Stephen knew, it was not correct etiquette for departing lady guests to shake hands with the footman, but since she appeared so anxious to do so he let her have her way. The next moment he felt a small piece of paper thrust hurriedly into his palm. It was a ten-shilling note. Stephen had received his first tip.

His own business at the cloakroom did not take a minute, and he carried his case out to the car, passing through the little booking-office. Cicely was at the ticket-window.

Apparently she did not see him as he approached, and he glanced with some curiosity at the nervous way in which her foot was tapping on the floor. It had seemed to him even while loading her luggage on to the car that she was in a highly nervous, almost an agitated state, and he wondered what there could be so upsetting about a journey to Folkestone.

'First single, Brighton,' he heard her say as he passed.

'Now, why the deuce,' remarked Stephen to himself, 'does a lady who wants to go to Folkestone take a ticket to Brighton?'

It was a somewhat thoughtful young man who rode back to Wintringham Hell and resumed his duties.

It was not the only surprise Stephen was to receive that afternoon. It often happens that a remote contingency which has occurred to one's mind and been brushed aside again in the same thought as too impossible for serious consideration, is fantastically fulfilled within a space of time incredibly short. As Stephen walked across the hall to answer the first ring of the front-door bell after his return, the idea leapt momentarily into his mind—supposing it were some person whom he had known in the old life! The possibility was not too remote. The band of people who visit country houses is not indefinitely large, and he had been a member of it.

The next instant he dismissed the notion as impossible. For coincidences like that one must depend on the theatre, not real life.

He swung open the door and found himself looking into the eyes of the girl whose photograph he had burnt not half a down hours before—Pauline Mainwaring.

For a moment Stephen could only stand in the doorway and stare at Pauline dumbly, while the blood mounted into both their faces. She had recognized him just as soon as he had recognized her; there was no doubt of that. But she it was who first recovered.

Even while Stephen's lips were framing an astonished and unorthodox 'Pauline!' and his mouth twitching into the rather shamefaced grin which the situation appeared to require, her face froze from surprise into scorn; she frowned angrily and, handing him the small case she was carrying, said in an imperious and exceedingly cold voice:

'Take this, please. The rest of my luggage is on the car.'

The next instant she had swept past him into the hall, and Stephen was left staring blankly at a small Russian leather jewel-case.

Not till then did he realize that Pauline had not arrived alone. A tall, fleshy man with a very red face, clad in an opulent fur coat, pushed past him in her wake, jostling him out of the way with a muttered: 'What are you mooning about, man? Look slippy with that luggage. My chauffeur wants to put the car away.'

Stephen walked down the steps in a daze, and in a daze directed the chauffeur to the back door. That Pauline, of all people, should turn out to be such a horrible snob! Should not only cut him, but administer the snub direct, at finding him in the livery of a footman! It seemed incredible. The very last thing in all the world one would have expected of a girl like Pauline.

Stephen, helping the chauffeur unload the piled luggage, let a heavy trunk drop on his foot. It hurt, but it woke him up. He shrugged his shoulders. Ah, well, one never knew one's friends till adversity appeared on the scene. That was an old tag, but it was a horribly true one. But for all that—Pauline!

'What's the matter, chum?' asked the chauffeur pertly. 'Look as if you'd got a pain.'

'Who was that man?' Stephen asked. 'Whose car is this?'

'Who's the boss? Sir Julius Hammerstein.'

'Hammerstein?' Stephen repeated stupidly. The name seemed familiar, but he could not quite place it.

'Yes, you know. The financier bloke. The girl's his feeancy.'

'Stephen started violently. 'His—fiancée?' he echoed mechanically.

'If you like it better that way. Yes, got engaged last week, they did. Don't you never read the papers? Been chasing him for years, they have, but she's caught him at last. Miss Mainwaring, or something. They reckon he's the richest man in London, or pretty near it. She's got the family and he's got the dibs, y'see; that's how it always goes. Well, good luck to 'er, says I. There's many had a shot at it and never brought it off, and she had to work hard enough for it, you can take it from me. I reckon I know Sir Julius pretty well, I do. We'll drink her 'ealth when you've taken these things in, if you've got a bit o' wet anywhere handy, hey?' And the chauffeur contorted his features into a prodigious wink.

Stephen could have dashed his fist into the man's grinning face. It was bad enough that Pauline should have done this thing at all, but that her affairs should be discussed like this—!

He hoisted an enormous trunk up on to his shoulder with a vicious thud and staggered into the house. He felt as if he must set himself some physical task almost beyond his powers to shut his mind to his thoughts.

IV STARCROSS IS UNEASY

B Y half-past six Stephen had more or less recovered his equilibrium. All those expected had arrived except one, and Stephen had had a busy time. Sir Julius had brought his own valet, but two other men had not done so and for these Stephen had had to unpack and put out on the bed their evening clothes.

He has seen Pauline once or twice and though he had watched her mournfully out of the tail of his eye, she cast not a single glance in his direction; he could hear her well-remembered tones, and now and then her laugh rang out lightly and happily as when he himself had been its favoured recipient.

He had just dropped into a chair in the pantry for a brief rest when the front-door bell rang once more.

'That'll be Mr Frederick,' said Martin, cocking a wise eye at the clock. 'Always last at everything, he is.'

Completely indifferent to anything about Mr Frederick beyond the pious hope that he had brought a man of his own with him, Stephen made his way once more to the front door.

A young man who had been standing on the step shot past him into the hall, and, in the same movement as, it seemed, began to divest himself of voluminous coats, mufflers, and other impedimenta.

'Catch hold of these, I say, do you mind,' he said, extricating himself from the last muffler and throwing it at Stephen. 'I've got a couple of cases in the car, and you might tell the chauffeur to trot it round to the garage when you've hoicked 'em out. Thanks!'

'Very good, sir,' said Stephen gravely.

The young man spun round sharply and stared at him. Then he caught him by the shoulders and turned him to the light.

'Good Lord!' he said, stepping back a pace or two. 'It is! Old Steve Munro, of Donnington's house!'

'I think you are mistaken, sir,' Stephen returned, not quite knowing whether to welcome or to curse this turn of fortune. 'My name is William.'

The young man smote Stephen suddenly and heavily in the chest. 'No, you don't. I recognized you at once. But, I say, Steve, old lad, what in the name of heaven are you doing in those togs?'

Deciding that things were hopeless, Stephen grinned. 'Being a foot-man, Freddie, if you must know,' he said, returning the other's buffet with interest. 'And don't hit me again, or I'll give notice.'

'I say, not really!' said Freddie, with an expression of extreme con-sternation. 'Not—'

'I don't usually allow my footmen to raise their fists to my nephews,

William,' observed a grim voice behind them.

Freddie whirled round. 'Hullo, Aunt Susan! I say, this is a pal of mine at Winchester—did you know? We can't possibly have him being a footman. We must—'

'If William wishes to leave my service, Freddie,' Lady Susan interrupted calmly, 'no doubt he will give notice in the usual way.'

'I must apologize, Lady Susan—I mean, my lady,' Stephen stammered, considerably embarrassed. 'Just by a bit of rotten luck—I mean, by an unfortunate coincidence—'

'In the meantime, Freddie,' Lady Susan continued superbly, completely disregarding him, 'I must ask you not to interfere with my servants while they are busy with the duties for which I employ them.' Stephen fled out into the night.

As he was unpacking Freddie's cases upstairs a few minutes later, that young man joined him in a state of considerable perturbation.

'Here, stop that, Steve,' Freddie said uncomfortably, perceiving what the other was doing. 'I'm hanged if I'm going to have you running about for me, at any rate.'

'With pleasure, Freddie,' Stephen grinned, subsiding into a chair. 'I'm about due for a rest, I must say, and it won't hurt you to do a little work for once.'

Freddie bent over the suitcase. 'Now, then, Steve,' he said, 'let's have it. Tell me what's happened and why on earth you're here like this.'

Bowing to necessity, Stephen embarked on a résumé of his history since they had last met, nearly ten years ago.

'But for goodness' sake, Freddie,' he concluded, 'do keep quiet about things. You've given me away to your aunt already. Don't butt in any more.'

'What, treat you like a real footman and send you running about for drinks and things and pretend I've never set eyes on you before?' said Freddie indignantly. 'I'm dashed if I will! What do you take me for? A beastly snob?'

Stephen forced a smile. Freddie's attitude seemed in such pointed contrast with that of somebody else. He put the thought resolutely away from him.

'It isn't that at all,' he pointed out patiently. 'It's simply that I'm a footman, and you're an employer; and if you don't treat me like a footman I shall get the sack and it will be your fault.'

'Sack, nonsense!' retorted Freddie warmly. 'My aunt isn't like that. She'd be much more likely to sack me out of her will if I did cut you. Not that I'm down for too much in any case,' he added frankly. 'Millicent's booked for most of the cash, being a Carey and all that, and the house; and I've a pretty good idea that Cicely'll get the jewellery.'

'Miss Vernon?' put in Stephen absently.

'Yes, and that's going to amount to something pretty tidy; the old lady simply teems with pearl necklaces and diamond brooches and all the rest of it—regular fortune. Still,' he went on cheerfully, 'my share of the spoils won't be any too dusty, you know. I'm her only nephew, although I am a Venables and not a Carey, and there'll be plenty to go round. Or so I've been given to understand, at any rate. Of course, she never has cottoned on to me much, not from a kid. I don't suppose I've been to stay here, for instance, half the number of times Cicely has, but—'

'Freddie!' Stephen interrupted suddenly, his thoughts very much elsewhere. 'Freddie, who is this fellow Sir Julius?'

During the last hour the conviction had been growing upon him that there must be more in this incongruous engagement than met the eye. The temptation to discuss it was irresistible.

'Well, between you and me, I think he's a pretty poisonous sort of blighter. And what Pauline Mainwaring can see in him simply beats me. Of course, he's rolling in wealth and all that, so I suppose—!' Freddie shrugged his shoulders expressively.

Stephen decided all of a sudden that he had no wish after all to discuss Pauline or her engagement, even with Freddie. Hurriedly pleading excess of work, he made his escape from the room.

His time during the next hour and a half was fully occupied. What with helping Martin lay the table, polishing silver, valeting the two men, making up the fires and giving a hand to anybody who wanted it in his spare moments, one would have thought that he had little time for reflection. Nevertheless, Stephen performed his duties like an automaton, his mind filled with one thought, and one only—why had Pauline promised herself in marriage to a man of the calibre of Sir Julius?

It was only as he was carrying a tray of cocktails up to the library before dinner that a possible explanation occurred to him: could it be that the man had some hold over her? He could not quite imagine anybody having a hold over Pauline, but what other reason could there be for her inexplicable action?

He looked at Sir Julius narrowly as he held the tray for him. The magnate was talking to one of the men with whom Stephen had been occupied, Henry Kentisbeare, an exquisite creature of about Stephen's own age, with a slightly languid air, who looked as if he had been melted down and poured into his clothes. Henry Kentisbeare, it was well known, did nothing for a living; but how could he? To dress like that is a whole-time occupation. He was enabled to devote proper time to it by consistently living on the resources of his friends.

Stephen smiled grimly to himself. Sir Julius was not the sort of person upon whom even such a practised exponent of the art as Henry Kentisbeare could live. His small eyes, set far too closely together in his fleshy red face, gleamed maliciously as he deftly parried the other's pointed hints for useful Stock Exchange tips. He took a glass from the tray, drained it and put it back again, without any other acknowledgement of Stephen's presence, and with not even a nod of thanks. What could Pauline have seen in such a man?

At the farther end of the room, Freddie was talking with two other men. As Stephen approached he beamed expansively.

'Hullo, Stephen, old lad! I say, I want to introduce you to Colonel Uffculme and John Starcross. This is the chap I was telling you about,' he added to the other two.

Stephen writhed. His position would really become impossible if Freddie made a habit of this sort of thing. He meant it awfully kindly, of course; but it was the very last thing in the world that Stephen wanted.

If Stephen was embarrassed the Colonel was no less so. 'Uh-huh!' he grunted, and took refuge in his handkerchief.

The other man promptly held out his hand. Stephen had heard of John Starcross. He had sprung into fame a few months ago, on his return from a long and dangerous feat of exploration in Central South America, and no country-house gathering was now complete without him.

'I think it's extraordinarily sporting of you,' he said with a frank smile.

Stephen hurriedly put a glass into the outstretched hand. 'Very kind of you to say so, sir,' he mumbled, blushing hotly.

'We were talking about witchcraft, Steve, old lad,' Freddie remarked chattily, tapping a book which he was holding. 'Extraordinarily interesting. This book I've just found in here gives all sorts of spells and things to—'

'Very sorry,' Stephen interrupted awkwardly. 'Frightfully busy. Must run.' He took himself and his tray hastily out of the room. It was so like dear old Freddie to try to draw him into a conversation about witchcraft, of all remarkable things, in an effort to make him feel at home!

Dinner, and his duties of waiting at table, came to Stephen as a positive relief. He was kept so much on the alert that he had no time even to think. This was fortunate, for not by so much as a look or a glance did Pauline show herself aware of his identity; and Stephen went to a good deal of unnecessary trouble to avoid her eye. He was also exceedingly busy trying not to observe the airs of complacent proprietorship which the unpleasant Sir Julius was so tactlessly displaying.

With Lady Susan and Millicent there were ten people at the table, Miss Rivers not being present as the couples were already even. Lady Susan sat at one end, Freddie Venables, as the only male relative, at the other. On Freddie's left was the fluffy little lady to whom Stephen had first opened the door. Her name was Miss Cullompton, but everybody called her Baby. Not that Miss Cullompton was of tender years or anything near it, admitting openly to twenty-four of them; but she cultivated a lisp and an expression of childish innocence because it suited her blue eyes and her little round face, and her success in her pose was officially recognized by the nickname which her friends had given her.

On Freddie's right, between him and Henry Kentisbeare, sat a young and distant cousin of Millicent's and Lady Susan's, Miss Annette Agnew, aged nineteen, very pretty, very natural, very direct and very modern. It is almost superfluous to add that Miss Agnew and Miss Cullompton did not like each other one little bit.

During the first part of the meal Stephen was so absorbed in his duties, and so anxious not to pour the soup down anyone's back or deposit the fish in Lady Susan's lap, that the conversation had flowed unheeded past his ears. With the return of his self-assurance the spoken words began to penetrate to his understanding.

Freddie, it appeared, was still obsessed with the subject of witchcraft. In fact he now seemed to have reached the stage of putting forward witchcraft as an interesting after-dinner diversion in preference to bridge.

'Well, why not?' he was saying happily. 'There's a topping spell I saw for making a person disappear. I vote we have a pop at it. I say, thanks most awfully, old lad,' he added gratefully to Stephen, who was offering him a dish of potatoes. Stephen cursed him silently and withdrew the potatoes before Freddie could help himself.

'What a divine idea, Freddie!' exclaimed Miss Collumpton rapturously, with a sympathetic little side-smile at Stephen which told him only too plainly that the ineffable Freddie had already made his story common property to everybody. 'How divinely thrilling! Oh, yes, do let's!'

'What awful rot!' observed Annette instantly, with all the scorn of her nineteen years. 'Don't be such an idiot, Freddie. Disappear, indeed! This is the twentieth century, not the twelfth.'

'Yes, but it's rather fun,' Freddie protested. 'Get a bit of a thrill, I mean, and all that. I've been at some jolly exciting séances, I can tell you, and this looks a spot better still.'

'Freddie, your being childish.' This from Lady Susan.

'What's the idea?' Pauline smiled down the table. 'Are you looking for a new sensation, Freddie?'

'Something like that,' Freddie admitted. 'What do you say, Sir Julius?'

Sir Julius smiled grimly. 'I get all the thrills I need in business, Venables.'

'I remember,' observed Colonel Uffculme to his neighbour, 'when I was in Bengal in '93, Miss Carey—or was it '94? Let me see, it was the same year as—' The Colonel and Millicent were out of the conversation for the next ten minutes.

Henry Kentisbeare succeeded in looking as if the sight of a witch would only bore him to tears, but John Starcross seemed uneasy. 'That sort of thing may be dangerous,' he said to Freddie. 'Better leave it alone, if you ask my advice. I've seen some very curious things indeed, and in my opinion it's playing with fire.'

The discussion raged furiously.

'I've never met Mr Starcross before,' Annette confided to her neighbour. 'What does he explore, Henry?'

'Goodness knows! He goes away for irregular periods, I believe, and comes back with interesting stories about how the natives of Central America shingle their hair and all that sort of thing; but I'm sure I could do it just as well myself without leaving the country at all.'

'Don't try to be cynical, Henry,' said Annette frankly. 'It's too frightfully unoriginal.'

'It is getting a bit cheap,' Henry admitted.

'Well, what about it?' Freddie was saying to the table at large. 'I'm sure we could have a jolly good Witches' Sabbath in the drawing-room. Simply made for Witches' Sabbaths, in fact. Shall we have a pop at the disappearing stunt or not?'

'No!' replied Annette immediately. 'Let's play bridge.' But the loud chorus of approval which instantly arose from all the other younger members of the party easily drowned not only her dissent but any murmurs of a similar nature which might have issued from their elders.

'Right!' said Freddie with satisfaction. 'Then that's settled.'

John Starcross looked as if he was about to say something, but before he could speak Lady Susan had risen. The next moment the ladies filed out of the room. And somewhere the gods who arrange these things burst into happy and expectant laughter; but of course nobody heard them. Nobody ever does.

Stephen was busy for a minute or two after their departure. Then occasion sent him out of the room and into the hall. As he closed the door of the dining-room behind him a figure stepped from the last of the broad stairs, hesitated a moment and then walked swiftly towards him.

It was Pauline.

She was wearing a dinner-gown of some soft black stuff, and Stephen thought he had never seen her looking more lovely. Her red lips were just parted, and there was a faint flush in her cheeks.

But he did not check his pace. It did not occur to him that she wished to speak to him. He merely thought that their paths had happened to cross at an awkward moment, and walked a little more rapidly.

'Stephen!' she said in a low voice, evidently understanding what was in his mind.

He hesitated, and she hurried across the space between them to lay her hand on his sleeve and stop him going. 'Stephen, I'm a pig! Will you ever forgive me?'

'Oh, that's all right,' Stephen said awkwardly. 'That's all right, Pauline.'

She grasped his sleeve more firmly as he tried to edge away from her, and spoke in a rapid, passionate voice. 'It isn't all right! You're a brick to say it is, but I shall never forgive myself even if you do. I can't imagine what made me do such a thing. It was the—the shock, I think. I simply couldn't look at you at dinner, I was feeling so ashamed of myself. I've been waiting here ever since we came out to apologize to you.'

'Pauline!' said Stephen in much distress. His eye fell on the single large diamond that glittered on the hand which was holding his sleeve, and he looked away hastily.

Pauline noticed the direction of his glance and coloured slightly. 'I think it was splendid of you to take on a job like this,' she hurried on. 'You're a lesson to some of us, at any rate. Freddie was telling us your story in the drawing-room just before we went up to dress.'

'Curse Freddie!' said Stephen in heartfelt tones.

'Not at all. I'm only too glad he did.' She paused, and seemed to be deliberating. 'Look here, Stephen,' she went on rapidly the next moment, 'we can't talk here. When can we have a long talk? There are hundreds of things I'm dying to ask you. Where can I find you?'

'Well, I look like being pretty busy,' Stephen smiled, 'but you can usually find me in the butler's pantry. I believe I'm to get Wednesday afternoons off, by the way, but I don't know whether I shall get tomorrow. Still, I ought to be able to manage a couple of hours or so.'

'We'll go for a walk together,' said Pauline with decision. 'Shall we?'

Stephen smiled at her joyfully. Such a question hardly seemed to need an answer from him.

It was a singularly cheerful young man who hurried on his way a minute later. His thoughts as he cleared away the debris of the meal, polished the silver and generally worked like a slave during the next hour or two (single-handed, in the convenient absence of Martin), were in pleasant contrast with those which had been occupying him before.

V THE LIGHT THAT FAILED

THE interior of Wintringham Hall had been very little modernised. All the downstairs rooms, the hall, the dining-room, the drawing-room, the morning-room (commonly known as the oak-room, and Lady Susan's own special perquisite), the gun-room and the library—all retained their original oak panelling, now black with age and polish, and their wide-open fireplaces, from which broad chimneys, wide enough to accommodate the old-time chimney sweeper's devil, rose sturdily up the outside walls of the house.

It is true that electric light had been installed, but even this was not quite as modernly infallible as it might have been. There being no electric light in the village, and the nearest town being over five miles away, it had been necessary to put in a plant to manufacture it on the premises; and it is well known that plants have their drooping moments. As Stephen was sitting in the pantry an hour or so after his interview with Pauline, the electric light above his head suddenly extinguished itself.

'Where was Mr Martin when the light went out?' observed Stephen humorously. A few pithy remarks from his superior had recently enlightened him regarding the etiquette of the back stairs, which appeared considerably more rigid than that of the front. It would be far, far more pardonable, he had gathered for example, for him to address his younger mistress as 'Millie' than for a footman to speak to his butler without the customary prefix of 'Mr' before his name. Butlers are very touchy about such things as that.

In the darkness he could hear Martin's bland laugh. 'Ha ha! Very funny, William. But you'll have to stir yourself, my lad. There's lamps to be taken to the drawing-room, and candlesticks to be left in the hall for the bedrooms.' He struck a match and pointed to a row of lamps standing ready on a shelf. They began to light them together.

'Does this often happen, then?' Stephen asked with interest.

'Often enough, William. Often enough.' It seemed to Stephen as if Martin was by no means displeased at the prospect of extra work for his underling; his voice held a silky, purring note. Stephen felt his dislike of the man instinctively deepen, though it was impossible to say why. 'The chauffeur, George, he's supposed to look after it, but there won't be any more electric light tonight, I'm thinking. Now, William, off you run with these two to the drawing-room first of all, and then this one for the hall. After that we'll see.'

'But not very well,' Stephen laughed as he hurried off.

His entry into the drawing-room was hailed with relief and, from Freddie, loud and embarrassing gratitude. It appeared that the failure of the light had interrupted the preparations which were being made for casting the spell.

It had also rather spoilt the entrance of Miss Cullompton, who had been upstairs to array herself fittingly for the ceremony. Her frock at dinner had been shell-pink, but this evidently did not coincide with Miss Cullompton's ideas about what should be worn when communicating with spirits. She had been upstairs for three-quarters of an hour, and certainly she had succeeded, with the help of a black velvet gown and floating, gauzy scarves, in making herself look uncommonly delightful; but the thoughtlessness of the electric light had undoubtedly detracted from the effect.

Stephen sniffed to himself as he saw her retire, with considerable petulance, into a far corner of the room. Like Annette Agnew, Stephen did not find himself overburdened with affection for Miss Cullompton.

As he was setting the solitary lamp a few minutes later in the middle of the vast hall, where it made a little oasis of yellow light which only seemed to render the surrounding shadows still deeper, there was a knock at the door.

A girl was standing outside, in the act of paying a taxi-man. She turned as Stephen opened the door, but it was too dark for him to see her distinctly.

'Oh, would you mind telling Miss Carey that I've come back, please,' she said in an agitated voice. 'The yachting trip's been cancelled at the last moment, and I want to know—Oh, perhaps you could ask her to come out, and I'll wait in the hall.'

'Certainly, madam,' Stephen said, standing aside to allow her to pass and taking the small suitcase she had in her hand. 'It is Miss—?'

'Miss Vernon.'

'Oh, yes; of course. I will tell Miss Carey, madam.'

He went into the drawing-room and delivered his message in a low voice. Millicent hurried out at once.

'Of course, you must stay here, Cicely!' Stephen heard her exclaim as soon as the other had made her explanation, in tones inaudible at the distance at which he was respectfully standing, but unmistakably agitated. Stephen wondered what could have happened to upset her so much. Until seeing her at the station, he had not thought her a girl to be easily thrown off her balance.

'Well, fancy that!' Millicent was twittering. 'Poor Mrs Seymour! An operation, you say? How dreadful for her! But I'm so glad you came back here, dear. William, will you take Miss Vernon's case upstairs, please? The room next to mine. You don't mind having a tiny room, do you, dear? Baby Cullompton's got yours. Oh, and will you find Miss Rivers, please, William, and tell her that Lady Susan wants her. She'll be in her room.'

'Well, how extraordinary, Cicely! But what about all your other luggage, dear?' she continued. 'Gone on to Folkestone, has it? Oh, you poor thing! Never mind. I can lend you anything you want, and—'

Stephen passed out of earshot. It must be a very dangerous operation, he reflected, to cause such uneasiness. So her luggage had gone on to Folkestone, had it, while she herself, so far as he knew, had been to Brighton? Why Brighton? It seemed a curious way of proceeding to Folkestone.

Stephen shrugged his shoulders. After all, it was none of his business. Then the idea of the exquisitely-dressed Cicely Vernon appearing in some of the garments affected by Miss Carey suddenly occurred to him, and tickled his fancy so deplorably that the matter of tickets to Brighton was driven out of his mind.

In spite of Millicent's assurance, Miss Rivers was not in her room. Having tapped respectfully three or four times, Stephen stroked his hair with his left hand in perplexity. It was just little matters like this, he foresaw, which were going to make the job of being a footman not quite so easy as it sounded.

Where on earth might Miss Rivers be expected to be when not in her room? Not having the faintest idea, he proceeded to seek out the lady's maid, Farrar, and delivered his message to her.

'Miss Rivers?' repeated that acidulated female sourly. 'I haven't seen her. I don't know where she is if she's not in her room, nor I wouldn't like to say, neither.' It could quite easily be gathered that Farrar had no particular love for Miss Rivers. 'Never mind,' she added, softening as she caught sight of Stephen's unhappy expression. 'I'll find her for you, William, and send her along to the drawing-room.'

Stephen thanked her fittingly, and hurried back to the pantry to collect more lamps and candlesticks. Stephen was beginning to look forward rather actively to his bed.

But bedtime was not for him yet.

When he had at last completed the temporary lighting arrangements, it appeared that a tray containing siphons, decanters and glasses must be taken into the drawing-room.

'Ten o'clock drinks, William,' Martin leered at him as he dropped into a chair in the pantry. 'Ten o'clock drinks. I've got 'em all ready for you on the tray.'

'Thank you,' Stephen sighed wearily.

'And after you've done that, you'll be finished for the night. I can't ask you to have a smoke and a chat with me this evening, though,' Martin continued with dignity, 'having a previous engagement, so if you're tired, William, you can get straight to bed.'

'That'll suit me down to the ground,' Stephen agreed. 'I am a bit weary. You wouldn't like to carry that tray into the drawing-room for me, I suppose?'

Martin's expression changed to a frown. It was clear that his dignity was badly upset. 'No, I would not, young man. And just because I talk to you friendly-like, I'll trouble you not to forget that you're the footman and I'm the butler.'

'I'm very sorry, Mr Martin,' Stephen returned, rising from his chair and doing his best to conceal a smile. 'I should hate to forget that.'

'I can see there's lots of things I shall have to speak to you about, William,' Martin pursued severely. 'Lots of things! Poking your nose into things that don't concern you's one of them. I don't hold with footmen being so friendly with guests in the house, for instance; not at all, I don't. Talking to young ladies in the hall and arranging to go for walks on your afternoon off! I don't hold with it, William, and that's a fact.'

Stephen carries his tray into the drawing-room in a state of some emotion.

'Here's the very chap!' Freddie exclaimed instantly. 'Shove that tray down, old man, and come here. We were trying to decide who's to read the spell. As a thoroughly disinterested party, I vote you for the job. Any objections, anyone?'

VI THE SÉANCE

STEPHEN looked helplessly at Lady Susan—or at where Lady Susan was sitting by the fireplace, dimly visible in the ill-lit gloom which the dark walls only seemed to make more deep. Loud approval of Freddie's suggestion made itself heard on all sides. Lady Susan said nothing.

Stephen approached her in desperation. 'Have you anything for me to do, my lady?' he asked.

Lady Susan looked at him. 'You heard what Mr Venables said, William. Apparently you are to take your orders from him.' Her tone was uncompromising enough, but Stephen could swear that he caught a glimpse of a twinkle in her eyes. 'If we are to submit to this tomfoolery, my footman may just as well turn himself into a wizard for the occasion.'

'Bridge!' wailed a voice from the end of the room. 'Somebody come into another room with me and play bridge. Freddie, do stop this rot. I want to play bridge. Tell him to play bridge with me, Aunt Susan!' Miss Annette Agnew was voicing her lack of interest in the matter in hand.

'I'm afraid I have no control over Freddie,' replied Lady Susan.

'It's only her toothache making her fractious again, Aunt Susan,' observed Freddie blithely. 'Disregard the woman!'

The Colonel, who was sitting by the side of his hostess, snorted emphatically. 'When I was a young man—' he began, and went on at some length.

'And when I'm an old one,' muttered Freddie, throwing a rug over a statue which stood at the end of the room by the door, 'I hope I'll be a silent one.'

'Freddie, what are you doing now?' asked Pauline. She was seated with Sir Julius on a deep, wide couch that stood in front of one of the windows, and Stephen noted with satisfaction that they sat well back in the corners with a considerable space between them.

'Covering up this old girl,' replied Freddie, indicating without respect the life-size reproduction of Artemis which he was busy upholstering.

'But why?'

'Because she's probably a malign influence.'

'Oh, what rot this is!' came the wailing voice again. 'Bridge, for the love of Allah! Bridge!'

'Did you ask Miss Rivers to come to me, William?' Lady Susan asked.

'No, my lady,' said Stephen, who was hovering uneasily by the door, not knowing in the least what he ought to do. 'She was not in her room, but Farrar promised to find her and send her to you.'

'Farrar!' observed Lady Susan. And that disposed of Farrar.

Pauline glanced at him with a smile, and Stephen felt absurdly heartened.

The door opened, and Millicent entered with Cicely. She went across at once to Lady Susan and began to explain the circumstances.

Cicely followed a trifle diffidently. She was wearing a light scarf of crêpe de Chine round her neck, and coughed once or twice; but Stephen noticed that she seemed very much more composed.

'I do hope you don't mind my coming back, Lady Susan,' she said, in a somewhat husky voice.

'Of course not, my dear,' Lady Susan returned with unwonted warmth. 'Only too glad to have you. Your cold seems much worse.'

'It is, a little,' Cicely admitted.

'I think it must really be a touch of hay fever,' Millicent explained volubly. 'She felt it coming on this afternoon, on top of her cold, but hoped that walk would put her right. Isn't it a nuisance for her?'

Cicely, standing in the shadow, coughed her acquiescence in this sentiment. She had not changed her dress, either for this reason or because she could not bear to be seen in one of Millicent's, and she kept her scarf pressed to her mouth.

'We'll, sit down somewhere out of a draught, dear,' Lady Susan urged kindly. 'By the way, has Millicent explained this absurd game that Freddie insists on our playing?'

'Oh, I expect Cicely knows all about séances,' Millicent said nervously, but nevertheless took the opportunity of drawing the girl into a farther corner to discuss it.

'It isn't a séance,' put in Freddie, who had caught the last words. 'It's a Witches' Sabbath. I'm surprised at you, Millicent. Now then, are we all ready?'

'Oh, won't anyone play bridge with me?' Annette cried.

'Shut up, Annette!' drawled Henry Kentisbeare, who had been sitting beautifully on the arm of her couch. He rose and strolled towards the circle. 'Freddie wants to play ghosts. Don't interfere with his little amusements. Come along!'

'I won't! I'm going to stay here and sleep till it's all over. It's no good looking at me like that, Freddie; nothing'll induce me to play ghosts with you. Chuck me a cushion, somebody!'

As if with a common thought, Freddie and Henry each snatched up the largest cushion within reach and hurled it at Miss Agnew. One enveloped her face, the other landed with a thud on the wall just above her, dropping neatly on to her head.

'Oof!' observed Miss Agnew in somewhat muffled tones. She rose with dignity, disposed the cushions on the couch and reclined upon them, yawning ostentatiously. 'Wake me up when Freddie comes to his senses,' she said loftily, and set herself to the manufacture of several creditable snores.

Annette was not the only person who did not appear to share Freddie's ideas as to fitting entertainment of his aunt's guests. Stephen had been watching Miss Cullompton with a good deal of secret amusement. She was seated in a little triangular cosy-corner behind the enormous grand piano, and since he entered the room she had not spoken a single word. This was so unlike Miss Cullompton that Stephen had been speculating as to its reason.

It was not very difficult to find. After all, it is enough to make everybody a little sulky to go to the trouble of making oneself look really charming only to meet with no recognition whatever. No wonder Miss Cullompton patted her velvet skirt a trifle viciously and spoke no word.

'Come on, Baby,' Freddie urged.

'I'd rather not, if you don't mind,' Miss Cullompton replied coldly. 'This sort of thing always gives me a headache.'

Freddie, who was perhaps a wiser man than he appeared, accepted this decision and set about finding a suitable volunteer for his disappearing act. Annette was out of the question, Miss Cullompton no less so; Pauline did not appear anxious to leave either her couch or this sphere.

'Ask Henry,' she suggested. 'Or perhaps Mr Starcross would.'

'But I must have a girl,' Freddie pointed out. 'The people who work witches' spells for them are frightfully particular about that.'

'What about Millicent?' suggested Lady Susan unkindly.

'Oh, Millicent's wanted to play soulful music,' Freddie replied at once, and received a grateful glance from his cousin.

Millicent rose at the hint and seated herself at the piano.

'I'll disappear for you if you like, Freddie,' said Cicely, stepping huskily into the breach.

'Will you? I say, that's topping. Thanks awfully. Now then, what about a few precautions to see you don't hop off somewhere while nobody's looking? I know you far too well to trust you, Cicely. Henry, come off that couch and stand by this window, so see she doesn't make a dive through it.'

Henry Kentisbeare left his seat with every sign of reluctance and took up his stand before the window in question. 'Freddie,' he remarked mildly, 'do you know that you're getting a bit of a nuisance?'

The lack of enthusiasm among his fellow-players did not appear to damp Freddie in the least. 'And you, Starcross, might pull up your chair in front of the French windows, will you? You might close them while you're about it, too.'

'Really, Freddie!' Pauline laughed, and again smiled at Stephen.

The explorer shut the windows as bidden and pulled a chair up to them. 'Look here, Venables,' he said awkwardly, as if speaking almost against his will, 'before you go any further, I want to say that I don't altogether like this. You can laugh if you like—'

'Certainly not!' murmured Freddie, who would never have dreamed at laughing at one of his aunt's guests—at least, not openly.

'You can laugh, but I must tell you that I've seen some very queer things in this line before now. Very queer indeed! I do warn you that, for anything any of us know, you may be playing with fire.'

'Oh, I think we might risk that,' Freddie returned, politely but lightly. 'Eh, Cicely?'

'I'll take the risk,' Cicely smiled. 'At any rate, it would cure my hay fever.'

John Starcross shrugged his shoulders, as if the responsibility at any rate rested no longer upon him, and sat down before the closed French windows.

Freddie was busy setting a small chair in the exact centre of the room. 'Now then, Cicely, if you'll sit on that, we'll get on with the doings. Ready, Stephen, old lad?'

'But who's going to guard the door into the hall, if you want all the exits guarded?' Henry Kentisbeare wanted to know.

'I am,' replied Freddie with dignity. 'Come on, Steve!'

Stephen allowed himself to be led forward and stationed, facing Cicely but some distance away from her, in front of a table laden, in the old-fashioned way, with silver objects d'art. He felt extremely unhappy, but anyhow it was better than the prying curiosity of Martin and his blandly veiled insolence.

'Here's the book,' said Freddie, 'and this is the bit you're to read. See it? Here's a torch for you, but mind you don't shine it on anything else. I've got a luminous watch, and I'll give Cicely five minutes; then we'll light the lights. Strike up, Millicent!' He pushed a tiny torch, no thicker than a pencil, into Stephen's hand and ran off, twittering with excitement, to turn out the lamps. Stephen's last glance before the room was plunged into darkness was at Pauline, and they exchanged a smile of amusement. Millicent began to play a succession of solemn, dirge-like chords.

'I say, not five minutes!' protested Henry Kentisbeare. 'Two.'

'Three, then,' Freddie conceded. 'Let her rip, Steve.'

From Miss Agnew's end of the room a prolonged snore rose above the music.

Feeling exceedingly foolish, Stephen began to read out the gibberish. He had scarcely completed half a dozen sentences when a sharp tap suddenly interrupted him. He jumped—and then smiled at himself for doing so. Somebody was evidently being funny. He stopped reading and listened.

Stephen was not the only person to be startled.

'Did you hear that?' asked somebody a little shakily.

'Hush!' whispered Freddie, his voice almost choked with excitement. 'Half a minute, Steve. Is anybody there?' he asked in loud, gruff tones.

'Yes,' said a voice from the hall. 'It's me. I think Lady Susan wants me.'

There was a sound of pent breath being expelled. Someone giggled.

'Oh, Miss Rivers,' said Freddie disappointedly. 'All right,' he called out. 'Come in!'

The door opened, and for a fleeting second a figure seemed to be silhouetted against the very dim light from the hall lamp. The door closed again softly.

'Sit down, Miss Rivers,' Freddie said. 'We're in the middle of something rather exciting. There's a chair on your left. That's right. All serene? Carry on, then, Steve.'

Plan of the drawing-room at Wintringham Hall during the holding of the séance. 1. Cicely; 2. Sir Julius; 3. Pauline; 4. Stephen; 5. Henry Kentisbeare; 6. Freddie; 7. Miss Rivers; 8. John Starcross; 9. Lady Susan; 10. Colonel Uffculme; 11. Millicent; 12; Annette Agnew; 13. Miss Cullompton.

It might have been thought that the anti-climax would have dissipated the slight eeriness which had already begun to make itself felt, but Stephen was conscious as soon as silence was restored of a strange feeling of expectancy. In some curious way there was a distinct sensation of strain. It was as of what had hitherto been only a silly joke held a promise of real drama. He shook himself impatiently. This was foolish; he was allowing an unnatural situation to affect his nerves.

Switching on the torch again, he began in a carefully normal voice to read the nonsensical passage through to the end.

As his voice ceased, Millicent slightly increased the loudness of her funereal chords. At the same time, just audible above the sombre music, came a low, shuddering moan.

'What—what was that?' whispered somebody.

Straining his ears into the darkness, Stephen took half a dozen noiseless steps towards where Pauline was sitting. By good luck he felt the end of the couch before blundering into it and bent down. 'It's me,' he whispered, in a voice which could not have carried farther than the person to whom it was addressed. 'Stephen!' A soft hand touched his, and his fingers closed over it.

'Hush!' Freddie was saying. 'Don't move, anybody. We mustn't '

A loud rap, proceeding apparently from the empty space above their heads, cut him short abruptly. Stephen felt Pauline start, and gripped her hand more tightly. The rap was repeated, and again.

'Somebody being funny,' remarked the voice of Henry Kentisbeare, but his tones lacked conviction.

'Shut up, Henry!' quavered Freddie. 'Is—is there anyone there? Rap three times for yes.'

A trio of raps answered him almost before his voice had ceased. The piano stopped playing.

Stephen strained his ears. At first he could hear nothing; then it seemed as if he caught the sound of a stealthy footstep. He leaned forward.

Yes, he could hear it distinctly—somebody was moving about the room!

'Look here, we'd better stop this.' The voice of Starcross cut sharply across the tense silence. 'I don't like it.'

'Shut up!' Freddie hissed, adding more loudly, 'Can you speak?'

The next instant Stephen's hair rose on his head, and a cold shudder of sheer terror passed down his spine, for a booming voice, speaking as it seemed out of the empty nothingness overhead, answered, 'Yes!'

Pauline's hand gripped his own so fast that it almost hurt him, and he could feel her trembling all over. For the moment he forgot his new position, and shouted towards Freddie: 'This is past a joke. Turn the lights up, Freddie!'

Other voices were shouting also, but Freddie's rose above them all. 'Don't spoil it!' he was crying. 'Don't move! This is wonderful. Don't spoil it!'

As if in agreement, a veritable cascade of raps sounded through the room, seeming to Stephen's bewildered ears as if they came from all points of the compass. One of the women shrieked. The next moment followed a silence almost more pregnant with fear.

'Who are you?' asked Freddie hoarsely. 'Who—?'

A terrible scream drowned his words, rising to an ear-splitting crescendo, and then ceasing abruptly, as if choked in mid-career. The next instant there was an appalling crash from the direction of the fireplace which made everything in the room rattle. Almost at the same moment Stephen detected, faint but pungent, the unmistakable odour of chloroform.

Still gripping Pauline's hand, he took a step forward. 'Freddie,' he shouted above the din of voices, 'there's something wrong. I—'

'Don't spoil it!' Freddie was wailing. 'Do keep calm!'

Stephen freed his left hand and felt in his pocket for matches, but before he could extract the box the problem was solved for him. The electric light suddenly burst into full blaze.

Nearly blinded, people blinked at each other fearfully and half ashamed of their panic, till a hoarse cry from Starcross startled them once more.

'Miss Vernon!' he exclaimed. 'Where is she?'

All eyes turned to the chair in which Cicely had been sitting. It was empty.

CHAPTER VII
WHERE IS CICELY?

FOR a moment there was a stupefied silence. Then:

'She—she's gone!' squeaked Freddie in a ludicrously high voice, his eyes almost popping out of his head as he stared at the chair on which

Cicely had been sitting.

'What—what was that terrible crash?' quavered Millicent from the music-stool. Her face was quite chalky.

'I suppose it was that picture,' remarked Sir Julius calmly, pointing at a large gilt frame which lay, face downwards, on the floor in front of the fireplace.

Millicent followed the direction of his finger with starting eyes. 'Grandfather's portrait,' she muttered, 'from over the mantelpiece. Whatever made it—?' She shivered and made a palpable effort to pull herself together, then rose, a little unsteadily, and made her way to Lady Susan's side. 'Are you all right, Aunt Susan?'

'By the mercy of God, yes!' replied the old lady grimly. 'By all rights I ought to be dead—and if I were, somebody would have murdered me. A joke carried to that extent—' She fixed her penetrating glance upon Freddie.

'I wasn't doing anything, Aunt Susan!' he expostulated.

'You weren't? Well, somebody was.'

'But what on earth happened to Cicely?' asked Pauline. She too looked decidedly shaken, but was recovering rapidly.

Stephen swept a thoughtful look round the room. Somehow it seemed of the utmost importance to examine the positions of all the others. Those footsteps he had heard …

He frowned. Two people besides himself were not in the same places as before the lights went out. Miss Cullompton had left her corner and was standing near the door; her face was no longer petulant, she looked highly alarmed, even terrified. And Henry Kentisbeare was seated nonchalantly on top of the piano instead of lounging in front of the window. Stephen did his best to photograph the scene on his mind. He had an idea it might be interesting later.

All this happened in less time than has been taken to read it. Hardly more than three seconds after the light appeared, Miss Cullompton quavered: 'What—what's this funny smell?'

'Chloroform,' replied John Starcross shortly. He looked narrowly at Henry Kentisbeare. 'There's been some hanky-panky going on here.'

'That dreadful scream!' muttered Millicent, and shivered.

'Where is Cicely?' asked Pauline again, and again nobody answered her.

'Why did you leave your place, Henry?' Freddie asked suddenly, still standing as if petrified by the door.

'To tell you the truth, Freddie, I was a trifle bored. Also I wanted to sit down.'

'I suppose it—it must have been Cicely who made those awful knocks,' put in Miss Cullompton, still somewhat unsteadily.

'Very naughty of her,' said Lady Susan tolerantly. 'Very naughty indeed. She might have frightened me to death. No wonder she's hiding.'

'Hiding?' repeated John Starcross thoughtfully, as if the idea had not occurred to him.

Henry Kentisbeare stifled a yawn with elegance. 'What else? Doesn't it occur to you that Miss Vernon is pulling our legs rather neatly?'

'No, I'm afraid it doesn't,' Starcross replied shortly.

'What's the idea then, Starcross?' asked Colonel Uffculme, speaking for the first time. 'Got anything up your sleeve?'

'No. Simply what I said before, that there's been some hanky-panky.'

'The chloroform, you mean?' said Stephen. 'And that scream?'

'Exactly.'

Henry waved a delicate hand in the air. 'Blinds, my dear fellow. Blinds, of course. She's having the laugh over us delightfully. First she made exciting noises, and now she pretends to have been spirited away. Confess you were startled, Freddie.'

'I was,' Freddie did not hesitate to admit. 'Dashed startled, old lad. Still, you must be right. She's hiding somewhere.'

'Well, thank goodness, somebody's beginning to get some glimmerings of sense at last,' remarked Annette with much scorn, apparently addressing the ceiling. 'Fancy letting Cicely put the wind up you like that. Pull yourselves together, my children. We'll get a little bridge soon with any luck.'

'You don't agree, Mr Starcross?' asked Pauline, seeing the explorer's serious expression.

'Well—is chloroform the kind of thing that one usually carries about with one on the off-chance of pulling one's friends' legs with it?' asked Starcross dryly.

'What are you hinting at?' grunted Sir Julius. 'Let's have it in plain words. Do you believe Miss Vernon has been forcibly kidnapped, Starcross?'

'I've known more curious things happen than that,' replied the explorer, in the same dry, unemotional tone.

'Oh, Mr Starcross,' fluttered Millicent, 'I'm sure—in this house of all places—really!'

'I shouldn't distress yourself about it if I were you, Millicent,' advised Lady Susan laconically.

'Then you don't agree with Starcross?' Sir Julius asked his hostess.

'That one of my guests has been forcibly abducted under my very nose, Sir Julius?' Lady Susan said stiffly. She did not like this Stock Exchange knight and took no pains to disguise the fact. If it had not been as the fiancé of Pauline Mainwaring, he would never have set foot inside her house. 'I should have thought the question unnecessary.'

Sir Julius grunted noncommittally.

Pauline turned towards Stephen. 'What do you think about it all,

Stephen? she asked, in friendly tones. 'I was holding your hand, so I know that you had nothing to do with it, whatever it was.'

Stephen knew instinctively that Pauline meant her words to be a public declaration of the unaltered friendship between herself and him, and his heart warmed with gratitude. She smiled at him as if to say that she had guessed his thoughts and that they were correct.

'Well,' he said, answering her question, 'all I can tell you is that I heard footsteps and of course a certain amount of whispering; and that doesn't help us either way.'

'Did you hear any sounds of a struggle?' Starcross asked.

'No, nothing; but there was such a noise going on at the end that perhaps that isn't surprising.'

Colonel Uffculme was ponderously examining the fallen picture. 'Cord's a bit frayed,' he announced a little doubtfully. 'Coincidence, I suppose.'

'Those bangs on the wall brought it down, naturally,' observed Henry Kentisbeare wearily. 'What else?'

'But they came from the other side,' objected Starcross.

'They came from every side. Certainly that one.'

'But what about that—that dreadful voice?' asked Millicent, who still looked considerably shaken. 'Will anyone own up to that?'

'You can hardly expect him to do that, Millicent,' rejoined Lady Susan tartly, 'now he sees what a fool he made of himself and not of us.'

'Oh, do hurry up and look for Cicely.' This from Annette. 'Of course she's hiding under your noses somewhere, and I know we shan't get any bridge till she's found.'

'Really, I believe the horrible child must be right,' Freddie smiled. 'Anyhow, what about having a look for her?'

'I think she's behind the window curtains,' Pauline agreed. Already the atmosphere was rapidly becoming more normal; only John Starcross still looked profoundly uneasy. 'Don't you, Stephen?'

'There don't seem to be many other places,' Stephen smiled. For the moment he had forgotten that he was a footman, unconsciously he had dropped easily into the role of guest.

Miss Rivers took advantage of the diversion to approach her mistress. Stephen glanced at her carelessly. She was wearing a rather baggy little black frock and looked exceedingly inconspicuous. Stephen wondered why she affected those heavy horn spectacles when pince-nez would have suited her so much better, and why she dragged her hair back so ruthlessly from her forehead; she might have been quite moderately good-looking with a little more trouble, whereas at present she looked so ordinary that one could hardly say five minutes afterwards exactly what she did look like.

'Will you want me any more this evening, Lady Susan?' she asked, in a low voice.

'I did want you about an hour ago,' returned Lady Susan, 'but apparently I wasn't allowed to have you. No, I shan't want you any more. You'd better go to bed; you're looking pale.'

'Thank you. Yes, I have a slight headache.'

'No wonder, after all this tomfoolery,' Lady Susan agreed. 'Screams and raps and chloroform and disappearances indeed! It's a miracle that I'm still alive. I shall go to bed myself soon.'

Cicely turned out not to be in the cushioned recess behind the window-curtains.

Stephen looked thoughtfully round the room. Its dark panelled walls appeared to offer no hiding-place; the polished parquet floor strewn with big rugs afforded no clue whatever. His eyes roamed towards the ceiling. Suddenly he started. Bunched on the gilt frame of a big picture, on the farther wall opposite the fireplace, reposed a crêpe de Chine scarf. Stephen recognized it at once as the one which Cicely had been wearing.

'Great Scott, Pauline!' he exclaimed, catching her arm in his excitement. 'Look at that!' He pointed at the wrap.

'Stephen! How on earth did it get there? Look, Freddie!'

Everybody stared at the mysterious scarf. Everybody, that is, except Sir Julius. Stephen, dropping his eyes for a moment, became aware of those of the financier fixed upon him from under raised brows, and he realized that he was still holding Pauline's arm. In some confusion he withdrew his hand.

Freddie had pulled the scarf down, and a voluble discussion was in progress as to how it had reached its resting-place.

'She threw it away when she got up to hide, of course,' Henry observed languidly. 'It just happened to stick up there.'

'But would it carry?' asked Starcross, eyeing the flimsy material doubtfully.

'Rolled up into a ball, yes.'

'Hum!' Starcross examined the ceiling with a thoughtful eye.

'Frightfully prosaic, Henry,' Freddie commented, with regret, 'but I suppose you're right.'

'I always am, you know,' Henry remarked, complacently.

'I say!' Freddie exclaimed. 'I know where she is. Inside the piano, by Jove! Come off it, Henry, and let's have a look.'

Henry regarded his friend with a pained expression. 'Really, Freddie! The inside of a piano, I would have you know, is stuffed with works. There's no room for a cat to hide. And we know the works are there, because Miss Carey has been playing it. And lastly, the lid's locked, because I tried it myself before I got up here.'

'You're a disappointing sort of blighter,' Freddie observed, turning away to search elsewhere.

'Oh!' said Millicent suddenly. 'I wonder if she's in the cupboard! I heard someone moving about quite near me.'

Balancing the door into the hall was another on the same side of the room. Stephen had thought it a dummy, but he now saw there was a lock with a key in it. Millicent turned the key and threw open the door, disclosing a shallow cupboard. Across the top half were two or three shelves laden with china and dusty ornaments; in the bottom was a dust-sheet and one or two folded rugs. In any case, there was no sign of Cicely.

'Well, I did think she might be there,' said Millicent, and nobody was so unkind as to point out that the door had been locked on the outside.

'Annette, you lazy person!' Pauline called across the room. 'Come and help us search.'

'Oh, what a nuisance you people are!' said Miss Agnew wearily. 'You can all have your legs pulled if you like, but I don't see why I should have mine. However—' She rolled reluctantly off the couch, searched ostentatiously underneath it, looked inside a flower-vase, into one or two ash bowls, inside Miss Cullompton's wrist-watch and behind a picture. 'I can't find her anywhere,' she said tolerantly, in the tones of one addressing a small child, and returned to her resting-place. 'Let's tell her we give up. I do want one rubber before bedtime.'

'Oh, you and your bridge!' laughed Pauline, and went off to look again under the corner-seat where Miss Cullompton had been sitting. Stephen, incidentally, was looking under the corner-seat too.

'Well,' said Freddie a minute later in puzzled tones from the other end of the room, 'well, I thought I knew this room pretty well, and we've searched every inch of it. There's no getting away from the fact—Cicely is not here!'

'I was beginning to arrive at that conclusion myself,' Pauline agreed. 'But if she isn't here, where is she?'

'She must have got out somehow when we weren't looking, don't you think?' suggested Millicent brightly. 'You see, she could quite well have—'

'I know where Cicely is,' said Lady Susan.

'You do, Aunt Susan?' Freddie said with interest. 'Where, then?'

'Oh, I'm not going to tell you. If the child's clever enough to take you all in like this, certainly I won't give her away. You'll have to find her for yourselves. Though I must say,' added Lady Susan thoughtfully, 'that I can't think how she, let us say, managed it.' The old lady darted a glance, faintly interrogative, at Millicent, but the latter met it with one of complete perplexity.

'You mean, she isn't still in the room, Lady Susan?' asked Pauline.

'I didn't say so, my dear, did I? But I'll give you one hint, if you like, as I don't want to be kept up till all hours while you look for her. If she isn't in the room, then she must be outside it. See what you can make of that.'

Stephen stepped forward. 'I think, if you do not require me any more, my lady—' he said, formally.

Lady Susan looked at him with a grim smile. 'I haven't required you at all, William,' she said candidly.

'Oh, you're not going, Stephen,' Pauline cried. 'You don't mind if he stays a little longer, do you, Lady Susan? It's such ages since I've seen him.'

Stephen intercepted another unloving look from the financier, who had returned to his former position on the couch. 'I'm sure,' he began in formal tones, 'that—'

'Oh, rot, old lad!' Freddie chipped in irrepressibly. 'You don't want to push off yet. You don't mind him staying, do you, Aunt Susan?'

'It doesn't seem to matter in the least whether I do or not. But perhaps if you intend my footman to spend his evenings in here with us in future, you could lend him a dress-suit for further occasions, Freddie?'

'Rather, Aunt Susan!' beamed Freddie, apparently taking this remark at its face value. 'I'll see about it tomorrow, that's all right, then. Now, what about this matter of Cicely?'

Stephen received a broad wink from the speaker; it occurred to him once again that Lady Susan's nephew was possibly not quite such a fool as he looked.

'Well,' said Pauline, 'what shall we do? I think it's up to us to find Cicely, wherever she is, don't you, Baby?'

'I suppose so,' said Miss Cullompton languidly. 'Though personally I think she's kept it up long enough. It'll stop being a joke and begin to get boring soon.' Since recovering from her alarm, Miss Cullompton had reverted in some degree to her former mood. She had not spoken much, and she wore a look of patient long-suffering. She also stood about a good deal in extremely graceful postures.

'Miss Vernon!' called out a suddenly peremptory voice. 'Miss Vernon, will you come out, please!'

All eyes turned to the speaker. It was John Starcross. 'I'm not satisfied,' he explained brusquely. 'I'm sorry, Lady Susan,' he went on, answering the unspoken question conveyed by the old lady's raised eyebrows, 'but I'm not. If Miss Vernon is hiding for a joke, then let us confess that she's had the better of us and let her come out. If not—' He shrugged his shoulders.

'If not, what, Mr Starcross?' asked Lady Susan, without enthusiasm.

'Then we shall have to get busy indeed,' Starcross replied imperturbably. He raised his voice again: 'Miss Vernon! If you've heard what I said, please come out and put an end to this farce!'

There was no response.

'That's all right,' Freddie observed happily. 'All goes to prove what we were saying. She's hiding, but not in here. That's what you said, didn't you, Aunt Susan?'

'Something not unlike it, Freddie, yes.'

'Well, let's see; nobody's gone out of here since the lights were turned up except Miss Rivers, so she must somehow have got out in the dark. I expect she went out of that window there, if the truth were known, after Henry left it.'

'I'm quite sure she didn't,' said Henry Kentisbeare.

'Well, if she didn't go out of the door, or through the French windows, she must have done,' said Freddie with an air of finality.

'I'm afraid she can't have,' Stephen observed, examining the window in question. 'It's fastened on the inside.'

'Oh!' said Freddie, somewhat abashed. 'Well, what about the French windows, then?'

'The same, as I've already taken the trouble to prove,' said Starcross. 'They, too, are fastened on the inside. Go and see for yourself. She couldn't possibly have gone out that way. Besides, nobody passed me.'

'Well, she must have got out somehow,' retorted Freddie, unperturbed. 'After all, she could easily have slipped through the door, I suppose.'

'Not very easily,' said Pauline. 'I was sitting opposite the door, and I'm sure it only opened that time Miss Rivers came in, Freddie. That's the only time I saw the light from the hall.'

'Well, anyhow,' said Freddie desperately, 'if she isn't in this room she must have got out of it. I don't care whether she could have done or whether she couldn't—she must! At the present moment she's either in the house somewhere, or in the garden, probably watching us through the windows and laughing like anything. So we'd better split up and search for her.'

'Oh, bridge!' wailed Annette suddenly. 'Do someone play bridge with me.'

'You can't play bridge now, infant,' Henry said tolerantly. 'You've got to come along and help us play hide-and-seek with Freddie and Cicely.'

'I won't!' cried Annette mutinously. 'I won't! I want to play bridge.'

'Well, you children can do what you like,' said Lady Susan, rising to her feet. 'Personally, I'm going to bed. Colonel, perhaps you'd like to take Sir Julius along to the smoking-room. There will almost certainly be pandemonium in here and everywhere else.'

Colonel Uffculme did not look in the least as if he wanted to take Sir Julius along to the smoking-room, nor did Sir Julius look as if he wanted to go. But they both went at once.

Freddie was organizing his search-party. 'Millicent can be in charge of the house contingent, and I'll look after the garden. Henry, you join Millicent, and Starcross, you'd better do a bit of exploring outside. You'd better stay in the house, Pauline, and so had Baby. Stephen, you can come along with us, old lad. As for Annette—'

'As for Annette,' that young lady supplied for herself, 'she's jolly well going to stay here. Run along and play, little children; and when you've finished and want somebody to teach you the grown-up game of bridge, come back for Auntie Annette. Good-bye!'

'All right, then,' Freddie agreed, making the best of a bad job. 'You stay here and watch for Cicely to come popping down the chimney or out of the grandfather clock or somewhere.'

The two parties separated, Millicent leading her charges, including an extremely reluctant Henry, into the hall, and Freddie throwing open the French windows for his party.

'Hullo, Pauline!' said Freddie, as he watched his contingent file into the garden. 'You're one of the house-party.'

'Thank you, Freddie,' said Pauline very innocently, 'but I think I'd rather come to your garden-party, if you don't mind. I want a breath of fresh air after all that excitement.'

VIII OUT OF THE DARK

IT was a long time before Stephen got to sleep that night. Indeed, it was a long time before he got to bed at all. For Cicely continued to remain mysteriously undiscovered. Neither the search-party in the house nor that in the garden could unearth the very smallest clue as to her whereabouts.

When at last the decision was reached to abandon the search, it was agreed that Cicely had scored over them very considerably indeed. Nobody doubted for a moment that the whole thing was merely a very cleverly contrived joke on Cicely's part, even if it was felt that to keep it up till past midnight was prolonging even the best of jokes a little unduly.

Nobody, that is, except John Starcross. He, for his part, did not attempt to conceal his anxiety. Not once, but half a dozen times during the search in the garden did he tell Stephen in worried tones of his firm conviction that there was a great deal more in this affair than had appeared on the surface; hanky-panky was the expression he used, and he used it a great number of times. What exactly he had in mind Stephen could not quite make out, for Starcross could know nothing about that mysterious ticket to Brighton; but it seemed as if the theory of abduction was only one of several possibilities, all unpleasant, which Starcross was fearing. Once, indeed, he had gone so far as to suggest that the police should be rung up and asked to keep a look-out for Cicely at the neighbouring railway stations, but before Stephen's blank amazement he admitted that perhaps this was stretching matters a little too far.

Stephen suspected that he was made the recipient of these confidences because nobody else would listen to them (indeed Starcross had gone so far as to remark candidly that he and Miss Mainwaring were the only two who seemed to have a grain of sense between them), and he did his best to receive them politely; but the idea of somebody being abducted (for that, after all, was what it appeared chiefly to amount to) from a drawing-room full of people under cover of a fatuous experiment in witchcraft seemed too ludicrous to merit serious consideration.

However, although his private knowledge was already helping him to form a theory of his own, Stephen had been sufficiently impressed to have a further look round the then empty drawing-room (Annette having apparently abandoned all hope of bridge and retired to bed in despair) on coming in from the garden with Pauline half an hour or so later; though what he expected to find by that time he would have been hard put to it to say—certainly not Cicely's lifeless corpse concealed in some hiding-place where nobody had thought before of looking.

Pauline and he had pottered round together for some minutes, look-ing under chairs and couches which had been carefully looked under before, peering into the dark recesses of the chimney and trying the door of the cupboard, now re-locked and lacking its key; but nothing in the way of a clue, however small, had been brought to light.

There had been one rather eerie moment, Stephen smiled to remember, when Pauline had stated positively that she had heard something moving in the room—a kind of bump or muffled thud; but though they had listened in dead silence for at least a minute, the sound, whatever it had been, was not repeated, nor was Pauline able to say even from what direction it had appeared to come. They had switched out the lights, made their way into the hall, and there said good night to one another.

And those few minutes had really been the only opportunity he had had of discussing the matter or anything else with Pauline. It had been impossible in the circumstances for them to wander away alone together and have the heart-to-heart talk for which he, at any rate, was longing. Interruptions from the others were constant, and besides, the business on hand was too obtrusive to allow much room for more private affairs, and Pauline had seemed extraordinarily keen upon finding Cicely.

Stephen could not help feeling now either that she was a good deal more impressed than she would admit by the explorer's pessimistic views or else that she had had some theory of her own which she was extremely anxious not to prove, but to disprove. Stephen was quite sure as he looked back on what had happened that Pauline was definitely worried about something. He would ask her about it on their walk tomorrow.

Their walk!

Stephen's heart jumped. How extraordinarily sporting she had been that evening! Nobody could have made a fuller and more honourable apology for what she had done, and ever since she had gone quite out of her way to prove both to him and everybody else that they were firm friends—though that, Stephen recognized ruefully, was all they could ever be to each other. But Sir Julius hadn't liked even that. He had looked at Stephen once or twice as if he would like to eat him.

Stephen smiled into the darkness. There might be trouble from that quarter before long, and Stephen was in a mood rather to welcome trouble. In the meantime he had the memory of the warm hand-clasp Pauline had given him when they parted.

He turned on to his back and gave himself up to the memory of it. Pauline had smiled at him in the old way and held out her hand with that air of frank camaraderie which had always seemed to be her own particular hallmark; he had taken it, and then she had—

A sharp, shrill noise suddenly cut across the thread of his thoughts. It was a woman's hoarse scream, and it seemed to come from the direction of the drawing-room. A moment later it was followed by another.

Stephen jumped out of bed and huddled on his dressing-gown. The butler's pantry in which he slept was situated across a little passage which ran along the side of the dining-room remote from the hall and led into the conservatory that separated the billiard-room from the dining-room and the staircase. The quickest way into the drawing-room, which lay on the farther side of the hall, was through the service door into the dining-room, round the screen of old Spanish leather which masked it (and which Stephen blundered into and all but upset in his flurry), through the dining-room and across the hall.

This course Stephen took. He took it rapidly, but he was not the first to reach the drawing-room. The lights were on when he hurried in at the door, and Henry Kentisbeare was already staring out of the open French windows, clad in silk pyjamas and a magnificent crimson dressing-gown.

'I heard screams,' Stephen said abruptly.

'Marvellous!' commented Mr Kentisbeare. 'So did I. That, in fact, is why I came down. Not, as you might have imagined, to shoot glow-worms.'

Stephen flushed with annoyance. He had already taken a dislike to this immaculate, languid, ironical young man. Now he experienced a feeling of definite hostility.

'Well, what about it?' he asked shortly.

'What, indeed?' said Mr Kentisbeare dreamily, staring out through the French windows.

Stephen stifled an intense desire to lay violent hands on him. 'Did you open those windows?'

'I did not. That is what makes it all so curious. Ha! Our exploring friend, still on the job!'

Starcross had come into view and was entering from the garden. He was still fully dressed.

'Did you two men hear a scream a couple of minutes ago?' he asked in brisk, business-like tones.

Mr Kentisbeare rolled his eyes up to the ceiling. 'Oh, no,' he murmured. 'It was the nightingales.'

'Yes,' Stephen said curtly. 'Two screams, in fact. Were you in here, sir?'

'No, unfortunately not. And, for heaven's sake, don't call me "sir" when we're alone. I told you I thought there was some hanky-panky going on, and, by Jove, I was right. I always act on my instincts, so I decided to spend the rest of the night prowling round the house and grounds, just to see if anything happened. By a piece of infernal bad luck, I was right on the other side when I heard those screams.'

'And this is the first time you got here?'

'Exactly.'

'Then who opened these windows?'

Henry Kentisbeare waved an airy hand. 'It's no good looking at me. I didn't. I should say that—'

'Hullo, hullo!' remarked a voice from the door. 'What's all the excitement about?' Freddie strolled towards them, wearing a dressing-gown which positively outdid Henry's.

'You heard those screams, too, then, Freddie?' asked Stephen.

'Yes, and—I say, what a ghastly smell!'

Stephen started. So absorbed had he been in the problem of those open windows that he had never noticed the sickly odour which pervaded the room.

'Chloroform!' he exclaimed.

'By 'Jove, yes!' said Starcross, sniffing. 'Unmistakably. And surely it's stronger than it was before?'

'A jolly sight,' Freddie agreed, poking about the room. 'Hullo, who upset the music-stool? And there's a chair upside-down, too. What on earth's been happening in here?' He pottered busily round, lifting the lid of the grand piano as if hopeful of finding some explanation entangled among the works, moving furniture and peering into the empty cupboard.

'Doesn't it occur to you, by the way,' observed Henry, 'that the smell of chloroform is probably just the same as before, but strikes us as stronger because we've just come in?'

'No, it doesn't,' said Starcross abruptly. 'The room's been aired since then, and the smell ought to have gone entirely.'

'I can't understand about this furniture,' Freddie remarked, looking about him in bewilderment. 'Somebody seems to have been having a free fight in here.'

'You're right, Freddie,' Starcross assented. 'And while we're standing talking, goodness knows what may be happening elsewhere. Look here, you men, you'd better understand once and for all that there is something fishy going on, and we'd better be pretty smart on the track of it. If those windows are open, somebody must obviously have gone out through them. Come along, all of you, and search the grounds. Quick!'

Henry rolled his eyes despairingly, but did not demur. All four of them hurried out into the open. Stephen's last vision, as he disappeared into the darkness, was of Henry Kentisbeare delicately picking his way across the terrace, the skirts of his dressing-gown held on high with both hands.

For half an hour Stephen plunged aimlessly across flower-beds and into rose-bushes. He knew nothing of the grounds, and even if he had it could hardly have been expected that he would find anything. Returning disconsolately to the house, he found Pauline alone in the drawing-room, in a loose wrapper and bedroom slippers.

'Pauline!' he exclaimed in surprise.

'Oh, thank goodness you've come back first, Stephen. What has been happening? I heard people rushing about, so I slipped down. I got here just in time to see you four disappearing through the French windows, but I didn't like to obtrude just then because'—she glanced down at her wrapper and her bare feet in the fluffy little slippers and coloured faintly—'well, because!'

Stephen told her in a few words what had occurred, and her expression grew graver. 'Come in the next room, Stephen,' she said. 'We can't talk here. The others will be back at any minute. This is serious.'

She led the way into Lady Susan's morning-room, and Stephen followed. It was so delightfully like Pauline not to worry about empty conventions when something really important was at stake. She was just natural, Stephen thought, and that is such a very rare thing in these days.

'Well, Pauline?' he said as he closed the door behind them and switched on the light.

Pauline busied herself with pulling the heavy curtains over the windows. 'We don't want to advertise our presence here to all the world, after all,' she smiled.

'It's awfully sporting of you,' Stephen said warmly.

'Not a bit. I shouldn't be here if the occasion wasn't important, but I must tell you what's in my mind, and I probably shan't get a chance tomorrow morning.' She sat down on the arm of a chair and looked at him earnestly. 'Stephen, tell me—what did you make of that business this evening?'

Stephen's hand strayed up towards his unsmoothable hair, a sure sign that he found the question a difficult one. 'Well, I don't know,' he said slowly. 'At first, of course, I thought that she was pulling our legs like everybody else. But now—! What do you think about it, anyhow?'

'Oh, I thought the same as you. I know Cicely pretty well, and she's just the sort of person to take advantage of an opportunity like that for playing a practical joke. She's very quick, you know, and full of fun. I like her awfully. But I shouldn't say she's got an awful lot of ballast, so to speak. I mean, she might hide herself on the spur of the moment, but I'm quite sure she wouldn't keep it up all this time.' She paused and reflected for a moment. 'Quite sure!' she added.

'But look here, Pauline,' Stephen said suddenly, 'how do we know she is keeping it up all this time? She's probably in bed and laughing in her sleep about us by now.'

Pauline shook her head. 'No, I peeped into her room before I came down. It's only two doors away from mine. The bed was empty.'

'The deuce!' said Stephen blankly.

'Stephen,' Pauline continued with energy, 'I'm convinced that Mr Starcross is right after all. There is something peculiar going on. The smell of chloroform and that scream weren't blinds at all. They were the real thing!'

'But how could they have been?' Stephen protested, clinging desperately to logic. 'You don't mean to say that you think Cicely was actually chloroformed in that room under our very noses and forcibly carried off somewhere, do you? There wasn't even any noise of a struggle. How could she have been?'

'I don't know,' Pauline replied helplessly. 'All I know is that something like that must have happened. I feel it in every bone. And those two screams just now and the open French windows! Surely they proved it, Stephen?'

'You don't think,' Stephen said slowly, 'that Miss Vernon is keeping it up, do you? If she wanted to, you see, she could easily have gone along to the drawing-room after we'd all gone to bed, screamed twice and run out into the garden, couldn't she? Really, Pauline, I'm half-inclined to think that's what must have happened. In fact, it's the one explanation I can see. Don't you think you've been underrating her sense of humour, and she might have done that?'

'No, I don't, Stephen!' Pauline retorted with decision. 'I don't think anything of the kind. I'm quite convinced that Cicely's in danger of some kind, and it's up to us to get her out of it.'

Stephen stared at her in perplexity. 'But what can we do? We've searched the grounds, but that wasn't any use. What can we do?'

'We ought to do something.' Pauline said restlessly. 'I'm sure we ought. Oh, dear, how mysterious it all is! She couldn't have been hidden in that room, Stephen. We went over it with a toothcomb.'

'Look here, Pauline,' Stephen said abruptly. 'You've got something up your sleeve, haven't you?'

'What do you mean, Stephen?'

'Well, it's rather difficult to explain, but I can't help feeling that you've got some sort of a theory which you're hoping very hard isn't the right one—some idea that you're trying rather desperately to persuade yourself can't be true. Am I right?'

'Yes,' Pauline said slowly. She swung a small slippered foot and looked at him with perplexed eyes. 'It's really too absurd, knowing Cicely as I do; but Mr Starcross put it into my head when he said something about ringing up the police, and I simply can't get it out—although I'm convinced there's nothing in it. Cicely, of all people! It's so absurd that I absolutely refuse to put it into words; but perhaps you can see what I mean?'

'I think I do,' Stephen said thoughtfully. 'And in that connection there's something I ought to tell you, Pauline. It may mean nothing at all, but on the other hand, it may mean quite a lot.' He recounted the story of the ticket to Brighton and Cicely's remarkable agitation.

'Oh, dear!' Pauline said, with a helpless little laugh. 'That seems to make it more hopelessly complicated still. Of course you're thinking that she's gone of her own free will—not for a joke, but for some mysterious purpose of her own?'

'Something like that,' Stephen admitted.

Pauline meditated. 'It's possible, but—oh, there are so many things that might have happened! What do you think we ought to do about it?'

'Well, really, Pauline, I don't see what we can do tonight. It's past two o'clock, you know, and you're missing all your beauty sleep. It's perfectly topping to talk to you like this, but I really think you ought to be getting back to bed, old girl.'

'I suppose I ought to,' Pauline agreed reluctantly. 'But—' She broke off suddenly, looking at Stephen's dressing-gown. 'Stephen! Come here this minute!'

'What's the matter?' asked Stephen, hastening to obey this imperious command.

Pauline caught at the hem of his dressing-gown. 'You hopeless man! You're absolutely sopping! What on earth do you mean by staying here talking when you're wringing wet through?' She jumped to her feet and felt his arm. 'Even your sleeves. Run along and change this minute.'

'What is the meaning of this?' demanded an angry voice behind them.

They turned about in haste. Sir Julius Hammerstein, the very last person Stephen wanted to see at that moment, had come through the open doorway.

'If there is any meaning in it at all, Sir Julius,' Stephen began stiffly, 'it is not—'

'Don't be absurd, please, Julius,' Pauline interrupted him in cold tones.

Sir Julius's fleshy face took in a more purple tinge. 'Absurd, indeed?' he said harshly. 'I find you and this—this fellow, whom I understand is a footman here, shut up alone together at two o'clock in the morning, both of you in your—'

'That will do, Julius,' Pauline cut in icily. 'I know you haven't the instincts of your title, but I did hope you had learnt its manners. I'll speak to you in the morning, when I hope you will have come to your senses.' She turned to Stephen and held out her hand. 'Good night, Stephen,' she smiled. 'Think over what I've been saying. And don't forget out walk tomorrow!'

'Rather not!' Stephen smiled back.

Pauline swept past Sir Julius into the hall. He waited, barring the doorway, until she was out of earshot; then he turned back to Stephen.

'And my advice to you, young man,' he said malevolently, 'is to stick to the sphere you've sunk into, and try not to run with the hare and hunt with the hounds. And if I find you shoving your nose into anything that happens to concern me, you'll wish you'd never been born before I've finished with you. Do you get that?' Sir Julius was distressingly vulgar in wrath.

But Stephen was not concerned at the moment with vulgarity. Something very much more interesting was engaging his attention.

'Sir Julius,' he said, 'what are you doing fully dressed at two o'clock in the morning? Why haven't you been to bed?'

For a moment Sir Julius appeared to be deprived of his voice. The next instant it returned with full force, and the uses to which he put it were neither pretty nor refined.

Stephen waited until the storm had subsided. Then he remarked with bland politeness: 'That is the sort of thing one expects from your type, no doubt. So having got it off your chest, perhaps you'll answer my question. Why haven't you been to bed tonight of all nights?'

Sir Julius opened his mouth as if to repeat his remarks. Then he appeared to think better of it. He looked at Stephen narrowly for a moment, turned on his heel and walked away without a word.

It was a very thoughtful young man who made his way back to the butler's pantry and bed a few minutes later.

IX THE TELEPHONE CALL

AFTER four hours' sleep, Stephen was early astir the next morning. His work before breakfast kept him almost too busy to think of the happenings of the previous night, and certainly too busy (or so he pretended with secret delight) to gratify any of Martin's exuberant curiosity. Some rumour as to extraordinary occurrences was already circulating in the servants' hall, and the housemaid was a-twitter with excitement over the fact that Miss Vernon's bed had not been slept in, and Miss Vernon herself was nowhere to be seen. Stephen assimilated this piece of information, and looked at it in the light of Pauline's intuitive conviction of the night before. Undoubtedly things did look distinctly bad.

On presenting himself to help John Starcross with his morning toilet, Stephen was told that 'Good Lord, he didn't want any of that sort of nonsense!' Colonel Uffculme also dismissed him with gruff embarrassment which afforded Stephen no little amusement. The poor Colonel was obviously bewildered by the situation; he recognized Stephen's birthright as a sahib, and yet he was not accustomed to admitting other people's footmen to terms of social equality with himself. He compromised by trying to ignore as much as possible the fact that Stephen existed at all.

Henry Kentisbeare, on the other hand, had no scruples in making use of his services, and Stephen found him more trouble than the other two men would have been together. It seemed to him that Henry was maliciously revenging himself thus for Stephen's most unfootmanlike behaviour over the open French window in the early hours that morning. Stephen's dislike of Henry Kentisbeare looked as if it was to be returned with interest.

As he had expected, he saw nothing of Pauline during the morning and no word from her except a smiling 'Hullo, Steve!' as he passed her in the hall on her way to breakfast.

As he was busy polishing silver in his pantry in the middle of the morning there was a knock at the door. Martin was occupied elsewhere, and imagining that it was one of the underservants with some message for him, Stephen called out a cheerful 'Come in!' To his astonishment, the person who obeyed his summons was Miss Baby Cullompton.

'Good morning, Stephen,' she said with a gracious smile, and immediately pouted. 'Oh, I suppose I oughtn't to have called you that; but you don't mind, do you?'

Stephen did not respond to the pout. He had never found himself attracted by the fluffy little ladies of the Baby Cullompton type, and in any case he did not want her in the pantry.

'My official name is William, madam,' he replied with stiff correctness, wondering why on earth he had been favoured with this call.

'Oh, but this isn't an official visit,' said Miss Cullompton winningly. 'And please don't call me "madam". I want us to be—friends.' The way in which she paused before the last word was miraculous.

59

'Oh, yes,' replied Stephen vaguely, who did not want them to be—friends.

'I felt I simply had to come and tell you how much we all admire you for your courage in taking a post like this,' pursued Miss Cullompton languishingly. 'We think—I think—it is so wonderfully plucky of you.'

'You're very kind,' said Stephen politely, taking up another fork and rubbing it briskly.

Miss Cullompton clasped her hands. 'Stephen,' she said in a tragic voice, 'are you very fond of Pauline Mainwaring?'

'What?' Stephen exclaimed, starting so violently that he dropped the fork.

'Oh, you are! You are!' cried Miss Cullompton in high glee. 'Oh, how wonderfully romantic!'

Stephen stooped with a very red face and retrieved the fork. Aloud, he said nothing, but he was thinking quite a lot.

'Oh, Stephen, do tell me all about it!' Miss Cullompton implored.

'I'm afraid I don't understand what you mean,' Stephen muttered.

'Oh, yes, you do. Now, don't be silly, Stephen. I'm simply dying to help you, you know. What are you going to do about it? Surely you're not going to let her marry that dreadful Sir Julius without raising a finger, are you?'

'I'm afraid, Miss Cullompton,' Stephen said deliberately, 'that I cannot discuss my private affairs with you, still less those of Miss Mainwaring.'

An unpleasant expression made itself apparent in Miss Cullompton's too innocent eyes.

'I shouldn't advise you to take that tone, Stephen,' she said slowly. 'It's hardly wise, you know. People who quarrel with me generally regret it in the end; and I might be very useful to you if we were—friends.'

She paused for a moment, but Stephen did not reply.

'For instance,' she went on slowly, 'I might be able to give you a hint—just a hint, mind—about something very important indeed!'

Stephen made an effort to control his temper and speak with the politeness due from a footman to a guest of the house. 'I must repeat,' he said firmly, 'that I cannot discuss any of my private affairs with you, Miss Cullompton, much though I appreciate the compliment you pay me in wishing to do so. And I should like respectfully to point out that the butler's pantry is hardly the place for a lady such as yourself, and that I might get into very serious trouble if anybody found you here. You will understand, I am sure, madam.'

Miss Cullompton nodded slowly and her eyes were no longer in the least innocent. 'Very well, Stephen,' she said sulkily. 'Yes, I understand. Very well!'

Dear me! Stephen reflected, as the door closed at last behind her. A most unpleasant little person, I'm afraid, and a singularly pushy one into the bargain. Now, what on earth can have been her little game? And what was all that about a very important hint? I wonder! Was I altogether wise in choking her off like that? Oughtn't I to have played her a little first?

Stephen had no time to debate these interesting questions just at the moment, for scarcely had Miss Cullompton disappeared when Martin entered with his soft, stealthy tread.

'Very nice,' he purred, rubbing his hands together and looking at Stephen with his large head on one side. 'Very nice, I'm sure. So the ladies of the house are visiting us in our pantry now, are they? Dear, dear, dear! Now, what could be the reason of that, I wonder, William? What could be the reason of that?'

'Ask me another, Mr Martin,' Stephen replied cheerfully, polishing away with vigour. 'Would you like me to hand a little notice in the door— "No admittance except on business"? I will with pleasure.'

'Very funny, William. Most humorous, I'm sure.'

'Thanks for the compliment,' Stephen replied, concealing his irritation with the man under a cloak of fatuous badinage. 'It's nice to meet with appreciation of one's little efforts.'

Martin shook his head reprovingly, rolling his eyes up to the ceiling. 'And getting into trouble already,' he remarked smoothly. 'As if there wasn't enough trouble in this house already, to be sure, what with unholy carryings-on and making lady guests disappear and footmen invited into the drawing-room, I don't know what things are coming to. Indeed, I don't.'

'What do you mean, Mr Martin?' Stephen asked carelessly, disregarding these barbed shafts. 'I haven't been getting into trouble, at any rate.'

'Getting into trouble before we've been in the house twenty-four hours!' Martin amplified, shaking his head paternally. 'Dear, dear, dear! Complaints already from a very important gentleman. Very serious complaints, too; oh, very serious. Compromising a dear little lady's good name, indeed! Oh, most disgraceful!'

'Now, then, stop that, Martin,' Stephen warned, flushing angrily, and quite forgetting the deference due to a butler from a mere footman.

'Such a dear little lady, too,' Martin continued, shaking his head harder than ever. 'Oh, such a—'

Stephen caught him by the shoulder and shook him in spite of his vast bulk. 'Do you want my fist in your oily face?' he said with ill-suppressed wrath. 'If not, I warn you—drop that!'

'Oh, what a terrible temper!' Martin sighed, but there was a distinct look of alarm on his large yellow face.

The sound of the telephone intervened to save the situation and Stephen hurried out into the hall to answer it, vaguely aware as he did so that his anger had almost certainly cost him his situation. Martin would hardly be the person to take that sort of behaviour from his footman without reprisals.

'Hullo!' said a tremulous feminine voice through the telephone. 'Can I speak to Lady Susan, please?'

'What name, please?' asked Stephen.

'Never mind the name. Just tell Lady Susan an—an old friend.'

By a lucky chance Lady Susan was crossing the hall with Millicent that very moment, and Stephen was enabled to deliver the message.

Lady Susan went to the telephone. 'Yes?' she said briskly. 'What old friend is it?'

Stephen saw her listen for the answer and an expression of surprise and incredulity appear in her face.

'Good gracious, my dear!' she exclaimed. 'You gave me quite a shock!' She turned to Stephen, who was on the point of retiring from the scene. 'Bring me a chair, please, William.' In the same breath she added over her shoulder to Millicent: 'It's Cicely!'

'Cicely?' Millicent repeated in amazement. 'Good gracious! But—' She broke off with an ineffective gesture. Her agitation was extreme, and she had gone as white as a sheet. Stephen looked at her in surprise. If Lady Susan had received a shock, Millicent appeared to have received a far greater one. She sat down heavily in the nearest chair, her handkerchief to her lips and her starting eyes glued upon Lady Susan.

'Yes?' the old lady was saying. 'Yes?—What, my dear?—What?— Whatever are you talking about?—But good gracious—! Speak up, I can hardly hear you. But what is this nonsense you're telling me?—Disappeared?—Oh, come, my dear! You can't expect to pull my leg like that. You—? My fault?—My dear, you must haunt Freddie, not me; he instigated the whole thing. Really, I never heard anything like it!—I knew you were fond of a joke, but really—! What's that? You'll—? Cicely, you'll make me cross in a minute—No, don't hang up! Wait a minute. I—'

She began to agitate the receiver. 'Oh, is that you, Exchange? Lady Susan Carey speaking. I was cut off in the middle of a conversation just then. Will you give me the connection again, please?' She waited a moment. 'What? You can't trace the call? But I tell you I was in the middle of a conversation, girl! But—oh, drat the woman!' She hung up the receiver and turned to Millicent with a smile of blended amusement and irritation. 'Sorry you've been trrrroubled!' she mimicked.

'But, Aunt Susan!' articulated Millicent, who had never removed her eyes from the old lady's face. 'Cicely—what did she say?'

'Such a ridiculous rigmarole!' snorted Lady Susan contemptuously. 'Really, I don't know what Cicely Vernon takes me for, but—' Her eye fell on Stephen, who was hovering by the dining-room door, listening with all his ears. 'Are you waiting for anything, William?' she inquired ominously.

'Er—no, my lady,' Stephen stammered. 'I thought perhaps I might be able to—to—'

'Well, I don't want you any more,' Lady Susan interrupted him briskly. 'You can go.'

'Very good, my lady,' said Stephen unhappily, and went. It was a maddeningly tantalizing moment at which to have to take his departure, but evidently Lady Susan did not intend him to know what Cicely had said.

It was in a state of some relief, however, that Stephen returned to his pantry. He was thankful to perceive that Martin was no longer there, so that he would have an opportunity of reflecting over some of the things with which his brain was buzzing. There is nothing to stimulate mental activity like the polishing of silver.

In the first place, then (ran Stephen's thoughts), Cicely Vernon is all right, and Pauline's anxiety on her behalf was without foundation. Whether she had done what she had as a colossal joke, or whether she actually had at one time been in some kind of danger, it was quite clear that that mystery, at any rate, was at an end and Cicely safe. Stephen felt convinced that his explanation of those two screams in the night had been the correct one. As for his natural curiosity, that must wait. Doubtless Pauline would be able to relieve it in any case on that walk of theirs in the afternoon.

Inevitably his thoughts turned to Sir Julius.

What could Pauline have seen in the man? A conviction which had been gathering gradually and unnoticed in his mind sprang suddenly into full consciousness—Pauline would never, never of her own free will have consented to this outrageous engagement: somehow or other, by some underhand trick or outright threat, it had been forced upon her!

Unconsciously Stephen set his jaw. If that indeed were the case, then things were going to hum.

He was glad that he and Sir Julius were now open enemies. There was no need to disguise either his feelings or his intentions.

Enemies! Stephen smiled ruefully. It was true, as Martin had said, that he had not yet been in the place twenty-four hours, and yet in that time he seemed to have made no less than four enemies, of varying degrees of bitterness. Indeed he appeared to have done little else since he arrived but make enemies; the thing was becoming almost a hobby. It never rains but it pours, evidently, he reflected.

Still, things might be worse. Henry Kentisbeare counted very little either way, and Baby Cullompton still less; the enmity of Sir Julius he welcomed. But Martin certainly was unfortunate. Martin could make life very difficult if he chose to do so. And it was practically certain that he would choose to do so. Yes, it was distinctly unfortunate that Martin should be such an unpleasant person, and still more unfortunate that Stephen should have lost his temper so far as to offer to introduce his fist to the butler's oily yellow face!

At this point Stephen laughed aloud. It had suddenly occurred to him that to punch Martin's face must inevitably feel like punching a pat of butter; and a pat of butter must be such a very difficult thing to punch.

He redoubled his polishing efforts. It was as sure as fate that Martin would return as soon as he could, his resentment tactfully subordinated for the time being to his curiosity. Martin would never get him dismissed, he felt sure, till he had done his very utmost to pump all possible information out of him. And Stephen did not want to be pumped in the least.

He was embarking on the last half-dozen tablespoons when there was a knock at the door.

'Come in!' he called out, not without apprehension this time, but with relief at the thought that Martin, at any rate, did not knock.

A black, close-cropped head was thrust round the door and Stephen recognized the friendly grin of Johnson, Sir Julius Hammerstein's wiry little Cockney chauffeur, who had first given him the news of Pauline's engagement to the financier. 'Busy, chum?' asked the little man, with a glance at Stephen's polishing rag and powder.

'No, rather not,' Stephen replied cheerfully. 'Come in and take a chair.'

The chauffeur did so, a neat little figure in his dark-green livery and black leggings. 'I was getting a bit lonesome out in the garage,' he explained, 'and seeing as 'ow I'd nothing to do for the time being, like, I thought I'd come along an' see if there was anybody to have a bit of a chat with.'

'That's right,' Stephen said heartily. 'Come in here whenever you like, and if Martin doesn't like it, he can lump it.'

Johnson grinned appreciatively. 'I never do get on with butlers some'ow,' he confided. 'Bit too much of the dignified stunt about 'em for my liking. I'll give you an 'and with that silver, if you like, chum.'

'Oh, that's all right,' said Stephen, who had taken a liking to the little man, in spite of the unfortunate circumstances of their first meeting. 'I've nearly finished, as a matter of fact.'

They chatted on indifferent subjects while Stephen finished off the tablespoons.

He straightened himself up with a sigh of relief and sat down for a moment on the edge of the table. 'Johnson,' he said suddenly, on the inspiration of the moment, 'what sort of a fellow is that Sir Julius of yours?'

The chauffeur winked. 'There's lot of people asked me that question, mate, ladies as well as gents, and I tell 'em all the same thing—I ain't got no fault to find with 'im.'

'But other people have, eh?' Stephen asked quickly.

Johnson winked again. 'Well, what do you think? A chap can't do what he's done without comin' up against people, can he?'

'Is he straight?'

'Well,' said Johnson slowly, 'I'll tell you something, chum, which I wouldn't tell many people: if you got your savin's tucked up in any of his companies, you sell 'em out quick as you know how and buy war-bonds—see?'

'Ah!' Stephen breathed. Without a word, he took a decanter and glasses from a cupboard behind him, poured out a stiff drink and handed it to the chauffeur, and splashed a little soda into his own glass. 'Here's how!' he said hospitably.

Johnson smacked his lips appreciatively. 'That's good stuff! And look here, chum, I'll tell you something more, seein' as you're a good sport and can keep your mouth shut. But this mustn't go any further, mind!'

'Of course not.'

'Well, Sir Blinkin' Julius won't be my employer much longer, an' that's a fact. I've been lookin' out for another berth, an' I start there the week after next.'

Stephen leant forward eagerly. 'And why are you leaving him?'

Johnson wiped his mouth with the back of his hand. 'We showvures get in the way of hearing things,' he said cryptically. 'Mind you,' he continued the next moment, 'I'm not saying whether it's true or not, though I've got me own opinion. I know this won't go any further, chum, but it's my idea that if Sir Julius can't lay 'is 'ands on a precious lot o' cash during the next week or two, 'e's going to find 'isself in quod! You mark my words!'

X A PAWN IN THE GAME

AT three o'clock Stephen met Pauline by appointment in the hall and they set out together. Sir Julius was not in sight, but Stephen had an uncanny feeling that from some hidden place his eyes were upon them; though this may only have been guilty conscience.

Pauline was wearing a brown coat and skirt which suited her tall, slim figure to perfection, and a little brown felt hat with a gay feather. Stephen, in his best remaining suit, with his flunkey's coat and stockings for the moment forgotten, felt himself a man again.

'Stephen,' Pauline said impulsively as soon as they were a hundred yards from the house and entering the park which separated it from the main road, 'Stephen, I've been longing for this moment.'

'So have I, Pauline,' said Stephen in heart-felt tones.

Pauline ignored the obvious meaning in his words. 'Because of what I was saying to you last night,' she continued in a worried voice. 'I was right, Stephen, I'm convinced if it.'

'About Cicely being in danger?' Stephen said in surprise. 'But she's all right, you know. She rang Lady Susan up this morning.'

'Exactly!' Pauline said seriously. 'And that's just what I've been longing to talk to you about—the extraordinary story she told Lady Susan.'

'Lady Susan told you what she said, then?' Stephen asked.

'Yes, she did. She told me and Millicent, under pledges of the most fearful secrecy.'

'Then—then do you think you ought to tell me, in that case?' Stephen hesitated.

A faint colour showed in Pauline's soft cheeks. 'I happen to know that she won't mind you knowing,' she replied serenely. She did not think it necessary to add that the old lady had informed her that she was at liberty to tell one person and one only, without stipulating who that person should be. There was very little that escaped Lady Susan's sharp old eyes, in spite of their sixty-seven years.

'Oh!' said Stephen, remembering vividly his peremptory dismissal from the hall that morning. 'Good! Well, what was it? I was in the hall at the time, but I couldn't make very much out from what Lady Susan said.'

'I'm not surprised in the circumstances. Well, according to Cicely—shall we go straight on or turn up to the left here through the wood? The wood looks nice and shady, doesn't it?—according to Cicely, she really did disappear last night, through the spell!'

'What?' Stephen exclaimed.

Pauline laughed uneasily. 'It does sound rather curious, doesn't it? But that's what she said. She was de-materialized or something extraordinary, by that spell you read over her, and has been translated to some other sphere, or some nonsense like that. She is very unhappy, can't get back, blames Lady Susan for the whole thing, and threatens all sorts of extraordinary penalties if Lady Susan doesn't hold another séance to materialize her back again—and that's the whole thing in a nutshell!'

'Jumping Jupiter!' commented the astonished Stephen.

'That, and more,' Pauline agreed. 'Well, what do you make of that interesting story, Stephen?'

'What can one make of it? I never heard such balderdash in my life.'

'I think we might take that for granted,' Pauline said dryly. 'I wasn't suggesting that the story itself deserved any serious consideration.'

'Sorry!' said Stephen humbly.

Pauline laughed, and touched his arm for an instant with her gloved hand. 'Now I'm getting horrid again! But really, Stephen, I'm so worried over the whole business. And nobody else seems to be in the least, except Millicent. She's going about with a face like a Scotch Sunday, though I don't think there's any need to do that. Lady Susan, on the other hand, takes it as a joke, though in rather bad taste; and whatever it may be, I'm quite sure it isn't that. Honestly, Stephen, I'm frightened!'

Stephen's reply was a practical one.

They were in the shade of the wood by this time, and he took Pauline's arm and tucked it through his own. He knew he had not the faintest right to do anything of the sort, he knew it was an unfair thing to do, he knew it was an unsporting advantage to take. And he did it.

Pauline did not appear to object.

'I think you're right, Pauline,' he said. 'There is something funny going on. And there's an object in this extraordinary message, if we can only make out what it is. By Jove, I wonder! Do you think it was Miss Vernon at the telephone?'

'Oh, yes; there's not much doubt about that. Lady Susan said she recognized her voice at once, though it was very faint.'

'Oh! Well, failing that, have you any theory about it?'

Pauline shook her head helplessly. 'None! All I can make of it is that, for some obscure reason, they want another séance to be held.'

'Why "they"?' Stephen asked quickly. 'Who are "they"?'

'The people who carried Cicely off, of course.'

'Then you haven't any doubt that she was carried off?'

'You mean, whether she's acting of her own free will? No, I've thought that over and I'm quite sure she isn't.'

'Humph!' Stephen ruminated for a moment. 'You know, it seems almost incredible to me that she could have been carried off. I've been thinking things over too, and there's one thing I think someone ought to do at once, and that's to find out a little information about the people with whom Miss Vernon was going yachting, and especially about the yachting trip itself.'

'Whatever for?' Pauline asked in surprise.

'I just want to test an idea. It's so vague that it's hardly worth mentioning; but I wish you'd get hold of the people's name and address for me. Will you?'

'Of course I will, if you really want it; but—'

Stephen hastened to change the subject. 'By the way, what did you make of that scarf she was wearing, Pauline?'

'Being up on the picture? Yes, that's the only real, tangible clue, isn't it? Well, all I can say is that I don't know what to make of it! How could Cicely's scarf have travelled between her and the top of that picture, only a few feet below the ceiling? Well, it can only have been thrown up there, or dropped down; so obviously it must have been thrown. But why, I certainly can't say.'

'No,' Stephen agreed. 'There doesn't seem to me much help there.'

They walked on for a few minutes in silence. Stephen retained his hold of Pauline's arm, and could only infer that Pauline herself must have forgotten all about it, for she made no attempt to withdraw it.

'Pauline,' Stephen said suddenly, 'supposing—just supposing—that Cicely was carried off by your mysterious "them", do you think anybody in the house is a party to it? Any of the guests, for instance?'

Pauline turned an anxious face towards him. 'Oh, Stephen, that's just what's worrying me so. You see—how could she have been carried off without the connivance of some person in that room?'

Stephen nodded slowly. 'Yes, I see that. But—well, who?'

'Who, indeed?' Pauline sighed.

'And what could be the object? You think that Cicely was carried off for—well, for her own sake, so to speak?'

'Possibly,' Pauline said doubtfully. 'But somehow I don't think that. I feel sure that there is something very much bigger behind it all, and that Cicely is only a pawn in some rather important game.'

Stephen whistled. 'I say, that's a bit on the fanciful side, isn't it, Pauline?'

'I suppose it is,' Pauline admitted with a little smile. 'But it's what I feel, all the same. And then there was that extraordinary voice that said "Yes!" Really, it nearly terrified me to death at the moment. What on earth do you make of that, Stephen?'

'I've been thinking about that,' Stephen agreed. 'It seemed to me, you know, that it must have come through a megaphone. It was so very loud. Besides, a megaphone would disguise the speaker's voice.'

Pauline looked thoughtful. 'You think the speaker—well, wanted to disguise his voice?'

'I'm quite sure he did.'

'But how could it possibly have been anybody in the room?' Pauline objected, referring rather to the implication in Stephen's words than to what he actually said.

'Goodness knows!' said Stephen helplessly. 'But it must have been the same person who was doing those raps and everything.'

'Do you think it was Henry or Baby? They were the only ones we know who moved.'

'It might have been. Again, goodness knows!'

Pauline sighed. 'I should like to get to the bottom of it. Well—Stephen!'

'Yes?'

'Let's join forces! Let's join forces and see what we can find out between us. You're the only man I can trust, and—' She checked herself, but the words were out. 'You're the only man I know well enough,' she amended hastily, 'and I mean to look into things myself, but a girl can't do much alone. Will you help me?'

'I will indeed,' Stephen said fervently. 'You bet I will!'

'Well, I've got an idea. Something very strange happened in that room last night after we'd all gone to bed. It's just possible that something else might happen tonight. What do you say to going down there when everybody's in bed and keeping a watch for a little while, in hiding?'

'That's a jolly good idea,' Stephen agreed with enthusiasm. 'Of course I will.' He would have kept watch for three weeks on the North Pole, if Pauline had suggested any necessity for it.

'No, not alone, silly!' Pauline laughed. 'Both of us.'

'Oh!' said Stephen, his thoughts flying to the entry of Sir Julius upon their conversation in the early hours of that morning. 'Yes, rather. Of course. If you think it advisable, from—from your own point of view, Pauline,' he added lamely.

'And why shouldn't it be?' Pauline asked haughtily.

'Well,' said Stephen, still more lamely, 'I don't want you—that is—'

Pauline cut him short with a laugh. 'I apologize again, Stephen. I am getting a pig, aren't I? That was a thoroughly horrid thing to say, and silly as well. Of course I know what you mean. About Julius. Well, I don't think you need worry about that.'

'You—spoke to him this morning?' Stephen ventured.

'I did, Stephen!' Pauline said, with a grimness in her young voice which reminded Stephen irresistibly of Lady Susan. 'I don't think we need worry about that point of view.'

'That's good,' said Stephen mechanically. He was wondering whether to divulge to Pauline the information he had received that morning from Johnson. It is a ticklish thing to tell a girl that her fiancé, if he is not extremely careful, may possibly be finding himself soon in prison. It is still more ticklish when one happens to be in love with the girl oneself.

Before he could decide, Pauline had gently disengaged her arm from his and was pointing to a log which lay a little back from the path, just visible from the angle at which they were passing amid a dense mass of tall undergrowth. 'Let's sit down for a few minutes, Stephen,' she said. 'We've come about a mile, and we ought to be turning back soon. Besides, I want to ask you all sorts of questions about yourself, and a log seems rather a nice thing to do it on.'

Nothing loth, Stephen followed her and made a path for her to reach the log from the back, where the undergrowth was a little less thick. They sat down in the green twilight. Pauline pulled off her gloves and laid them on the log by her side. Then she turned towards Stephen with an abrupt movement.

'Now, then,' she said, 'tell me all about yourself, Stephen, that I don't know. Every little bit!'

Now, it had been Stephen's intention to tell his story to nobody on this earth. He was not in the least proud of it, and the way in which he had lived like a prince on the capital he had inherited, instead of investing it and eking out the frugal proceeds with good, honest work, seemed no longer the fine gesture it had appeared at first, but a thing of quite incredible stupidity. He had given the outline to Freddie because—well, because it didn't seem to matter then whether one told Freddie or not; but he had made up his mind with invincible determination that nothing would ever induce him to say one word of it to Pauline. It would seem too much like a cheap appeal for sympathy. Yes, Stephen's determination on this point had been of rigid steel. Yet in less than ten minutes, with the aid of a stream of harassing questions, a steady flow of irresistible coaxing, a warm tide of sympathy and oceans of native intuition, Pauline was in triumphant possession of the whole story and the steel of Stephen's resolve lay ignominiously snapped.

'I see,' Pauline said thoughtfully, when she had gleaned the last straw of the story. 'I see.'

'What do you see?' Stephen asked, with an attempt at lightness. He was feeling decidedly embarrassed by the recital which had been forced from him, and felt the situation to be more than a little strained.

Pauline turned her head away and gazed in the opposite direction. 'Something that I—didn't see before,' she said in a low voice.

'And what's that?' Stephen asked fatuously. 'What silly sort of idiot I am?'

Pauline shook her averted head speechlessly. A little quiver shook her, and she fumbled hurriedly in her bag to extract a handkerchief. With a sudden stab Stephen realized that she was crying.

His first impulse was to take her in his arms. Instinctively he moved to do so, but as if divining his intention, Pauline jumped suddenly to her feet and took a few hasty steps towards the path. Stephen realized that she was trying to conceal her tears from him and, taking refuge as the kindest thing in pretence of ignorance, stared gloomily before him in silence. A moment or two later Pauline surreptitiously wiped her eyes and returned her handkerchief to her bag. The whole incident had not lasted more than a minute.

'Well, I suppose we ought to be thinking about getting back,' she said with forced cheerfulness, turning round to him again.

'I suppose so,' Stephen assented miserably.

Pauline also seemed reluctant to move. She hesitated a moment and then took a step or two towards the log. At the same instant the sound of voices reached Stephen's ears, and he caught her hand and drew her quickly back. Stephen had no wish that anyone but himself should see any possible tell-tale marks on Pauline's face. 'Let's wait till these people have gone by,' he said, and she nodded silently as she resumed her seat.

A moment later Freddie and Baby Cullompton strolled leisurely into sight along the path.

Freddie had a loud voice and he was making no effort to subdue it. 'Oh, I don't think you need worry about him,' Stephen could hear him saying. 'He's all right.'

Baby Cullompton said something inaudible.

'Oh, no,' Freddie reassured her. 'He's perfectly harmless. I told you we were at school together.'

Stephen stiffened. They were talking about him. Disregarding the old adage, he strained his ears.

The two were almost abreast of them now, and Miss Cullompton's reply was perfectly audible. 'Well, I think he's dangerous,' she said. 'Really I do, Freddie. I was frightened to death.'

'Poor little girl!' Freddie replied fatuously. 'No wonder, too. Well, it's all right now, isn't it?' He slipped an arm round her waist and drew her closer to him.

'Oh, Freddie, you oughtn't to do that, you know!' sighed Miss Cullompton, and laid her head on his shoulder.

They passed slowly out of sight.

Exchanging the slightly superior smiles of those who have witnessed the love-making of others, Stephen and Pauline sought the path. But there was a constraint upon them. Their conversation as they walked back began by being artificial, became spasmodic and finally lapsed altogether. Both were busy with their thoughts, and in Stephen's, at any rate, the mystery of Cicely's disappearance was not just then playing a leading part.

Did Pauline know about Sir Julius's impending financial troubles? Was the information which Johnson had given him so secret that even the magnate's own fiancée had no inkling of it? That was the question which was hammering on Stephen's brain during the return journey. And if she did not, ought he to let fall a warning hint?

Stephen had long ago discarded the fleeting suspicion that Pauline might be doing anything so crude as to marry Sir Julius for his money, inevitable though this conclusion seemed to be to the rest of the world. Having pondered and pondered the thing again, he was now utterly convinced that there was far more behind this impossible engagement than anyone but the two principals themselves could conceive.

Unquestionably the man must have some hold over her, for, otherwise, would she not without hesitation have broken her engagement to him after the discourteous—more, downright vulgarly rude way in which he had addressed her in the small hours of that same morning? It was impossible to imagine Pauline submitting tamely to that sort of thing without some very strong reason.

Should he warn her, then? It was a ticklish question. Pauline was so infernally proud. She might well resent the criticism of her fiancé that would of necessity be implied. Was there no way of finding out things for himself—of testing the truth of Johnson's information and getting a peep at the hidden reasons which lay behind the engagement?

Suddenly Stephen's heart gave a jump. Pauline's father! He was a dear and kindly, if somewhat feckless old man, and since the death of his wife Pauline had been the apple of his eye. True, Stephen did not know him very well, but well enough when such tremendous issues were at stake. Why not beg a day off at the earliest possible opportunity, go up to London and lay the whole thing before the old man? There and then Stephen registered his decision, and felt absurdly comforted by it.

As they crossed the gravelled sweep in front of the house, Stephen caught sight of Bridger a few yards away, bending over a flower-bed.

'Half a minute, Pauline,' he said. 'That's my man—or was till yesterday. He got wind that I'd lifted a job here, and managed to get himself installed as under-gardener. He's a great fellow. I must just have one word with him—won't keep you a minute.'

He ran across and thumped the other on the shoulder. 'Hullo, Bridger! Well, how goes it?'

Bridger straightened up with a grin. 'Afternoon, sir. Nicely, thank you. You all right, too, sir?'

'Oh, fine! A better footman you've never seen in your life, Bridger, believe me. This is my afternoon off.'

There was a pluck at his sleeve. 'Won't you introduce me, Stephen?' said the voice of Pauline.

Stephen flushed with pleasure. The action was as like Pauline as that of yesterday had been unlike her.

'Rather!' he said enthusiastically. 'Bridger, this is Miss Mainwaring, who used to be a friend of mine in the old days and isn't cutting me now.'

Bridger, who had seen the lady's photograph on his master's mantelpiece a hundred times and knew perfectly well what he had thought about her, grinned sheepishly.

Pauline held out her hand. 'I am so pleased,' she said, with her peculiarly sweet smile. 'Stephen has told me all about you. I think you're simply splendid—both of you!'

The sheepishness of Bridger's grin increased perceptibly, to Stephen's secret delight; Stephen had hardly ever seen Bridger grin at all, certainly he had never before seen him looking sheepish. He eyed the slim, outstretched hand as if it were some peculiarly deadly species of stinging-nettle. Then he wiped his own on his trousers, grasped the other gingerly between his finger and thumb, and gave it one hearty shake.

'Pleased to meet you, miss,' he mumbled, and was her abject slave from that moment.

'Pauline,' said Stephen in heart-felt tones, as they crossed the gravelled sweep again a moment later, 'Pauline, you're a b-r-i-c-k—brick!'

'Don't, Stephen!' Pauline exclaimed quite sharply. 'I'm not. I'm a horrid pig. It's little enough that I can do to make up for it, too. Oh, if you only knew me as I really am!'

'I think I do, Pauline,' Stephen said in a low voice as they mounted the steps. 'At any rate, better than you do.'

The front door was open, and they passed through into the hall. As they did so, Millicent popped out of the morning-room like a haggard jack-in-the-box.

'Oh, it's you, Pauline!' she exclaimed, disregarding Stephen. 'Oh, dear, I am so glad you've come back. The most dreadful thing's happened since you went out!' The poor lady seemed quite distraught. Her eyes bulged, and she breathed as if she had been running a race.

Pauline did not waste time. She caught her by the arm and shook her slightly. 'Pull yourself together, Millicent, at any rate,' she said urgently. 'You'll be hysterical in a minute. What's happened?'

Millicent made a palpable effort to obey. 'We've had a letter from Cicely,' she said jerkily.

'A letter?'

'Yes. Oh, it's dreadful! We were all sitting in the drawing-room, when suddenly down came this piece of paper, fluttering from the ceiling. Just fluttering down! It fell into my lap.' She shuddered uncontrollably. 'We all saw it coming down, and Aunt Susan thought it was something blown in from the window. But it wasn't. It couldn't have been, because—'

'Yes, yes,' Pauline said impatiently. 'But never mind that now. What did the letter say?'

Millicent shuddered again. 'Oh, it's all so dreadfully uncanny. It said that Aunt Susan must see that a séance was held again this evening and that Cicely was brought back again to earth, otherwise something terrible would happen.'

Stephen stifled an insane desire to laugh. At first sight the incident struck him as rather more funny than tragic, but there was no doubt that Miss Carey did not regard it in that light.

'Was the note in Miss Vernon's handwriting?' he asked.

Millicent stared at him as if she were seeing him for the first time. 'Yes, it was. There can be no mistake about that. None at all. Oh, dear, oh, dear!'

'Who read it besides you and Lady Susan?' Pauline asked.

'Nobody else. Of course we don't intend to tell the others, but as Aunt Susan told you about the other thing, I thought—' She broke off, looking vaguely at Stephen.

'Oh, he's all right,' Pauline said. 'I told him about the telephone message. Now tell me this, Millicent, who was in the drawing-room when this happened?'

'Everybody! It was just after lunch, while we were having coffee. Only a minute or two after you'd gone upstairs. I meant to catch you when you came down, but I missed you. I've been waiting ever since for you to come in. Aunt Susan only laughs, you see, and I'm so terribly—' She ceased abruptly, and her hand flew to her mouth; a look of sudden alarm showed in her pale, slightly prominent eyes.

'William,' said a smooth, oily voice, 'I was to tell you that Lady Susan wishes to speak to you in the morning-room the moment you came in.'

Stephen turned round. Martin was regarding him with a barely concealed leer of malevolent triumph.

XI THE COLONEL'S THEORY

L ADY SUSAN appeared quite unperturbed by any recent unconventional events in her household. She sat at her writing-table, a little, spare, fierce figure, and eyed Stephen grimly.

'William,' she said, 'I have had serious reports of you. You have been in my house a bare twenty-four hours, and already I have received no less than three complaints about you. Two of my guests have apparently been compelled to speak to me about you, and your direct superior in the household, Martin, has given me an extremely bad account of you indeed.'

Martin assumed an expression of portentous though complacent gravity and allowed his eyes to roll towards the ceiling; it was clear that he had striven to wean this young man from his evil predispositions, and striven earnestly and long, but, alas, in vain.

'Have you anything to say?' Lady Susan added after an impressive little pause.

Stephen looked at her helplessly. 'I've done my best, my lady,' he said helplessly, 'but—' He hesitated. He could guess the identity of the two guests, while Martin must have given his mistress an account of events so cunningly blended of truth and falsehood that anything he might say in his defence would only make matters worse. He remained silent.

'I'm sorry, William,' Lady Susan went on more kindly. 'I hope you would settle down here and develop into a good servant, but as things are I have no alternative. It is not for me to say whether the complaints are justified or not; the point is that there should never have been grounds for them to be made at all. It is impossible for me to retain you in my employment any longer. Martin, you have a month's wages for William ready there?'

Stephen started. He had expected a severe reprimand, of course, but the idea of dismissal had never occurred to him. He looked at Lady Susan helplessly. It was useless to appeal to her, he knew, but matters could not have turned out with more exasperating awkwardness. Not only would he be deprived of Pauline's company, but they would now be unable to carry out their joint investigation together. The whole thing must be abandoned. It was maddening! And then the dreary round of searching for another situation …

In a daze he watched Martin triumphantly counting out the money on the table in front of him. Martin had a right to his triumph; he had scored with a vengeance. Mechanically he swept up the notes and silver and turned to the door.

'Good-bye, William,' said Lady Susan calmly.

'Good-bye, my lady,' Stephen mumbled as he opened the door.

'Mr Munro!' said Lady Susan silkily.

Stephen paused, his hand on the doorknob. Something in Lady Susan's tone struck him as peculiar. He looked round. She was smiling at him with considerable amusement.

'Yes, Lady Susan?' he said.

'Have you any immediate plans?'

'No, I can't say that I have, Lady Susan.'

Lady Susan's smile broadened. 'How fortunate! I'm having a small house-party here and I was rather in need of another man, to balance my companion, Miss Rivers. Would you care to join us?'

Stephen looked at her for a moment as if he could hardly believe his ears. Then he found her smile involuntarily reflected on his own face and heard his voice saying, apparently of its own volition: 'Lady Susan, you're a sport! Thank you most awfully. I should love to.'

Lady Susan turned to her yellow-faced servitor, now yellower than ever. 'Martin,' she said serenely, 'please get a room ready for Mr Munro, and see that his things are taken down there. You'd better see Miss Millicent about it.'

'Very good, my lady,' said Martin as blandly as ever; but the look with which he favoured Stephen as he passed him was not a loving one.

'What have you been doing to my excellent Martin?' Lady Susan asked, with a twinkle in her eye, as the door closed behind the smooth exterior of her seething butler. 'I'm afraid you've been rubbing him up the wrong way.'

Stephen laughed joyously. The reaction after the abrupt dispersal of all his hopes was correspondingly severe. 'I really can't blame him if he doesn't love me, Lady Susan. I'm afraid I offered to punch his face this morning.'

'Well, I dare say it might have done him a lot of good. Still, I don't think you must make trouble with Martin. He may not be a particularly pleasant companion perhaps, but he's an admirable butler; I've had him nearly seven years now, and never had to complain once of anything in his department.'

'The feud is at an end from this minute,' Stephen smiled. 'But really, Lady Susan, I must thank you for—for asking your late footman to stay on as a guest. It's extraordinarily good of you.'

'Not in the least,' retorted Lady Susan briskly. 'It was a purely selfish motive. I shouldn't have asked you if I hadn't wanted you. Besides, your experiment interested me a good deal. It would never have succeeded, you know.'

'No,' Stephen agreed ruefully. 'I was beginning to recognize that.'

'You'd only have made the front of the house feel awkward and the servants' hall resentful, whether you found any personal acquaintances in either or not. Now, Mr Munro, I know all about your circumstances (you might as well publish them in a daily paper as tell Freddie) and I want you to look on this house as your own until you've found your feet: and no making any more absurd experiments in the meantime, mind.'

'Lady Susan!' Stephen stammered, quite overwhelmed by this kindness. 'I can't possibly—really—'

'Don't be foolish!' Lady Susan interrupted peremptorily. 'It may interest you to learn that you're no stranger to me. I knew your mother quite well when I lived in London, and I've had you many a time on my knee—when you were a little bit smaller. I didn't tell you all this before, because I wanted to see what sort of stuff you were made of. Now I've seen and I'm satisfied.' She clapped her hands suddenly. 'Don't stand there staring at me as if I were a ghost, Stephen! Run along to the drawing-room and have your tea. I'm having a tray sent into me here, so I'm not coming. They'll be interested to hear your news, especially'—she paused, and Stephen could have sworn she winked at him—'especially the excellent Sir Julius Hammerblower, or whatever his horrible name is. Run along!'

Being quite past speech by this time, Stephen ran.

His news, when he reached the drawing-room, was received with acclamation, in some cases almost hilarious. Freddie shouted his congratulations with deafening fervour, Starcross wrung him vigorously by one hand and Pauline by the other, Annette performed a war-dance in honour of Lady Susan, and Colonel Uffculme's grunts of approbation were positively alarming. Henry Kentisbeare, if he displayed no signs of exuberant joy, at least refrained from damping the proceedings in any way, shaking Stephen warmly enough by the hand (when the latter had one to spare) and only lamenting the fact that he would in future have to put his dress-clothes out for himself. Only two people stood conspicuously aloof from the general rejoicings. Sir Julius Hammerstein made no attempt to disguise his disgust with this boomerang-like result of his complaint earlier in the day to Stephen's mistress, and Miss Cullompton looked as if she were suffering from a surfeit of green apples.

Gradually the excitement died away and the topic of conversation, which Stephen's entrance had interrupted, was resumed. Stephen, unashamedly consuming a positively enormous tea in honour of the occasion, listened with interest. They were discussing Cicely's disappearance, and he was particularly anxious to hear what other people had to say about it.

Colonel Uffculme, it appeared, had a theory. Colonel Uffculme was the sort of person who always had a theory about everything, even about women—the most impossible of all subjects to theorize over. It is hardly necessary to add that Colonel Uffculme's theories were invariably wrong.

This one seemed to be no exception. 'Hypnotism!' he was saying importantly. 'Only possible explanation. I've been thinking about it, and it's the only possible one.'

'Hypnotism, Colonel?' cooed Miss Cullompton, her blue eyes alight with innocent interest. 'How terribly interesting! But how?'

'Mass hypnotism, m'dear,' replied the Colonel still more importantly. 'Indian rope trick, y'know. Same sort of thing exactly. I remember once when I was in Bengal—'

Freddie sighed, audibly. But one could not stem the current of Colonel Uffculme's reminiscences with a mere sigh. He embarked upon it with gusto.

To make a long story (a very long story) short, it appeared that in Bengal the Colonel had been a witness more than once of the celebrated Indian rope trick, and had with his own eyes seen the juggler's little boy disappear into thin air in broad daylight. 'In broad daylight, mark!' As everyone knew, that was done by mass hypnotism. It was by mass hypnotism, therefore, that Cicely Vernon had been apparently spirited away last night from under their very noses.

'I was sure of it all the time,' the Colonel concluded triumphantly. 'Told you so last night in the smoking-room in fact, didn't I, Sir Julius?'

'You did, Colonel,' replied Sir Julius calmly. 'Up till past one o'clock in the morning, if I remember rightly.'

Stephen started. So that was the explanation of Sir Julius being still fully dressed when he had burst in upon Pauline and himself at two o'clock. He must have reached his bedroom only a few minutes before the screams which had roused the others, and joined subsequently in the search, unknown to Pauline or himself.

But in that case, why had the Colonel also not come down? Perhaps he had, and Stephen had not seen him either. But was that likely? Was it likely that neither Pauline nor he should have seen either of them? And Pauline, now he came to think of it, had been waiting all the time in the drawing-room. And why had Sir Julius gone almost out of his way to establish in Stephen's hearing an explanation of his appearance, knowing perfectly well the suspicions to which Stephen had frankly given voice? Was it natural?

There was something fishy here, Stephen decided. He would have to look into this rather closely.

The rest of the party had no important suggestions to offer. Freddie was convinced that the whole thing was an elaborate hoax, and so were most of the others. Starcross said nothing, nor did Millicent, who had made her appearance to preside over the tea-tray a few minutes after Stephen's entrance. Both of them, however, looked extremely worried.

As Martin, swallowing his resentment has best he could, was indignantly removing the tea-tray, Stephen caught Pauline's eye, it was alight with excitement. She nodded her head significantly towards the garden and at once rose, to stroll out on to the terrace through the French windows. Stephen allowed a minute to elapse, then he followed her.

Pauline was waiting for him a little way along the terrace. 'Stephen!' she exclaimed, as soon as he reached her. 'I've had a tremendous idea!'

'You have? Good! What?'

'Why, doesn't it occur to you that in a house like this there might be a secret room—a priest-hole, or something like that? And, if so, why shouldn't it be in the drawing-room?'

'By Jove! That's a brain-wave, Pauline. What an idiot I am never to have thought of it! But how can we find out for certain?'

'Millicent!' said Pauline promptly. 'There's no time like the present. You stay here; I'll get her.'

She hurried back to the drawing-room, to appear a minute or two later with Millicent in tow. Beckoning to Stephen to join them, she led the unfortunate lady down a broad flight of stone steps on to the lawn, safely out of hearing of the house.

'Stephen and I have got an idea, Millicent,' she began without further preamble immediately Stephen caught them up. 'Tell me this—is there a secret room off the drawing-room?'

Millicent started. 'What—what makes you ask that?'

'There is!' cried Pauline triumphantly. 'You've given it away. Do show it to us, Millicent. Of course that's how Cicely managed to disappear. Oh, I do believe you guessed it all the time!'

'I didn't, Pauline,' Millicent said earnestly. 'Indeed I didn't. Because I'm quite sure that Cicely doesn't know anything about it. I—I suppose I ought not to be saying anything to you, because it's a very close family secret. Nobody's supposed to know anything about it except the Careys actually living in the house. It's a tradition. I'm quite sure Cicely didn't know about it.'

'But that's where Lady Susan thought she was, all the same,' Stephen put in shrewdly.

Millicent looked at him with vague alarm, and Pauline gave an almost imperceptible nod of her head back to the house. Stephen seized his cue and, with a muttered excuse, left them together. He realized clearly the purport of Pauline's unspoken message—that it was going to be difficult to get anything out of Millicent in any case, and in the presence of a practical stranger quite impossible. He lounged idly on the terrace, in sight if he should be wanted, and smoked a couple of cigarettes.

Pauline joined him there half an hour later.

'I got it all out of her,' she smiled. 'Poor old Millicent! It's really rather a shame, but still—! There is a priest-hole, just as I guessed, opening off the fireplace, Stephen. And I've managed to extract full details for opening it!'

'I say, that's great! When can we try it?'

'I don't know,' Pauline said a little doubtfully. 'We must wait till the coast's clear, I suppose.'

They turned and headed towards the open French windows.

'And you think Cicely will be inside it?' Stephen asked.

'I hope so,' Pauline said seriously.

The drawing-room was empty. As if by common consent they halted in front of the big fireplace, gazing curiously.

'It's there!' Pauline whispered, pointing to the ingle-nook on the left of the hearth.

'I say, Pauline,' Stephen urged excitedly, 'let's try now! The coast's clear enough, and I'll shut the door.'

'All right!' Pauline agreed recklessly.

Stephen hurried over and secured the French windows and the door into the hall. When he returned Pauline had done something mysterious to the fireplace, and, beyond the ingle seat, there was now exposed a short flight of half a dozen worn wooden stairs.

Feeling as if they were a couple of children, Stephen caught Pauline's hand and led the way up them.

'Oh, Stephen,' Pauline whispered as she followed him, 'isn't this absurdly exciting?'

They found themselves in a little bare room, dusty, airless and pitch dark. Stephen struck a match and looked round. The place was not more than eight feet square, and quite empty. Wherever Cicely might be, she was certainly not there.

'Dash!' Stephen observed, with acute disappointment.

Pauline darted forward in the last flickering light of the match and snatched up something which was lying on the floor by one of the walls. 'Stephen!' she exclaimed. 'Cicely has been here! This is her handkerchief. I can recognize it by the scent.'

'Her handkerchief?' Stephen repeated, hurriedly striking another match. 'Good! Well, that's an infallible clue, at any rate.'

'We're in the track, Stephen!' Pauline exclaimed jubilantly. 'We're on the track.'

Stephen took the small white square from her and sniffed it gingerly. 'Humph! You must have an uncommonly good nose, Pauline, I'm quite sure I couldn't tell this from any other sort of scent.'

'But then you're a man, Stephen,' Pauline pointed out with a tolerant little smile. 'It's Reine des Fleurs, two guineas a bottle—Cicely's worst extravagance, I happen to know. She always brings it over from Paris herself.'

'I see.' Some of the enthusiasm had gone out of Stephen's tones; he spoke thoughtfully.

'What's the matter, Stephen? You ought to be dancing with excitement over this clue. I am. Why so pensive?'

'Well, I was just wondering about its exact value. I mean—has Cicely got a monopoly of Reine des Fleurs, or whatever it is? How do we know that nobody else is using it, too? Don't think I'm trying to crab your discovery. I'm just trying to work out exactly how far we can rely on it.'

'All the way,' Pauline said with decision. 'Reine des Fleurs is a very uncommon scent. I've got hundreds of scented friends, and not one of them but Cicely ever uses it. I don't think they even know of it. She keeps it a close secret, and only told the name to me as a great favour and on condition that I never used it myself. Don't be pig-headed, please, Stephen. I'm sure there can't be the least doubt about this hanky being Cicely's.'

Stephen struck another match and smiled at Pauline. 'Good! All the better. I only wanted to examine all possibilities. Oh, but look here, Pauline! Here's an idea! Supposing this handkerchief was put here as a blind!'

'Good gracious! Who by?'

'Why, the people who are so anxious for Cicely not to be found. Your mysterious "they".'

'That is possible,' Pauline admitted, with a serious expression. 'I never thought of that. Do you really think so, Stephen?'

'Oh, no, not necessarily . It's only a possibility that we ought to bear in mind. You see, they must have known that this place would be searched sooner or later, and—'

Pauline caught him suddenly by the arm. 'Hush!' she breathed. 'Somebody's coming into the drawing-room.' She darted across to the top of the flight of stairs and pulled a lever which projected from the wall. Hurrying noiselessly back to Stephen's side, she blew out the match in his hand. 'It's all right,' she whispered in the dark. 'I've closed the entrance up again. I don't think they can possibly have seen.'

'I suppose we shall have to stay here till they've gone,' Stephen whispered back. 'I wonder who it is.'

'Look, there's quite a big chink over there. We might be able to see.'

They tiptoed softly across to where a long narrow chink in the wooden side, which was apparently the back of the drawing-room panelling, formed a spy-hole sufficiently broad for two pairs of eyes—provided that their respective heads were in sufficiently close proximity. Stephen did not stop to analyse the slightly breathless feeling which invaded him as they applied their faces to the chink, an action which caused Pauline's hair to be pressed against his ear and even, when Stephen wilfully sought a better field of view, Pauline's soft cheek to be brushed gently against his own: it might have been the excitement of the chase, and, on the other hand, it might not.

It was Henry Kentisbeare who had entered the drawing-room. The little opening afforded both a perfect view of him as he glanced round the empty room and then made his way over to the bell by the fireplace. A minute later Martin made his appearance.

'Shut the door, Martin,' said Henry softly.

Martin shut the door. 'You required me, sir?' he asked urbanely.

'Yes. It seemed a good opportunity to pursue our conversation of this afternoon. Well, have you thought over what I said?'

'Certainly, sir.'

'That's good. And what's your decision?'

'It seems to me an interesting proposition, sir,' Martin replied carefully.

'You mean, you'll join us?'

'I think I should like to take a 'and in it, sir, yes.'

'Good man!' said Henry, with unusual elation. 'There's a pot of money in it, you know, if it's handled the right way.'

'That is what induces me to agree, sir,' Martin observed smoothly, 'against my principles though it is.'

'Never mind your principles, Martin. You'll forget that you ever had such things as principles very soon, I promise you.'

'It was a great shock at first, sir,' Martin remarked with a deprecatory air.

'You appear to have survived it,' Henry said dryly.

Stephen caught Pauline's arm in his excitement. She squeezed his hand against her side in her own.

'And we divide the emoluments, if I may so term them, as you were good enough to suggest, sir?' Martin was inquiring urbanely.

'That's right. You'll get a quarter of everything, and on top of that you get the advantage of what we've done already. That's fair enough, isn't it?'

'Very fair, indeed, sir.'

'The other party—we needn't mention any more names—has been trying to get the information we want, but in any case you must do what we arranged this evening during the second séance, if we can get one going again. You understand?'

'Perfectly, sir. And Miss—and the young lady will continue to play her part, so to speak?'

'That's what she's in with us for,' Henry replied shortly. He stroked his chin with a thoughtful air. 'Now, what about if things go wrong?'

'You mean, if'—Martin coughed gently—'if we are discovered?'

'Yes. One always wants a line of retreat properly planned out.'

'I think I can make a suggestion there, sir. There is somebody on the premises on whom it would not be difficult to shift the responsibility for anything of this nature.'

'How do you mean?'

Martin's face became blander than ever. 'I happen to know that a certain gentleman at present in the 'ouse has served a term of imprisonment. It was under another name and a good many years ago, but I may say that I recognized him at once. A nasty little matter of forgery it was.'

Henry whistled. 'Who is he?'

'Well, sir, you could hardly expect me to tell you that. I look on that as a private perquisite of my own. Knowledge of that kind may be very helpful at times, sir. Very helpful!'

'I see. You're bleeding him, are you?'

'Well, no, not exactly that, sir. In fact, I haven't yet approached the gentleman on the subject. But I hope to be putting a little proposition to him in quite a short time.'

Henry laughed. 'Your principles, indeed! It seems to me, Martin, that you're as thorough-paced a villain as—as anybody else at present in the house. Well, I think that's all. You know what to do, and if we want to change our plans in any way I'll let you know. I can always come to the pantry now that blighter's out of the way.'

Martin's face darkened. 'Yes, and that's another thing, sir. You mark my words, that young man is going to be a nuisance. I don't say he'll be in our way, but he's a Nosey Parker. Poking his nose in already, he is. We'd have a better chance if he were out of the way.'

'I'm inclined to agree. But there doesn't seem any prospect of getting rid of him. And, after all, what can he do? Oh, I don't think you need worry about him, Martin.'

'Very good, sir. Then perhaps I had better be getting back.'

Martin opened the door, paused a moment as if listening, and then walked ponderously out of the room. A minute later Henry followed him.

'Quick!' Pauline exclaimed. 'We must get down before anybody else comes. Oh, Stephen, what an amazing bit of luck!'

It took less than a minute to hurry down into the drawing-room and seat themselves decorously in two armchairs.

'We're simply smothered in dust,' Pauline remarked, patting vigorously at her frock. 'Oof, wasn't it terribly close in there?'

'Do you realize what we've done, Pauline?' said Stephen, marvelling slightly at the way in which the feminine mind can jump from the essential to the trivial. 'We've got our hands right on the heart of the mystery.'

'Yes,' Pauline said doubtfully. 'We know who's in it now, but we don't know why. And, oh, Stephen—Cicely!'

'Yes, I know,' Stephen agreed gravely. 'I'm afraid that's a bit of a shock for you.'

'It is. I could never have believed it of her. Never!'

There was a little pause. Then: 'Well, our next move's plain enough,' Stephen remarked briskly.

'What?'

'To discover the identity of Henry's "other party".'

XII THE WATCHERS

STRANGELY enough, Pauline and Stephen did not go on to discuss this new light which had fallen on the mysterious affair in any detail just then. The knowledge that Cicely must be playing an active instead of a passive part in what was now shown up as a conspiracy of a merely sordid description, oppressed the spirits of both of them. The motive behind the strange business still remained obscure, and Stephen was unable to see how the parties to it expected to turn it to financial account, or how the holding of another séance that evening would help them, unless it was to restore Cicely in the same miraculous way in which she had disappeared. One thing, at any rate, was obvious enough: if the plot was to be circumvented, and the villains of the piece baffled, no séance must be allowed to take place that evening. Both Stephen and Pauline agreed without hesitation to do their best to prevent it.

As things turned out, there was never any danger of anything of the kind. Henry, of course, urged it strongly at dinner, and he was backed up by Miss Cullompton and Freddie; neither Millicent nor Starcross expressed any opinion. The others might have been indifferent, but Lady Susan refused to entertain the suggestion in any circumstances whatever. So adamant and peremptory was she, indeed, that the conversation on the topic lasted scarcely two minutes. Pauline and Stephen exchanged smiles of secret amusement.

The party was now larger than on the previous evening, Miss Rivers being included to balance Stephen. As for the deficiency in the domestic arrangements caused by the late footman's elevation to the rank of guest, this had already been miraculously made good. Millicent and Martin, it appeared, had laid their heads together, a wire had been dispatched, and lo! a perfectly efficient parlourmaid was already installed by dinner-time—a large, Junoesque person of commanding, almost petrifying mien, certainly the equal of any footman ever invented. Money apparently can do these things.

The evening which followed was tame in comparison with the previous one. Annette got her bridge, Pauline sang a couple of songs, and Henry Kentisbeare hid his disappointment under a flood of jazz music at the piano, which incidentally he played extremely well. Stephen, looking round on the placid scene, was not by any means sure that he had been right after all. Might it not have been better to let the séance take place and so give himself a chance of finding out what really was going on behind the scenes?

As the party was dispersing for the night, Pauline found an opportunity to draw Stephen aside. 'Don't forget we're keeping watch down here tonight, Stephen,' she whispered. 'There's always the chance something may happen. Meet me down here when the coast's quite clear—say in an hour from now!'

Stephen nodded in silence, and made his way up to his new bedroom.

The next hour passed quite impossibly slowly. He changed from evening dress into a lounge suit, and then felt constrained to turn out his light in order to avoid rousing suspicion. For fifty minutes he had to sit in his bedroom in the dark, unable even to read. However, the thought that at the end of that period he would not only see Pauline again, but would be sitting next to her for perhaps an hour in the delightful intimacy of a dark room, was a singularly comforting one.

At last a cautious match showed the hands of his watch pointing to the time limit. Full of excited anticipation, he took off his pumps and, carrying them in his hand, stole noiselessly down to the drawing-room. Less than a minute later Pauline appeared. She too had changed her evening frock for something darker and less conspicuous.

'Where shall we hide, Stephen?' she whispered. 'Isn't this thrilling? I'm positively aching with excitement all over.'

Stephen shut the door silently behind her and, boldly taking her hand, led her through the darkness to where a large couch stood across the corner of the room immediately on the left of the door.

'I thought we might get behind this,' he whispered back. 'We want to be under cover in case the lights are turned up, you see, and this gives a fine view of the fireplace as well as the door.'

'Yes, that's a good place. Let's dump a few cushions there first, though.'

They collected half a dozen cushions, and Stephen pulled the couch aside for Pauline to get round behind it. Then he put it back in position and scrambled over the low back. There was just room for the two of them in comfort in the angle, and it was all very nice and cosy.

'Well, here we are,' said Pauline softly, when they were settled.

'Here we are,' Stephen agreed. 'And what next?'

'Goodness knows. But let's hope it's something worth waiting for. It would be an awful anti-climax if it wasn't.'

Stephen was of the opinion that the waiting alone was worth a considerable amount; but he did not express it. Instead he said something exceedingly irrelevant.

'Lady Susan was wearing her pearls tonight,' said Stephen surprisingly.

'Yes, she was. Why?'

'Nothing in particular. It just occurred to me. She wasn't last night, as far as I remember. Does she usually?'

'No, I don't think she does.'

'Pretty valuable, I should think, aren't they?'

'Very. But not much compared with the rest of her jewellery. She's got some simply wonderful diamonds, you know.'

'And she's leaving the lot to Cicely,' Stephen observed thoughtfully. 'Humph!'

'Is she? I didn't know that.'

'So Freddie told me.'

'What have you got in your mind, Stephen?' Pauline asked curiously.

'Nothing. I was only seeing if one could get a pointer that way. I've been going over every item of information that I've got about Cicely.'

There was a little silence. Then it was Pauline's turn to be irrelevant.

'Poor Millicent's taking all this dreadfully to heart, I'm afraid,' she remarked.

'Yes,' Stephen agreed. 'She looks worried to death.'

'I'm quite sure that she firmly believes Cicely's own ridiculous explanation—that she was removed by supernatural means, you know.'

'Oh, surely not!'

'I'm positive she does. She wouldn't admit it for the world, but she was telling me quite seriously upstairs before dinner that she really thought we ought to hold that séance this evening, just in case.'

'In case Cicely could be spirited back by the same energetic witch who took her away?' Stephen laughed.

'Something like that. She said one ought to leave no possibility unexplored, however absurd it might seem, because one never knew.'

'Did she? I say, Pauline, hasn't it struck you that Lady Susan seems to be taking all this very calmly?'

'Yes, it has. In fact, I meant to mention it to you. It's my belief, Stephen, that Lady Susan knows a good deal more about the business than she pretends.'

'Humph!' said Stephen doubtfully. 'She guessed that Cicely was in the secret room at the time of the disappearance, of course; but I don't see how she could know more than that.'

'I'm convinced she does!' Pauline said with decision. 'Just think—she's very fond of Cicely—much more than she is of Millicent—and she hasn't done a single thing. She doesn't even seem in the least alarmed. If she knew nothing, she'd have raised a regular hullaballoo by this time, called detectives in, had the house turned upside down, and goodness knows what. It stands to reason.'

'There is something in that,' Stephen admitted. 'But on the other hand, is she the sort of person to call the police in and make a fuss when there's any hope at all of things righting themselves if left alone? If she's as convinced as she appears that the whole thing's just an elaborate joke on Cicely's part, in distinctly doubtful taste, wouldn't she behave just as she has behaved? Oh, I don't know; it's easy enough to argue either way. By the way, are you casting Lady Susan for the role of chief villain of the piece?'

'I wouldn't go so far as to say that,' Pauline smiled into the darkness. 'But I do think, with Millicent, that we ought to explore every possibility, however absurd it sounds at first, because I've been quite sure all the time that there's a great deal more in this than anybody seems to imagine—except perhaps Mr Starcross.'

'Starcross!' Stephen repeated thoughtfully. 'Humph! Yes.'

'Stephen, I do wish you wouldn't say "Humph!" It always means that you've got something in your mind, and you never go on to explain it.'

'Sorry!' Stephen laughed. 'I only say "Humph!" when a possibility crosses my mind so ridiculous that it really isn't worth putting into words. But if you don't like "Humph!" I'll say "Yah!" or "Skiboo!" or anything else you prefer,' he volunteered kindly.

'You're rather a nice old idiot, you know, Steve,' Pauline remarked comfortably.

On this more personal note the conversation, which had been conducted throughout in low whispers, lapsed altogether. Pauline was apparently busy working out all the various interesting possibilities on which they had touched; Stephen was even busier with his own thoughts. Stephen's thoughts, by a curious transition, were no longer concerned with the business in hand, absorbing though it should have been; they centred entirely round the person of Pauline.

If their vigil that night were fruitless, he had decided to go up to London on the following day in order to carry out his intention of interviewing Pauline's father about her incongruous engagement. It was a task that would require every ounce of tact in his possession, and Stephen was very far from welcoming it, but as far as he could see it was the only possible means of discovering what might lie behind that affair; to approach Pauline herself on the subject would, of course, be worse than useless. In the meantime, he gave himself up to the enjoyment of the moment, with Pauline's warm presence at his side and the sound of Pauline's soft voice still in his ears. He began to wish that something would happen, so that he might have an excuse to take her hand.

Pauline appeared to be wishing the same thing, though perhaps not for the same reason. 'Oh dear, isn't anybody going to come?' she remarked after the silence had lasted some considerable time. 'How disappointing!'

It seemed as if they were both to be disappointed. It was now nearly three-quarters of an hour since they had taken up their positions, and a growing restlessness on Pauline's part showed that she at any rate was beginning to think of putting an end to their watch. She had, indeed, already risen on to her knees and was beginning to talk very firmly about Bed with a capital B, when a faint sound from the direction of the hall caught Stephen's ears. Hurriedly catching her arm, he pulled her down again beside him and whispered into her ear:

'Hush! There's someone moving about. In the hall.'

They listened, straining their ears. The sound was repeated, quite unmistakably this time. Without a doubt somebody was walking across the hall.

'Oh!' Pauline breathed. 'Do you think he's coming in here, Stephen?'

In an agony of apprehension, Stephen actually laid his finger on her lips, for scarcely had she framed the last word when the drawing-room door in front of them could be heard to open. Frozen like two statues, with every muscle rigid, they stared into the blank, unhelpful darkness.

As far as eyes went, both of them might have been blind. In that dead blackness, unrelieved by the faintest moonbeam from the still-curtained windows, absolutely nothing could be discerned. Only their ears were any guide to what was happening a few feet away from them.

The door closed softly, and the footsteps proceeded across the room, passing directly in front of them and obviously bearing towards the fireplace. Noiselessly Stephen's hand sought Pauline's and gripped it reassuringly. Pauline returned the pressure with interest, and Stephen could feel her quivering all over. It was not fright, he knew; simply almost uncontrollable excitement.

Just peering over the back of the couch, they followed the newcomer's progress with useless eyes. It was not until he had actually reached the fireplace, as a momentary clatter of fire-irons informed them, that their vigilance was in any way rewarded. For half a second there was the flash of an electric torch, against which Stephen received the instantaneous impression of a tall figure, shapeless in a flowing dressing-gown. The next moment the light vanished, and Stephen was really very little the wiser. There came a sound of ponderous creaking.

Stephen became aware of Pauline's lips at his ear. 'He's going up into the secret room,' she barely articulated.

Stephen nodded in silence.

Footsteps could be heard ascending the flight of wooden stairs.

Stephen turned to Pauline. 'We must find out who that is,' he whispered as softly as possible. 'I'm going up after him.'

'So am I, then,' Pauline whispered back.

Stephen was already climbing noiselessly over the back of the couch. 'No! You stay here, Pauline.'

He tiptoed across the room, halting warily a few feet away from the fireplace. There was no definite plan of campaign in his mind, and he did not want to be hasty. As long as the man was in the secret room he could not escape them.

He realized that Pauline was standing by his side, apparently prepared to follow him up the stars. He took her arm and drew her close to him.

'Go back, Pauline dear,' he whispered urgently. 'The chap may be dangerous.' He did not add that he was quite sure he would be armed.

'All the more reason for me to come too,' Pauline retorted.

'No!' Stephen's tone was suddenly peremptory. 'This is my job. You go over by the switch and turn it on when I bring him down.'

He did not stop to consider the briskness with which he had issued his demands. A plan had occurred to him; the only possible plan, as far as he could see. Kicking off his shoes, he advanced silently to the foot of the steps. Obviously the only thing to do was to dash up at top speed, take the man by surprise and grapple with him before he could fire, presuming he were armed, and then drag him down into the drawing-room. He leapt forward.

But the other was not to be taken so easily. Before Stephen was half-way up the short flight, a blinding light was flashed into his eyes and a heavy boot struck him square on the chest. He tumbled helplessly backwards, bumping his head nastily. Without a second's hesitation he picked himself up and plunged forward again.

This time, considerably to his surprise, he was allowed to reach the top of the flight. Bracing every muscle, he awaited the expected onslaught. It did not come. Cautiously he drew a match-box from his pocket and, careful not to look directly at the flame, struck a match.

He looked round him incredulously. The little room was empty.

'Pauline!' he called softly. 'Come up here!'

'Have you laid him out, Stephen?' Pauline asked eagerly, appearing a moment later. She looked round the little room by the light of Stephen's match. 'Oh! He's not here.'

'He's not,' Stephen agreed grimly. 'The blighter's got away. There must be some other exit from this place.' He began to examine the wooden walls, striking a succession of matches as he peered at them for signs of telltale cracks or hinges.

'What happened just now?' Pauline asked anxiously. 'I heard most alarming bumps and thuds.'

'That was me,' Stephen said ruefully, feeling the back of his head with a cautious hand. 'He had me properly. Flashed his light in my face while I was still on the stairs and then kicked me in the chest. I landed on something uncommonly hard, and by the time I'd got up here again he'd gone.'

'Oh, Stephen! Aren't you hurt?'

'Not as much as I ought to have been. Look here, Pauline, I can't find any signs at all of this other exit. It stands to reason there must be one, but it's uncommonly well concealed. These matches aren't any use either. I must get an electric torch tomorrow and examine it properly.'

'Tomorrow?' Pauline echoed disappointedly. 'Surely we ought to go on trying now, while the scent's so hot?'

'That's the trouble,' Stephen said, grinding an expiring match gingerly beneath his sock. 'The scent's too hot. He knows that we're after him now, and I bet he's safely tucked up in bed by this time, snoring away like mad and establishing an alibi as hard as he can. He was wearing a dressing-gown, you see, so he must be somebody in the house.'

'I suppose you're right,' Pauline said regretfully. 'It seems a pity, though. Of course he saw who you were when he flashed the light in your face?'

'Yes, dash it! That means he'll be on his guard against me. No hope of taking him by surprise now.'

'But he doesn't know about me.'

'That's true,' Stephen agreed.

They made their way back into the drawing-room, and Pauline touched the concealed knob which closed the entrance to the stairs.

'Another thing we'll have to do tomorrow is to find out what room lies above this one,' Stephen remarked, as they walked into the hall.

'I can in tell you that offhand. It's the big spare room.'

'Ah! And who's sleeping there now?'

'Baby.'

'Miss Cullompton?' Stephen observed with interest. 'Humph! I mean—skiboo!'

At the top of the stairs they parted and went to their respective rooms.

Stephen did not begin to undress at once. Setting a chair by the open window, he looked out into the night and began to meditate over the little adventure. It was delightful to be having adventures with Pauline. Suddenly he yawned; he must be more tired than he had realized. Adventures … Pauline … Sir Julius … Pauline's father …

A light tap at his door roused him with a jerk. He jumped to his feet and went over to open it. Pauline was standing outside, her cheeks flushed with excitement.

'Oh, Stephen, I am glad you haven't gone to bed. I simply had to come and tell you at once. I've made a tremendous discovery!'

'You have? Good! What?'

'Why, as soon as I got to my room I remembered that we hadn't put those cushions back from behind the couch, so I ran downstairs and did it. Then I thought I'd just have one tiny prowl round before going back, so I went along to the passage that leads to the big spare-room—you know, the one that Baby's sleeping in now.'

'I know,' said Stephen with feeling. 'I carried the lady's luggage up there.'

'Well, just outside Baby's door I stopped and had a look round—and what do you think I realized?'

'Goodness knows!' Stephen smiled. 'Tell me.'

'That I was smelling Reine des Fleurs!' Pauline exclaimed triumphantly. 'Do you realize what that means, Stephen? That Cicely is still in this house!'

XIII TRAGIC NEWS

STEPHEN came down to breakfast the next morning with his mind made up on one point. However pressing the mysterious happenings at Wintringham Hall, they must be allowed to slide for one day at any rate; his own affairs (or rather Pauline's affairs) must come first. He would go up to London, as he promised himself the night before, and seek an interview with Pauline's father.

There was no need to hurry. A train leaving the neighbouring station of Thornton at half-past twelve would get him up in plenty of time and still allow Pauline and himself an hour or two in which to examine the possibilities of the secret room. He announced his intention to Millicent at breakfast.

'Oh, yes,' said Millicent, even more vaguely than usual, for she looked as if she had not had a wink of sleep the previous night and was correspondingly distrait. 'Er—Collins,' she added to the grenadier-like new parlourmaid, who entered at that moment with some fresh toast, 'will you tell Parker to have the car round here at a quarter-past twelve to go to the station for Mr Munro, who has to go up to London on important business.' Millicent was one of those people who invariably enter into unnecessary explanations to servants.

'No, please don't trouble, Miss Carey,' Stephen interposed hurriedly. 'I'd rather walk. There's a short cut through the park, isn't there?'

'Well, there is,' Millicent admitted, 'if you really want to.'

'I do,' Stephen smiled.

'Then the car won't be wanted, Collins,' Millicent pointed out a trifle superfluously.

'Very good, madam,' replied the grenadier tonelessly.

Sir Julius, Stephen learnt, had breakfasted early and had already retired to the library, where he expected to be busy all the morning with the telephone. Freddie, Baby, Henry and Annette had arranged to play a foursome of golf, and departed immediately after breakfast. The Colonel retired with The Times, Millicent was busy with her household duties, and Miss Rivers was attending upon Lady Susan.

So far luck had been on the side of Stephen and Pauline; but there it deserted them. Starcross, who had nobody left to talk to, showed very plainly that he wanted to talk to them; and do what they could, they were quite unable to shake him off.

They expatiated on the beautiful walks which a solitary person might enjoy in the vicinity, and Starcross did not take the hint; they retired to the billiard-room, and Starcross followed them, so that they were compelled to play a fifty-up game which neither of them desired in the very least; they kept offering to lend him books, which they praised in the most extravagant terms, but Starcross could not be driven into the mood for reading. Finally Stephen said he had some letters to write and retired to his bedroom, and Pauline said she had some letters to write too and retired to her own. Ten minutes later they met in the drawing-room. After that they lost no more time.

'This is a bit better,' Stephen observed, flashing an electric torch over the dusty walls of the little priest-hole.

'Where did you get that from, Stephen?' Pauline asked with interest.

'Borrowed it off Freddie,' Stephen grinned. 'To take with me to London.'

'But whatever for?'

'Goodness knows! But it seemed to do for Freddie all right. Now then, what about this mysterious exit?'

'Wait a minute,' Pauline said, listening intently. 'There seems to be an awful commotion going on upstairs, doesn't there?'

From over their heads was audible the sound of scurrying footsteps, cries and general upheaval. They looked at each other in surprise.

'We'd better defer this for a bit, Pauline,' Stephen decided suddenly. 'If there's something comic going on we may be wanted, and it'll look funny if we're nowhere about. They know we haven't gone out, you see. We'd better get down before anybody comes into the drawing-room.'

'There seems to be a fate against our finding this other exit,' Pauline sighed, preceding Stephen down the little stairs.

They closed the entrance behind them and strolled nonchalantly into the hall. Miss Rivers was in the act of hurrying across it.

'What's all the commotion, Miss Rivers?' Pauline asked pleasantly.

The girl stopped and looked at them through her horn spectacles. She seemed doubtful for the moment as to whether she ought to answer.

'Lady Susan's pearls have disappeared,' she said after a little pause.

'Her pearls!' Pauline cried. 'But she was wearing them only last night.'

'Yes, and I put them in the safe in her room last night myself, where she keeps all her jewellery. This morning everything had disappeared.'

'Everything?'

'Yes, all her rings and heaps of other things. Everything except her diamond necklace, which Lady Susan herself had fortunately put in one of her dressing-table drawers only yesterday afternoon.'

'Great Scott!' Stephen commented. 'And the safe was broken into in the night?'

'No, it must have been opened with a key.'

'I say! Looks like an inside job, then? And the safe was in Lady Susan's room, you say?'

'Yes, but she's a very sound sleeper.'

'She must be. Oh, Lord, I'd better run up there.'

'Why?' asked Pauline.

'Well, the safe ought not to be touched. There may be fingerprints on it.'

'I don't think there are,' Miss Rivers observed calmly. 'I looked for them myself.'

'You did? Oh! Well,' said Stephen lamely, 'I think I'll go up in any case and see if I can be of any help. Somebody will he wanted to telephone to the police, for instance.'

'I was on my way to do that now,' Miss Rivers replied serenely, and continued her way to the instrument to do so. 'Now I begin to understand why Lady Susan is always praising that girl's efficiency,' Stephen observed to Pauline as, feeling quite chastened, he mounted the broad stairs at her side. 'She made me feel rather like a small child.'

'Don't you hate people who do that?' Pauline answered in singularly heart-felt tones.

On the landing they came across Millicent, scurrying apparently quite aimlessly up and down it with a white face like some bewildered sheep's.

'Have you heard?' she burst out as soon as she caught sight of them. 'Isn't it dreadful! Dear me, I don't know what's happened to this house. Things never used to happen like this. First Cicely, and now Oh, dear!' She wrung her hands helplessly.

'It's all right, Millicent,' Pauline said soothingly. 'It must have been an inside job, as Stephen professionally calls it, and the police are bound to find out who did it and get the things back again.'

Millicent stared at her speechlessly. Such an idea as that, one might have gathered, had never occurred to her at all.

But the dramatic moments of that morning were not yet over. Scarcely had Pauline spoken when the gaunt lady's maid, Farrar, made her appearance, hurrying down a passage which led from the servants' quarters. Stephen stared at her in astonishment. Her face was white and she looked almost as distraught as her mistress.

'Oh, miss!' she exclaimed the moment she came abreast of the little group. 'Oh, miss, I don't know how to tell you. Martin's been killed!'

'What?' Stephen exclaimed. 'Martin been killed?'

'Oh, help me, Stephen,' Pauline cried suddenly. 'Millicent!'

Stephen turned hastily round. Millicent was swaying on her feet, her face the colour of chalk. Pauline held her by the arm, but this last culminating blow of fate proved too much for the unfortunate lady. She fainted.

Stephen was just in time to catch her as she fell. He lifted her up and laid her on a couch which stood close by.

'She'll be all right in a minute,' he said to Pauline, who was bending anxiously. 'Shock, you know.'

'And no wonder, poor thing,' Pauline agreed, chafing Millicent's inert hands.

'Ought I to go and break the news to Lady Susan, would you think, sir?' asked Farrar nervously.

'No, I think you'd better not,' Stephen replied grimly. 'Your methods of breaking news seem a trifle blunt, not to say disastrous. We'd better wait until Miss Carey recovers, and then perhaps Miss Mainwaring will tell Lady Susan. Don't you think so, Pauline?'

'Yes,' Pauline assented briefly. 'I'll tell her.'

Stephen turned back to the lady's maid. 'How was Martin killed?' he demanded curtly. 'Do you mean that it was—?'

'Oh, yes, sir. An accident. A branch of one of those big elms in the park fell on him. His back's broken, the gardener says. He must have been killed at once.'

'Good heavens! When did this happen?'

'Just a few minutes ago, sir. The gardener heard the crash and ran down the path, and then came straight here. They're bringing him in now, sir.'

'Path?' said Stephen quickly. 'What path?'

'The path through that little wood at the back of the house, sir. That's where it was. Oh, dear—poor Mr Martin!'

Stephen looked at the woman curiously. From his brief previous acquaintance with her he would have been almost inclined to say that she was capable of no feelings whatever. Yet her present distress was obviously genuine. Indeed she looked as if she were on the point of fainting herself and only her greater powers of control prevented her from doing so.

'And you say it was the gardener who found him?' he pursued.

'Yes, sir. The new gardener.'

'Bridger?' Stephen exclaimed.

'Yes, sir. I think that is his name.'

Pauline looked over her shoulder. 'I think she's coming round, Stephen. Hadn't you better go downstairs while we see to her and I break the news to Lady Susan?'

'Very well,' Stephen nodded. 'Come out on the terrace when you're free, will you?'

Stephen was not sorry for the break. He badly wanted a word or two with Bridger. A branch of a tree—of course it must be an accident. Branches of trees do not fall to order. And yet it was certainly an extremely lucky accident for at least one, if not two, or even three people in the house. Humph!

Bridger was soon found. He had been helping the head-gardener to bring in Martin's body, and was still waiting at the back of the house. Stephen conveyed him into a secluded corner of the grounds.

'Bridger,' he said abruptly, 'what do you make of this?'

'Well, sir,' Bridger replied frankly, 'it's a wonder to me that it's never happened before. 'Alf the branches on most of these old elm trees are rotten; and when they do fall, they do it sudden like, elms do. No warning at all. Just drop off the tree like a plum. I wouldn't stand under one of 'em, sir; not for anything you like. Yes, it's a wonder to me that it's never 'appened before.' Which was perhaps the longest speech that Bridger had ever made in his life.

'Then you think it was an accident all right?' Stephen asked in a careless voice.

Bridger looked his astonishment. 'Why, what else could it be, sir?'

'Oh, nothing. I was just wondering. By the way, I suppose you don't happen to know what Martin was doing in the wood just then?'

'Why, yes, sir, as a matter of fact I do. He passed me on his way about an hour before and stopped to have a word. Very affable man, Martin was. And he 'appened to mention that he had to take a telegram into Thornton. Rather put out about it, he seemed. He must have been in there, and the branch fell on 'im on 'is way back.'

'Into Thornton!' Stephen exclaimed. 'By Jove, yes; I never thought of that. That's the short cut into Thornton, isn't it?'

'It is, sir.'

'Do you know, Bridger,' Stephen said rather solemnly, 'that I should have been passing myself under that branch only a very little time later?'

'Then you're lucky it fell when it did, sir,' Bridger remarked with a touch of grimness.

'His back was broken, wasn't it?' Stephen went on, with an involuntary little shudder.

'Yes, sir. And his head too.'

'Was it a very big branch?'

'It was that, sir. Nearly twenty inches through, I should put it. But it wasn't the main bit that caught him. The tree stands too far back from the path for that. It was one of the smaller bits, getting towards the end, but as thick as your thigh, for all that. It seemed to me from the way it got 'im as if he'd heard it coming down and tried to get away in time. An' he would have done too, if this bit hadn't happened to stick out some way—oh, a tidy three yards, I should say, from the rest. Just a bit of real bad luck.'

'I see,' said Stephen thoughtfully. 'Oh, by the way, Bridger, I've got a bit of news for you. This business had nearly put it out of my head. I'm not a footman any longer.'

They conversed for a few minutes on this change of fortune, and then Stephen made his way back to the house. Of course the thing must have been an accident. Bridger had made that as certain as anything in this world well can be. It was absurd to contemplate any other possibility. Yet Stephen, as he walked back to the house, found that he was unable to prevent himself from being occasionally absurd.

Pauline was already waiting for him on the terrace.

Stephen leaned his elbows on the stone balustrade at her side and gazed with unseeing eyes over the trim garden below. For a minute or two they remained in complete silence—the silence of people who know each other so well that words are merely an accessory rather than a necessity.

'How did Lady Susan take it?' Stephen asked at last.

'She didn't say very much; she's not the sort of person who would. But I could see that she was very upset.'

'And how's Millicent?'

'I've induced her to go to bed. She seems completely done in. She's never had anything of this sort in her life before, and this last shock, coming after the business of Cicely's disappearance and the theft of Lady Susan's jewellery, seems to have finished her off completely.'

'Pauline,' Stephen exclaimed suddenly, 'has it occurred to you that we might have been putting a wrong construction all this time on that conversation we overheard between Henry and Martin? Your mention of Lady Susan's jewellery made me think—supposing it was that they were referring to, and not Cicely at all! It was all very vague, you know, and could have applied equally well.'

'It's possible,' Pauline remarked pensively. 'It hadn't occurred to me, no; but it is possible. I wonder!'

'And has it occurred to you also, in that case,' Stephen pursued slowly, 'how very fortuitous Martin's death must be to quite a number of people in this house?'

'What do you mean, Stephen?'

'Why, supposing it were a plot to steal Lady Susan's jewellery, and Martin himself had carried out the actual theft, how very convenient to get rid of him immediately! Martin would be a slippery customer as a fellow-conspirator, I feel sure. And even apart from that, there's our ex-convict, isn't there? Supposing Martin approached him last night, as he more or less hinted to Henry, and gave away the fact that he hadn't divulged his information to anybody else. That gives the gentleman a very powerful motive for Martin's removal, doesn't it?'

'But, Stephen!' Pauline gasped. 'You're not suggesting that Martin was—was murdered, are you?'

'I don't see how he could have been,' Stephen admitted. 'All I'm doing is to face the fact that his death is an extraordinarily convenient one for certainly one person in this house and possibly several.'

'But—but we know that everybody was busy this morning.'

Stephen repeated her words in a slightly different form. 'We know that everybody has a cast-iron alibi,' he said thoughtfully. 'Yes, almost blatantly cast-iron.'

Again there was a short silence between them. This time Pauline was the first to break it.

'Who's that coming up the drive?' she remarked. 'On a bicycle. Isn't it a policeman?'

Stephen followed the direction of her eyes. 'By Jove, yes. It's an inspector. He'll be coming about Lady Susan's jewellery.' He glanced at his watch. 'Look here, Pauline, I think I'll get along to the station now. If I don't, I shall—'

'But you're not going up to London now, Stephen?' Pauline cried.

'Er, yes,' Stephen mumbled uncomfortably. 'Must. Got an appointment. But I'll be back before dinner, I hope. And if I don't get off now, probably that fellow will stop anyone leaving the house. Keep an eye on things while I'm away, won't you?'

He made a somewhat embarrassed exit. It was impossible to tell Pauline his real reason for going up to London, and he dreaded any questions which she might put to him about it.

He hurriedly collected his hat and stick, and made his escape through the gardens before the inspector could forestall him.

The little wood in which Martin had met his death lay in the middle of the park, only six hundred yards or so from the house. The path to Thornton and its station led directly through the middle of it. Stephen had not the least difficulty in finding the scene of the tragedy. Just beyond half-way through the wood the little path was completely blocked by the enormous arm of an elm tree, which sprawled and spread far into the undergrowth on both sides. In the direction of the house one gnarled branch lay along the path just as Bridger had described it, except that Stephen computed its length at a good five yards instead of three. Stephen's imagination gave it an ominous and fateful appearance as he stood and gazed at it, in truth it did seem as if Providence had long determined upon Martin's death, and had grown this unnaturally projecting bough as its own unescapable weapon.

Stephen glanced at his watch again. He had plenty of time to make the brief examination of the scene which he was longing to perform. Without hesitation he approached the end of the arm which had broken off the trunk, and was now lying only a couple of feet beyond it.

The wood was rotten enough in all conscience; much of the outside was quite soft, while for a width of about six inches across the very middle was nothing but mere dust. Stephen bent and examined the uneven surface of the break. The next moment he whistled softly and bent still lower. The top half of the break was decayed and weather-stained, as if it had been exposed for some considerable time; the lower portion was obviously freshly severed, with jagged splinters and signs of tearing. But between them, for a depth of perhaps a couple of inches, was a clean, smooth surface, which could only have been made by a saw!

Stephen straightened up abruptly. His instincts had been right. Martin's death had not been an accident.

But how could the bough have been timed to fall so conveniently? He examined the ground at that end, but could find no further clue, except that certainty was made still more certain by the discovery of fresh sawdust still clinging to the bark of the trunk. Not even knowing what to look for, he moved to the mass of foliage and twigs on the farther side of the path, and peered into it with close attention. The next instant he had found what he sought—two lengths of smooth pole, a couple of inches in diameter and perhaps five feet long, each splintered at one end and looking exactly like a stout clothes'-prop, forcibly broken in two.

With uncanny insight he saw in a flash how the whole thing must have been done—the cautious deepening with the saw of the convenient fissure already there, the waiting till the huge bough began definitely to sag, the hurried scramble down and hoisting of the clothes'-prop perpendicularly upright to stay the fall at the critical moment (risky this, but inevitable) with the knowledge that a pole so placed will support a quite incredibly heavy branch, the tying of a strong, thin, long rope round the centre of the pole, the hiding at a safe distance with the other end of the rope, and then—the sharp tug at just the right instant, the breaking of the pole, the instantaneous crash and almost certain death! Stephen drew a deep breath. It was so ingenious, and yet so simple.

But whose was the shadowy figure performing all these actions? That was the problem now. Nobody in the house-party, he knew. Whose, then? Yes, that was going to be very much more difficult to solve.

Scarcely knowing why he did so, Stephen plunged into the tangle, extracted the two pieces of broken pole, and concealed them carefully under a bush at some distance. Then he resumed his way to the station. He had found what he had wanted, and there was no object in further delay. He emerged from the little wood and continued across the park.

The picture haunted him—Martin, walking so unsuspectingly along the path on his way back from Thornton, and that sinister figure crouched in the thick undergrowth. It was really rather horrible. But suddenly it was replaced in his mental vision by another picture of such a totally different and startling description that Stephen stopped dead in his tracks and caught his breath. He saw himself announcing at the crowded breakfast-table his intention of pursuing that very path only a short time after that at which Martin had been killed. Supposing—supposing that his theory of the rope had been wrong—that the trap had been arranged to act in some way automatically! And supposing that the shadowy figure was that same one who had flashed his electric torch in his face last night and so learnt who was close upon his track! In that case, instead of Martin—

Some minutes later a thoughtful young man called in at Thornton post office and asked if there was a telegram for him. Against all rules and regulations one was handed to him across the counter. He slit it open absently and read its contents with apparent lack of interest. Yet in other circumstances Stephen would have found his telegram interesting enough, for it ran:

'Do not understand. Mr and Mrs Seymour left on yachting trip from Folkestone last week. Miss Vernon never invited. Her acquaintance with Seymours of the slightest—ADYE, SECRETARY.'

XIV MR MAINWARING'S AFFAIRS

MR MAINWARING, important to so many people only because he happened to be the father of his daughter, lifted the telephone receiver reluctantly. To tell the truth, Mr Mainwaring disliked the telephone, and more so than ever during these last few months. It seemed to him that anybody who had any particularly unpleasant news to communicate to him, always chose the telephone as the method of its conveyance.

As he listened, his brow furrowed into the lines of acute anxiety which had been growing so much deeper within the last year. 'Yes, Sir Julius?' he murmured a little breathlessly.

Suddenly his face cleared and he positively beamed into the instrument. For the moment he looked a different man, and an onlooker would have said that a load had at last been removed from his shoulders. 'You will?' he cried. 'Really, that is extremely kind of you. I don't know how to—'

The voice at the other end evidently cut him short, and he listened attentively.

'Yes,' he nodded. 'Yes, I will. Immediately, yes.'

A minute or two later he hung up the receiver.

That Mr Mainwaring was delighted there could be no doubt. He rubbed his hands together and walked briskly over to his writing-table on the other side of the room. Pulling open a drawer he extracted some papers, laid them on the table and took his seat in front of them. He drew a sheet of note-paper towards him, picked up his pen and dipped it in the ink.

'Mr Munro,' announced the butler at that moment.

Mr Mainwaring jumped up. 'Hullo, Munro!' he exclaimed, his kindly old face creased into a smile of welcome. 'How are you, my boy? Haven't seen you for quite a long time.'

They shook hands.

'I'm very fit, thanks,' Stephen smiled.

'If you've come to see Pauline, your luck's out. She's away. You know about her engagement, of course?'

'Yes,' Stephen returned. 'But I haven't come to see her, Mr Mainwaring. As a matter of fact I've only just left her; we're both staying at Wintringham Hall. I've come to see you.'

'To see me?' chuckled Mr Mainwaring. 'That's something quite new. Well, well, what have you come to see me about? Pull up a chair and make yourself comfortable.'

Stephen drew a large leather-covered armchair up to the writing-table and subsided into it. For a moment or two he was silent. He had not formulated any definite plan of campaign, and his mission was undoubtedly a ticklish one. Mr Mainwaring was the most charming of men, but even the most charming of men may be excused for resenting the interference in their most private affairs of a comparative stranger. Stephen did not quite know how to begin.

'Well?' asked Mr Mainwaring genially.

Stephen plunged straight for the heart of the trouble. 'It's about Pauline's engagement, sir,' he said bluntly.

Mr Mainwaring stiffened perceptibly. 'Pauline's engagement?' he repeated, in tones that were not at all genial.

'Yes,' said Stephen desperately. All idea at tact forgotten, he could think of nothing but to state the issue in the plainest possible terms. 'Do you know, Mr Mainwaring, that she hates the sight of this fellow, Sir Julius? I'm convinced she does. And I'm also convinced that he must have some sort of a hold over her. I don't know whether you know all this, but in case you don't I felt the only thing I could do was to come up to London and tell you, so that we can see whether there isn't some way of getting Pauline out of this mess.'

Mr Mainwaring made no attempt to conceal his astonishment. 'Has my daughter said anything to you on the matter?' he asked, not exactly coldly, but without warmth.

'No,' Stephen had to admit. 'Not a word. It's not the sort of thing I could ask her, and Pauline certainly isn't the kind of girl to volunteer anything of that nature. But it is so, nevertheless. And I've been wondering whether you could put your finger on the hold which this man has over her. It can't be money, of course; everybody knows that you are, comparatively speaking, a rich man.'

A slightly perturbed expression replaced the look of resentful bewilderment in the older man's face. He began to fidget absently with the penholder in front of him. For a full minute there was silence. Then: 'I'm not a rich man, Munro,' said Mr Mainwaring uncomfortably.

It was Stephen's turn to be surprised. 'You're not?' he cried.

'No. I was once, but I'm not now. After all, there's no reason why I shouldn't tell you. Everybody will know soon enough. To be quite accurate, a week ago I was on the verge of ruin.'

'Good heavens!' Stephen exclaimed.

Again there was a silence between them, while Mr Mainwaring continued to fidget with his penholder and Stephen eagerly reviewed the circumstances in the light of this unexpected piece of information.

'You never knew that Pauline didn't care for the man?' he asked at length.

'No. It never occurred to me.' All traces of resentment had left Mr

Mainwaring's voice by now; he spoke defensively, as if rebutting charges which were being brought against him by insinuation rather than by direct accusation. 'I thought it rather curious that she should have fallen in love with a fellow like that, but she never gave me the slightest inkling that she wasn't in love with him; and—well, to tell you the truth, Munro, I was only too glad at the prospect of a wealthy son-in-law. Pauline's material future was assured, at any rate. I—I wonder whether there is anything in what you say. It certainly is rather—disturbing.'

Stephen looked at the older man sympathetically. He knew that he adored his daughter and that the suggestion just made must have come as a great shock to him if, as he said, he had no inkling of the true state of affairs. But Mr Mainwaring's feelings must be sacrificed to the necessity of establishing the facts as they really were.

'You say that a week ago you were on the verge of ruin,' he said slowly. 'Has something occurred since then to put you on your feet again, and if so, has that something been brought about through the agency of Sir Julius?'

Mr Mainwaring glanced at him with suddenly haggard eyes. The purport of the question could not be misunderstood. 'Yes,' he admitted.

Again there was a little pause. 'I think you had better tell me everything, Mr Mainwaring,' Stephen said gently. 'I assure you that all I want is to get you and Pauline out of this trouble, and to do that we've both of us got to work hard and swiftly. And devilish cunningly!' he added with feeling.

'Very well,' the old man agreed in a low voice. 'I'll tell you.'

It was a hackneyed story that Stephen listened to, but its staleness did nothing to abate its poignancy. Mr Mainwaring's investments had, it appeared, like those of everybody else, dwindled very considerably since the war. He had become alarmed; unnecessarily, for he still had more than a competent income, but the idea that Pauline should be stinted of the style of life to which she had been brought up, or that he would not be able to leave her on his death as much as she had every right to expect, had acutely distressed him. To make good his deficiencies he had speculated.

Why do people, with the warning of so many others before their eyes, succumb to the lure of haphazard speculation? Mr Mainwaring's plunges had followed the same course as those of almost every other tyro. From more than a competence his capital sank to something less than adequate, from that to something approaching the disastrous; and for every loss he plunged the more wildly in the hope of regaining what he had sacrificed. Finally he had found himself with less than a tenth of what he originally possessed.

From Pauline all this had been carefully concealed. It was impossible, therefore, to reduce his living expenses in proportion to his income, with the result that he had been forced to live on his capital as well as speculate with it. At last had come the final throw. Acting on information which he had every reason to believe disinterested and reliable, he had invested almost every single penny that was left to him in a gold-mining company, confidently expecting his money to be at least doubled, if not trebled, before a year was out. That had been three months ago. Six weeks later there had been a call on the shares, which of course he had been unable to meet. It was useless to attempt to realize a portion in order to pay off the call on the rest, for with the news they had sunk to half their market value. As far as he could see he was faced with bankruptcy and ruin.

Then at last he had told Pauline. She had been very sympathetic and had seemed to mind it much less than himself. As for him, he had not tried to conceal his feelings. Bankruptcy! He had talked wildly about suicide (as he now admitted under Stephen's probing questions) as the only way of saving his good name; he had made all sorts of hysterical suggestions; he had been utterly distraught. Pauline had soothed him, promised that all would come right in the end, and generally mothered him.

And then he had met Sir Julius. He met him at a dinner-party to which both Pauline and he had been invited, and he noticed that Sir Julius seemed uncommonly interested in Pauline. Being almost desperate by this time, this fact had given him courage to approach the financier, make a clean breast of his troubles, and ask for advice. Sir Julius had been kind—oh, very kind! He had listened sympathetically, asked where the information had come from, made a note of the number of shares held, and promised to go into the matter and give his opinion as soon as possible; he held out a distinct hope that a way might be found out of the difficulty. The next news was Pauline's engagement.

Mainwaring had never dreamed of coupling the two ideas together. Now of course it was plain enough what had happened. Sir Julius had put a business-like proposition to Pauline, and she, with her father's threats of suicide ringing in her ears, had accepted it. What it must have cost her to do so, neither of the two men now discussing her action dared to think. The point was that she had done so. Sir Julius, after a decent interval, had kept his side of the bargain. He had rung up from Thornton only a minute before Stephen arrived, to say that he would take over the whole parcel of shares at the price originally paid for them (twice their present market value!) and pay the call on them himself. Oh, yes, Sir Julius emerged from the affair in a favourable enough light.

Did he, though? Stephen reflected, when Mr Mainwaring's voice had at last died into silence. Did he, though? It did not square with the information of Johnson, the chauffeur? It did not square at all. Unless—! Oh, Sir Julius was a very cunning man; very cunning indeed. It would be just like him to kill two such eminently satisfactory birds with one stone.

'What was the name of this gold-mining company?' he asked abruptly.

'The African and Eastern Gold Syndicate.'

'Well, I can find out the truth about them, at any rate,' Stephen said, jumping up. 'May I use your telephone a minute? I used to have a very particular pal indeed whose father's a big pot on the Stock Exchange. I haven't seen him for years, but I know he was going into the business. Anyway, I can soon find out.' He ran his eye rapidly down a column in the telephone-book. 'Ah, here we are!' He unhooked the receiver and gave a number.

'Can I speak to Mr Carson, please?' he said a moment later. 'Mr Peter Carson. Yes. Hullo, is that you, Pete? This is Steve speaking—Steve Munro.' A short stream of light badinage was hurriedly exchanged. 'Yes, but look here, Pete, I want to ask you something deuced important. Listen—what can you tell me about the African and Eastern Gold Syndicate? Are they any good or not?'

There was a perceptible pause before Mr Carson replied slowly: 'Why? Are you interested in them?'

'Yes,' Stephen returned guardedly. 'I am.'

'Well, Steve, I wouldn't say this to anybody in the world but you, because it's the deadliest secret there ever was and only half a dozen people are in it, but—you hang on to every one of them you've got, my lad, and thank heaven you've got 'em! If in three months they're not worth exactly ten times what they are now, I'll eat this blinking telephone for you—without salt or pepper!'

'Land of Hope and Glory!' Stephen shouted into the receiver. 'But— but they've fallen to half their value, Pete.'

'Oh, that's just eyewash,' returned the man of affairs with proper scorn. 'They're quoted at that, but they can't be bought—either for that or anything else. They're all in the hands of those half-dozen people, or precious nearly all. We've got as many as we could lay our hands on, but we'd be only too glad to buy more. At four times the quoted price, if you want to sell, old man.'

'Thanks,' said Stephen briefly. 'I don't. But look here, Pete, why are they going to bound up like this? I thought a call meant that things were pretty rocky.'

'Well, it's like this. Not long ago an extraordinarily rich vein of gold was discovered in some of the territory on which the company's got an option. It's being kept frightfully dark, and only the directors are supposed to know (my father's a director, by the way). The call's partly eyewash to frighten off the small investor, but it's really wanted to provide money for taking up the option. By the way, it's lucky I've got a room to myself here. My father would cut me off with fourpence if he knew I was telling you all this. You'll promise to keep it to yourself, won't you?'

'Rather! But—this call. It's a little embarrassing. You see, I haven't got the cash to meet it.'

'Then borrow it, old son,' returned Mr Carson laconically. 'How much have you got to find?'

Stephen covered the mouthpiece with his hand and turned to Mr Mainwaring, who had been following the monologue with every sign of approaching delirium. 'What's the total amount that you're liable for on the call?' he whispered.

'Two thousand four hundred,' Mr Mainwaring whispered back.

'About two thousand four hundred,' Stephen repeated into the telephone. 'Couldn't lend it me yourself, by any chance, could you, Pete? The security's good enough.'

'Search me!' said Mr Carson shortly. 'The firm'll buy some if you want to get rid of them, but you might as well ask me for two million as two thousand in the present state of affairs. Two pounds is nearer my mark, and that'd be a bit of a squeeze.'

'Oh! Well—do you know anybody else who could?'

'I do not,' said Mr Carson with decision. 'And if you take my advice, you won't come chatting about African and Eastern round this part of the world. They'll tear you in pieces if they know you've got any. Touch one of your aristocratic pals for the cash. That's my advice. Well, look here, Steve, old man, we must fix up an evening some time. When are you free?' The conversation passed from matters financial.

A minute later Stephen hung up the receiver. Instantly a stream of questions, as if pent up almost beyond human endurance, poured excitedly from Mr Mainwaring's lips. Stephen answered as best he could and explained the nature of the surprising information he had succeeded in obtaining.

Mr Mainwaring's joy was pathetic to behold. He wrung Stephen's hand, smacked him on the back, rang for the butler and ordered a bottle of champagne, thumped the desk, roared with laughter one moment and almost wept the next, and generally behaved like a man nearly insane with delight. Stephen saw that the strain through which he had been passing must have been almost unbearable; no wonder that the reaction from it was correspondingly severe.

'Yes,' said Stephen, coming with difficulty at last down to hard facts once more, 'but what about that two thousand four hundred we've got to find?'

'Borrow it, my boy!' beamed the old gentleman, exuding happy optimism once more from every pore. 'Borrow it!'

'But do you know anybody you can borrow it from? I don't, or I would like a shot.'

'Heaps!' said Mr Mainwaring confidently. 'Dozens of 'em. Borrow it fifty times over. That dam' scoundrel! God bless my soul, he nearly had me on toast, Stephen!'

Stephen noted with gratification his promotion from ordinary Munro to confidential Stephen. 'He's a clever man, is Sir Julius,' he replied dryly.

On consideration he had decided to say nothing, to Mr Mainwaring at any rate, of the Stock Exchange knight's financial straits. No good would be gained by doing so, and the information might turn out to be baseless after all.

'Told me not to lose a minute in getting the transfer of the shares through,' Mr Mainwaring was chuckling. 'I must set about it that very instant! Oh, he's a clever rascal. And it's all due to you, Stephen. I owe you a debt of gratitude that I can never repay in this life. And my little girl too—even more than me. Good heavens, when I think—! You'll be seeing her when you get back. You'll break the news to her yourself? I can give you that pleasure.'

'Certainly I will,' said Stephen fervently. 'But remember, sir, we're not out of the wood yet. When has that call got to be paid off by?'

'Eleven o'clock tomorrow morning,' replied Mr Mainwaring blithely.

Stephen whistled. 'I say, then, we've got to look nippy. Hadn't you better begin ringing up some of those friends of yours about lending you the money?'

But he did not at that moment, for the butler entered with a tray on which reposed a bottle of champagne and two glasses, and justice had first to be done to that. It was not yet four o'clock in the afternoon, and a curious time to drink champagne; but never had Stephen drunk a more heart-felt toast than the silent one which rose to his mind as the glass touched his lips.

After that Mr Mainwaring did begin to get busy with the telephone.

And then came a swift reversal of fortune. For nearly two hours the telephone was in constant use, while Mr Mainwaring's expression grew more and more uneasy.

'It's no good,' he said despondently to Stephen at last. 'Half the people I was thinking of are out of town and I can't get into touch with them in time, and the other half can't—or won't—lay their hands on any cash at such short notice. The best I've got is an offer of two hundred and fifty.'

Stephen glanced at his watch. He had told Pauline he would be back in time for dinner, and he would only just be able to do it. Besides, he was anxious to hear whether any further developments had taken place at Wintringham Hall, about which he had thought it best to say nothing to Mr Mainwaring.

'And there's absolutely nobody else you can try?' he asked.

'Nobody.'

'Well, there's only one thing to be done. You'll have to sell out enough shares to cover the call. That means about a quarter, doesn't it? You'll get twice as much as you paid for them, after all. I'll leave you a note of Pete's address, and you'd better ring him up first thing tomorrow morning.'

'Sickening!' commented Mr Mainwaring disgustedly. 'If what your friend says is true and I could only have raised that money, I'd have got back every penny of my capital and a bit more besides. Still, I suppose I can't complain. I deserve to have lost the lot, and that's a fact.'

Stephen hurriedly wrote down the address and, with a warm hand-shake, departed from the house under a further torrent of Mr Mainwaring's gratitude. Not a little pleased with himself and fortune, he returned to Wintringham Hall.

He had only just time to change for dinner when he arrived, and everybody else was upstairs except Lady Susan who, already dressed, was crossing the hall as he entered.

'Hullo, Stephen,' she said, a little mockingly as usual. 'You're a fine young man to run off in the middle of all our troubles here. What have you been up to, eh?'

An overwhelming impulse rushed over Stephen to share his great news with some other human being. Lady Susan, he knew, detested Sir Julius and would be only too delighted at this story of the financier's circumvention. Following her into the drawing-room, he proceeded at once to give her a brief and excited outline of it.

Lady Susan listened with a grim smile. 'You were wasted as a footman, Stephen. I saw that at the time. So this ridiculous Mr Mainwaring hasn't been able to get hold of his two thousand four hundred, or whatever it is?'

'No, but after all—'

'I'll lend it to him,' Lady Susan said abruptly. 'You can ring him up after dinner and tell him he can post his cheque tonight. I'll ring up my bank tomorrow and have the money transferred to his account so that the cheque will be met. I'm not doing it for his sake,' she added, cutting short Stephen's thanks. 'I'm doing it partly for the girl, who really is a refreshing change from the usual hipless, spindle-legged, powdered and painted creature whom Freddie brings down to show me; but mostly I'm doing it to complete your admirable work of discomfiting that dreadful Sir Julius Guggleheimer, or whatever his horrible name is. Now run up and dress, or you'll miss the soup!'

Immediately after dinner, while the men were still in the dining-room, Stephen slipped away into the library and put through his call to London. Mr Mainwaring's delight at the other end rendered him quite incoherent.

Nothing further, it appeared, had transpired at the Hall during Stephen's absence. The inspector of police had taken it for granted that Martin's death was accidental, and had given but a cursory glance to the scene of the tragedy. Stephen was content that this should be so. He was anxious to pursue his own investigations into the matter, which he could not help connecting in his mind with the mystery of Cicely's disappear-ance, and did not wish to be hampered by police inquiries. As to Cicely, nothing further had been heard of her.

Having completed his telephoning, Stephen wandered out into the garden. The moment he had been looking forward to all day had at last arrived.

Pauline was already waiting for him on the terrace. He took her arm with a little smile and led her away to a secluded summer-house, tucked away in a shrubbery out of sight of the house.

'Now then!' Pauline said, settling herself comfortably. 'I know you're simply bursting with news, Stephen, and I'm dying to hear it. What's it all about?'

'You,' Stephen replied abruptly, and paused.

'Me?'

'Yes. It wasn't for any reasons connected with Cicely that I went up to London. It was because I knew quite well that this engagement of yours was all wrong. Anybody with half an eye could see that you didn't even like the chap—let alone love him. I knew you couldn't be marrying him for his money and I was convinced that he had managed to get some sort of a hold over you. I most officiously made it my business to find out what it was.'

'Oh!' breathed Pauline, and was silent.

'It was only because I couldn't bear the idea of you making an unhappy marriage,' Stephen pleaded, uncertain whether to interpret her silence as a good or a bad augury as to how she would receive his news. 'You of all people! So I went straight to your father and put things to him.' He went on to give a somewhat halting description of the afternoon's events.

'So Sir Julius was playing a double game, you see,' he concluded. 'He was out to get both you and—'

'Is that you, Pauline?' said a harsh voice from the dusk of the doorway. 'Now, look here, my girl, this is the last time I tell you. I will not have—'

'One minute, Sir Julius,' Pauline said in an icy voice. She glided over to the doorway and slipped something into the man's hand. 'I've changed my mind. There's your ring. Will you go away now, please?'

'What the devil's the meaning of this?' Sir Julius blustered. 'You know perfectly well your father's—'

'Did you hear what Miss Mainwaring said?' Stephen interrupted in silky tones. 'Get out—before I start kicking you!'

Sir Julius paused a moment. 'I'll talk to you about this when you've come to your senses, Pauline,' he grunted and turned on his heel.

In silence they listened to his retreating steps.

Pauline turned to Stephen. 'Oh, Stephen!' she whispered, in a funny, broken little voice.

Stephane caught her in her arms as she swayed towards him. For the first time their lips met.

XV WHAT ANNETTE CON-FESSED

IT was half an hour before hard sense returned to Stephen. He had loved Pauline for months in silence; now he knew that she loved him, and silence was broken. There had been explanations, the unravelling of misunderstandings, very sweet and happy confidences; but what, Stephen now had to ask himself, did all that avail? The realization of Pauline's love was a wonderful one, but there was almost more bitterness than sweetness in the knowledge, for marriage was as out of the question as it ever had been. He could not even mention the word to her. A penniless young man, now without even a footman's wages to support him, can hardly begin to talk of marriage until some definite prospect discloses itself that he will ever be able to support a wife; and at present that prospect looked even more remote to Stephen than ever before.

He was trying, somewhat lamely, to hint some of this to Pauline, when once more they were interrupted. Somebody passed close to the summer-house, crying: 'Pauline!'

'That's Annette,' Pauline said to Stephen. 'I suppose I'd better see what she wants. Hullo, Annette!'

'Is that you?' Annette called out with evident relief. 'Good heavens, where have you been? I've been screeching for you for the last half-hour. You're wanted indoors, at a council of war. Seen Stephen anywhere?' Annette had never dropped the 'Mr Munro' mode of address for the simple reason that she had never used it; Stephen had jumped in her speech straight from William into 'Stephen'.

'Yes, he's here too, as a matter of fact.'

'Oh, is he—as a matter of fact? How lucky! For me, I mean.' Her broad wink at Pauline was fortunately lost in the darkness. 'By the way, Pauline, the gent your fiancé is roaming about looking like a Scotch Sunday in Africa. Black, and plenty of gloom, so to speak. Do you think you could do anything towards soothing him?' Annette very seldom troubled to mince her words.

'I'm afraid not,' Pauline smiled. 'You see, he isn't my fiancé any more.'

'Coo!' said Miss Agnew earnestly. 'Given him the bird?'

'Something like that,' Pauline admitted.

Annette seized her hand and wrung it violently. 'This is a far better thing that you are doing now than you have ever done,' she intoned dramatically. 'Certainly it's a far better one than getting engaged to the blighter. Congratulations, Pauline! I hate to see good material wasted.'

'What's all this about a council of war, Annette?' Stephen intervened tactfully. 'Am I wanted too?'

'You are. And by the way, we'd better hurry. Cousin Susan'll be grinding her false teeth with rage by this time. She sent me to look for you somewhere about yesterday. How time does fly, doesn't it, Stephen?'

'Annette, I don't think you were smacked enough in your youth,' said Stephen, as they walked towards the house.

'Well, don't you start remedying the defect, that's all. I warn you, I've got a hefty punch; and my kick isn't to be despised either.'

'Why does Lady Susan want us, Annette?' asked Pauline. 'Do you know?'

'Because she says you're the only two people here with a grain of sense between you, if you really want to know,' returned Miss Agnew crisply.

On this invigorating intelligence they entered the hall.

Lady Susan was waiting for them in her morning-room, alone. As they came in, she looked up and smiled grimly. Lady Susan knew perfectly well all there was to know about the slightly embarrassed couple who walked delicately into her presence. For the matter of that, Stephen wore his feelings plastered inches deep over his face every time his glance happened to alight on Pauline—which it did singularly often.

'Sit down,' she said briskly, 'now you have come at last. I've decided to take you two into my confidence. I'm going to tell you how Cicely disappeared the night before last.'

'You know, then, Lady Susan?' Pauline cried.

'Oh, yes; I know. You see, Annette told me.'

'Annette!' Pauline exclaimed.

'Where was she, then?' Stephen demanded.

'Behind me on the couch,' Annette returned with simple pride. 'Tucked away in the hollow, between the loose cushions and the back. We had all you people properly on toast, didn't we?'

'But she couldn't have got there!' Pauline objected.

'But she did!' Annette retorted. 'There's oceans of room in one of those big couches. If you don't believe me, shrink to Cicely's size and try yourself.'

'Then—then she did it for a joke?' Stephen said, trying to readjust his theories in the light of this information.

'She did it for a joke,' Annette agreed gravely.

'And she's kept it up all this time?' Pauline chimed in incredulously.

'That's just what I want to talk to you two about,' Lady Susan intervened. 'Four heads are better than two, and it's hardly a thing I could discuss with that ridiculous policeman who was asking me all sorts of absurd questions this afternoon. But first you'd better tell them exactly what did happen, Annette; let's get clear about that, anyhow.'

'Well, it was like this,' Annette explained. 'I was bored stiff with the idea of a rotten séance, as you might have gathered; I wanted to play bridge. But directly after the lights had gone down Cicely ran across and whispered to me to hide her, for a bit of a joke. I knew that trick with a big couch, so I pushed her in there and went off to add a bit of local colour to the proceedings, first whispering to Cousin Susan not to be alarmed at anything that happened, because it would only be me.'

'I will say that you showed some sense there, my dear,' Lady Susan commented, almost with approval. 'I don't think I'm easily alarmed, but really—!'

'Then it was you doing those raps, was it?' Pauline remarked.

'Yes. I thought I might as well give Freddie a thrill for his money. But I wasn't the only one. I did those single raps at the beginning, but somebody else was playing the same game, because certainly I didn't produce all those exciting noises that came at the end.'

'Ah!, said Stephen thoughtfully. 'And the scream—did you do that?'

'I did,' replied Miss Agnew proudly. 'And the chloroform, which I flatter myself was the crowning touch.'

'How on earth did you do that?'

'Well, I had a bottle of toothache stuff in my bag, you see. After I'd finished rapping, I went back to the couch to see that Cicely was properly mixed up with its innards. Then I had the brilliant brain-wave about the chloroform, pulled it out of my bag, extracted the cork, ran a few steps away from the couch, emptied the bottle, produced one of our most lifelike screams, found her scarf in my hand and tossed it wildly away, and ran back to the couch again—and where was Cicely when the light went up?'

'Well, I'll be hanged!' observed Stephen in heart-felt tones.

'Yes, pretty neat, wasn't it?' remarked Miss Agnew complacently.

'But what happened after that?' asked Pauline. 'Was she there all the time till we went out of the room?'

'She was. Lying as snug as a—as a perfect lady. It isn't till after you'd all gone that there's any mystery. What happened then was this. We waited till the room was empty, and then I got off the couch to have a look round. Cicely wanted to keep it up a little longer and slip into the garden and hide there for a bit, so I stood at the French windows for a minute to see that the coast was clear. Then I heard somebody calling me from upstairs—Baby, I think it was. I thought it would look less suspicious if I went up to join them, so I did, turning out the drawing-room light as I passed the switch so that Cicely could come out in the dark and not be seen through the French windows from the garden. And that's all I know about it. When I went back to the drawing-room about twenty minutes later, Cicely had gone; and from that moment to this I haven't the foggiest notion where she's been or what she's been doing.'

'And you knew where she was hiding all the time, Lady Susan?' Stephen inquired of his hostess.

'No, I didn't know she was on the couch at the time; Annette was thoughtful enough to come along to my room and tell me that when she went upstairs. At the time I imagined Cicely to be somewhere quite different.'

'Yes,' Stephen nodded. 'In the secret room.'

Lady Susan looked astonished. 'And what do you know about a secret room in my house, young man?'

'Quite a lot, Lady Susan,' Stephen laughed. 'As it happens, Pauline and I have been poking our noses rather deeply into this business. We both felt there was foul play at the back of it, and we joined forces to see whether we couldn't get at the bottom of the mystery.'

'Tell Lady Susan what we've discovered, Stephen,' said Pauline.

'Yes, tell Lady Susan,' agreed the old lady grimly. 'After all, it's her house, her guest, and, presumably, her mystery. Tell her, by all means.'

Stephen did so. He recounted the gist of the midnight conversation between Pauline and himself and the conclusions they had arrived at, and went on to describe their first visit to the secret room and the finding of the handkerchief which Pauline had identified as Cicely's, and then the watch they had kept that night with its dramatic sequel.

'Humph!' Lady Susan commented. 'The secret of that priest-hole is supposed to be confined, by family tradition, to the actual master and mistress of the house alone. Millicent knows about it of course, and so apparently does not only Cicely, but the greater number of my visitors as well. Well, that appears to explain what Cicely did after you left her, Annette, but not much more. I must admit that I'm uneasy about the child. Even yesterday I wondered that she could keep up a silly joke so long, but today I'm convinced it isn't a joke any longer. But apart from the mysterious gentleman who kicked Stephen downstairs, it doesn't seem as if there is any personal clue at all.'

Stephen exchanged glances with Pauline. He had purposely omitted from his narrative all reference both to his knowledge that Martin's death was not due to an accident, and to the telegram he had received that morning, and the inevitable deductions to be drawn from it; and he had also withheld the conversation between Henry and Martin which they had overheard from the secret room and also the rumours of Sir Julius's impending financial troubles. The former he had not even mentioned as yet to Pauline and he would certainly want to talk it over with her before disclosing it further; as for the two latter, he was not sure whether he ought to reveal them. Pauline nodded, and he gathered that she thought he ought to do so.

'We have got hold of a certain amount of information that seems to throw suspicion on one or two people, Lady Susan,' he said slowly, 'but I think it ought to be treated as highly confidential.'

'Quite so,' Lady Susan agreed briskly. 'Annette, run along now, there's a good girl.'

Amid heart-felt protests, Annette accepted her banishment. Stephen at once explained the conversation between Henry Kentisbeare and Martin, with its sinister implications, and what he had heard from Johnson, Sir Julius's chauffeur.

'And I want to thank you, Lady Susan,' Pauline put in, a little nervously, 'for offering to lend that money to Father. It was—'

'Stuff!' Lady Susan cut her short without ceremony. 'It was the least I could do to help Stephen in his brilliant attempt to get your ridiculous father out of his mess. Well, Stephen, so you think the egregious Mr Kentisbeare, and some other person unknown, are at the bottom of the trouble, and that they were trying, apparently with excellent success, to induce Martin to join them, do you?'

'It seems to point that way,' Stephen admitted. 'I propose to tackle Kentisbeare on the subject.

'Good! And if you take my advice, you'll look for the unknown in the person of Sir Julius Guggleheimer. Your news about him sheds quite an interesting light on the disappearance of my jewellery. Pauline, my dear, you'd better see about breaking your engagement with the creature.'

'I've already seen about it, Lady Susan,' Pauline smiled.

There was a knock at the door and Annette's head appeared. 'Sorry to disturb you, but I thought you might like to hear this, Cousin Susan. Sir Julius has fled! He left a message with Millicent that urgent affairs had called him back to London, and hopped it half an hour ago.'

'Thank you, Annette,' said Lady Susan. 'That is very interesting. Very well, my dear.' As the door closed, she looked significantly at the other two.

'Very interesting,' Stephen agreed.

'Well, that says good-bye to my jewellery,' Lady Susan observed with resignation. 'Of course that absurd inspector couldn't find any clue. Fortunately it's insured.'

'You seem very confident that Sir Julius took it,' Pauline remarked, a little defensively.

'I am, my dear,' Lady Susan returned simply.

There was a little pause.

'Another thing I think we ought to find out,' Stephen said in reflective tones, 'is whether that séance was premeditated or not. That seems to me very important.'

Lady Susan looked at him quizzically. 'Are you accusing my nephew of being mixed up in it now?' she asked.

'Freddie?' said Stephen, genuinely startled. 'Good gracious, no! It never entered my head.'

'But if I remember rightly, he was active in promoting the séance.'

'Yes, but it may have been suggested to him by somebody else.'

'Humph!'

'One thing's obvious enough, I think, Lady Susan,' Pauline put in. 'Whether the first séance was premeditated or not, the people who are at the bottom of the business certainly wanted a second one. We know that from the telephone message and Cicely's letter.'

'Oh, yes,' Stephen chimed in eagerly. 'Are you really sure, Lady Susan, that it was Cicely's voice over the telephone and Cicely's handwriting in the letter? That neither of them could have been faked, I mean?'

'Quite sure, Stephen. The voice on the telephone was very blurred and faint, but it was unmistakably Cicely's.'

'Of course there are only two possible deductions from that,' Stephen said slowly. 'Either Miss Vernon was acting under pressure, or else—' He paused.

'Yes?' said Lady Susan grimly. 'Or else what?'

Stephen tried a ranging shot. 'That she's in league with these people!'

'That I'll never believe,' Lady Susan said with emphasis.

'That's what I said—at first,' Pauline observed. 'But that conversation between Henry and Martin seemed to hint very definitely that she is.'

'Stuff!' was Lady Susan's uncompromising reply. 'Well,' she went on in a matter-of-fact voice, 'it seems to me the best thing to be done is for you two to pursue the investigations you appear to have been making. As you can see, it isn't a case in which we can call the police in, except as a very last resource. And in the meantime you may as well see if you can save me a private detective's fees. From what I hear of them, anybody with half a grain of common-sense could do that. Now, run along, both of you!'

On this somewhat ambiguous compliment, they left the old lady.

It had been Stephen's intention to take Pauline aside as soon as the interview was over and acquaint her with his discovery concerning the circumstances of Martin's death, but the sight of Henry Kentisbeare crossing the hall as they emerged from the morning-room drove the thought out of his head.

'Come on, Pauline,' he whispered excitedly. 'Let's take the bull by the horns and tackle this fellow now. After all, he's got the whole thing at his finger-tips, if only I can frighten it out of them.'

'Oh, yes!' Pauline whispered back. 'Do let's!'

'Kentisbeare,' Stephen called across the hall, 'can you spare us a minute? We'd like a word with you.'

Henry Kentisbeare, who was in the act of climbing the stairs, halted and turned round. 'With me?' he drawled. 'Certainly. What's it all about?'

Stephen opened the door of the library and looked inside. Fortunately it was empty. 'Come along in here,' he said, not a little peremptorily.

Henry raised his eyebrows, but consented to do so. Pauline had preceded him.

Stephen shut the door and leaned his back against it, looking as large and massive as he could. 'Now then, Kentisbeare,' he said without preamble, 'I'll trouble you to tell us exactly what the conversation was about between you and Martin in the drawing-room at six o'clock yesterday evening.'

XVI AN UNEXPECTED EXPLANATION

FOR a moment Henry Kentisbeare quite forgot to be languid. 'What the devil—?' With a palpable effort he pulled himself together and succeeded in recovering his poise. 'My good chap,' he said in slightly pitying tones, 'what are you talking about?'

'Don't take that line, Kentisbeare,' Stephen said sharply. 'It won't pay you. I warn you, your only chance is to make a clean breast of the whole thing. Otherwise I shall see that the matter is handed over to the police.' It was bluff, of course, but Stephen could see nothing for it except bluff.

It did not look as if it was to be rewarded. Henry gazed at Stephen for a moment as if he were some curious species of unknown animal, then turned to Pauline.

'Is the man mad?' he asked with interest.

'Far from it, Henry,' Pauline returned brightly. 'But I think you must be.'

Henry transferred his gaze to the ceiling. 'There appear to be delusions about,' he confided to it with gentle melancholy.

'I suppose you think I'm bluffing?' Stephen snapped.

'The thought had crossed my mind, I admit,' Henry continued to confide to the ceiling.

'Very well, then. I'll give you a short account of what took place at the interview. You asked Martin whether he had considered your proposition. Martin replied that he had done so, favourably. You were glad to hear this, repeated what you had already told him in the pantry, that there was a pot of money in it, and confirmed the arrangement by which Martin was to receive a quarter of all the emoluments (Martin's word) which accrued. You added further that you would do your best to urge a second séance that evening, during which Martin could carry out his part of the business, and assured him that the young lady would also continue to play her part. In return for these confidences, Martin mentioned the fact that there was an ex-convict in the house upon whom he intended to practise a little gentle blackmailing. You were both so complimentary as to exchange a few heart-felt remarks about myself. Now then—kindly fill in the gaps!'

Henry's face during this speech had been an interesting study in emotional expressions. His gaze had left the ceiling, fastened itself upon Stephen, while his eyes grew more and more round, his jaw had dropped lower and lower, and his eyebrows had lifted themselves almost into the roots of his hair.

He whistled softly. 'Well, I'll be smothered!' he observed incredulously. 'Were you in the room?'

'What I said was—fill in the gaps!' returned Stephen sternly.

Henry shrugged his shoulders. 'Well, as you appear to know so much, I suppose it won't matter your knowing a little more. Ask, therefore, and you shall be answered. But I rely on you to keep all this confidential, of course,' he added as an afterthought.

'Why did you want a second séance to be held that night?' Stephen demanded, disregarding this injunction.

Henry had quite recovered himself in this short space of time. 'So that Martin could look through the papers without any fear of being disturbed,' he replied gently, in the manner of one explaining to a small child that two and two, added together, make four. He also delicately stifled a yawn.

'What papers?' asked Stephen in surprise.

'Sir Julius's, of course!' Henry returned, no less surprised.

It was beginning to dawn on Stephen that he had been grasping this stick by the wrong end. He shifted the trend of his inquiries.

'Who was the "young lady" referred to?'

'Need we really go into that?'

'Certainly we need.'

Henry shrugged his shoulders again. 'Very well. But you'll note that this is under protest, won't you? Miss Cullompton.'

'Baby?' exclaimed Pauline.

'The same, dear lady,' Henry agreed with gentle irony, and bowed gracefully.

'What was the plot?' asked Stephen bluntly.

'But I thought you knew!' Henry was mildly astonished. 'I confess that your reference to the police rather baffled me, but—'

'What was the plot?'

'Why, to find out whether certain rumours which had reached our ears concerning'—he bowed to Pauline again—'your admirable fiancé's financial position had any basis in truth. It will be obvious to you that if Sir Julius, as our information went, was on the verge of bankruptcy, quite a respectable amount of pocket-money might be collected by "bearing" (I believe that is the right term) the shares in which he happens to be interested.'

'And you wanted Martin in with you, because no comment would he raised if he were discovered in Sir Julius's room?' Stephen exclaimed, seeing daylight at last.

'But this is genius!' Henry murmured. 'My—er—partner did attempt to interest you in the matter while you were still, so to speak, in the plush, but you discouraged her advances so firmly that she hardly liked to pursue the question.'

'So that's what she wanted!'

'Precisely. It never occurred to you? Well, well, we can't all be bright in the uptake, can we? So humiliating for the poor lady, too; she was so certain that she would be able to induce you to join us by what is known technically, I believe, as a heart-appeal. The line she proposed to take, I understood, was—'

'That's enough of that,' Stephen growled, flushing in spite of himself. 'And who was the "other party" in with you?'

'I told you. Miss Cullompton.'

'I understood there was another man in it?'

'Your information was seriously at fault, then,' Henry replied gravely. 'There wasn't. By the way, it may interest you to know that ours, on the other hand, was not. As one person with a proper regard for money to another,' he added, turning to Pauline, 'I feel impelled to tell you that your fiancé is not merely a man of straw; in all probability he will shortly be a man of oakum. The admirable Martin did succeed in discovering that much for the syndicate before his regrettable interview with that elm tree this morning. If I were you, I should stop bulling him and join us bears.'

'All right,' Stephen said shortly, in reply to this kind advice. 'You can go.'

'Now that,' said Mr Kentisbeare, 'is what I call extraordinarily kind of you,' and went.

'Lord, how I dislike that man!' said Stephen as he shut the door upon him. 'Well, what do you make of that, Pauline? It appears that we've been barking up the wrong tree.'

'I suppose he was speaking the truth?' Pauline meditated.

'Oh, I think so. He knew he was playing a dirty sort of game, you see, and was trying to bluff it out that there was nothing in it that a decent fellow shouldn't do. If he wasn't telling the truth, he's a most perfect actor, that's all I can say.'

'Well, what are we to do now?' Pauline asked helplessly. 'This simply cuts all what we thought was solid ground away from under our feet. Still, it does exonerate Cicely.'

'Does it?' said Stephen grimly, and went on to tell her about the telegram he had received that morning. 'So that yachting trip was a blind, you see,' he concluded. 'I had my suspicions before Cicely was taking a hand in the game herself; now I'm sure of it.'

'I'm not,' Pauline said slowly. 'I admit her disappearance may have been voluntary. She seems to have been looking for an excuse to disappear for a time, and when the yachting trip, for some reason, didn't suit her plans, she may just have taken advantage of the opportunity of the séance. But in spite of your telegram, I don't believe for a minute that she's had anything to do with what's happened since. For one thing, she'd know that a disappearance like this would worry Lady Susan badly, and I'm sure she wouldn't voluntarily do that.'

'Well,' Stephen said mildly, 'all that we shan't know till we find Cicely.

At any rate, we do know now where she was for part of the time, and that she hid there for a joke.'

'We shall have to think it all over. In the meantime, Stephen, don't you think we ought to he going back to the drawing-room? They'll be wondering what on earth has happened to us.'

'Not for just a minute, Pauline,' Stephen said seriously. 'There's something jolly important that I want to tell you first.' Without waiting for her reply he began to narrate the story of his investigations and conclusions on the scene of Martin's death.

'Oh, Stephen!' Pauline exclaimed when he had finished. 'Then Martin was—murdered!'

'So it appears,' Stephen agreed with gravity.

'And you haven't told the police about those saw-marks on the bough?'

'No-o,' Stephen said, a little uneasily. 'I ought to, I suppose, but you see I can't help feeling convinced that Martin's death is all part and parcel of the mystery about Cicely. Lady Susan naturally doesn't want the police brought into that, which they would certainly have to be if I told them about Martin. Besides, I must say that I'd like to have a shot at clearing the thing up myself first. After all, it was up to them to discover those saw-marks, just as I did.'

'Yes,' Pauline meditated. 'I think on the whole you're right. But I do not think that you ought to hold up your knowledge indefinitely. If Martin really has been murdered by the same people who carried off Cicely, his death ought not to go—well, unavenged.'

'Oh, of course,' Stephen agreed quickly. 'But till we know who did carry off Cicely (always assuming that she was carried off), we shan't know who murdered Martin; so we must concentrate on that first. I hadn't any particular liking for Martin, by the way,' he added, 'and I'm quite sure he hadn't any for me, but that doesn't mean that I'm not going to try and find out as hard as I can who killed him.'

'Of course,' Pauline agreed emphatically.

Stephen paused. He was wondering whether to tell her about that suspicion of his, that it might not have been Martin for whom death was intended. To a person as sanely matter-of-fact as Stephen himself, the theory had certainly appeared a little far-fetched when it first jumped into his mind, and certainly melodramatic; but it was an uncommonly interesting one for all that. He decided to mention it.

'Pauline,' he said slowly, 'do these facts suggest anything to you? I remarked at breakfast, in the presence of, so far as I remember, everybody staying in this house except Lady Susan herself, that I was going to walk to the station to catch a certain train. Everyone knew that I should therefore be passing through that little wood at a specified time. Only a short while before that specified time somebody else does pass through that wood.

A very cunningly prepared trap is sprung and the passer-by is killed.'

Pauline's face whitened as the purport of his remarks dawned upon her. 'Oh, Stephen!' she breathed. 'You don't think—?'

'Added to all that,' Stephen continued, 'the only persons we know to have an unassailable alibi are the Colonel, Sir Julius and Starcross.'

'Especially Starcross,' Pauline remarked with an involuntary little smile.

'Yes,' Stephen smiled back, 'we're not likely to forget his alibi. The others said they were going to play golf. But did they? Annette could tell us that, by the way.'

'As a matter of fact, I know,' Pauline said thoughtfully. 'They didn't. Half-way to the links Henry suddenly decided that he didn't want to play golf, and Baby agreed with him. Freddie and Annette, on the other hand, did. They had quite a fierce little argument about it. In the end Henry and Baby got out of the car to go for a walk, and Freddie and Annette went on to play a round by themselves.'

'That's interesting,' Stephen commented. 'Very interesting. Freddie had an alibi then. Humph!'

'What have you got in your mind, Stephen?' Pauline demanded. 'Something, I'm sure.'

'No, really nothing. I'm just suspecting everybody and everything at the moment. But we want more facts. And the first thing I must do is to tackle Freddie about that séance. If only it does turn out that somebody put the idea into his head, we really shall have a definite pointer at last.'

'Do you think it's any good keeping watch tonight, Stephen?'

'No,' Stephen said thoughtfully. 'I don't. I can't conceive any reason why the fellow should want to go to the secret room tonight, and there's no doubt that we thoroughly frightened him yesterday. He certainly won't be anxious to repeat the performance.' He did not add that he had already made up his mind to keep watch by himself; for though firmly believing in the reasoning he had just expressed, Stephen intended to take no chances. But that was no reason why Pauline should be burdened with an almost certainly fruitless vigil as well.

Pauline rose from the chair in which she was sitting. 'Stephen, we really must go back to the drawing-room.'

'I suppose we must,' Stephen agreed reluctantly. 'By the way, that's another thing we've got to do tomorrow—find the other exit from that secret room. I don't suppose it will lead to anything but it's one of the possibilities that mustn't be neglected.'

But Pauline was not interested at the moment in secret rooms. She laid her hands on Stephen's shoulder and smiled up into his face.

'Then I'll say good night to you here—dear,' she said softly.

XVII MILLICENT'S STORY

LATE that night Stephen sought Freddie's room. Freddie, in the act of donning the coat of a pair of silk pyjamas that would have made Joseph turn green with envy, looked round inquiringly.

'Come in! Oh, it's you, old lad. And you've come. Well, well, how goes it?'

'Very nicely, thanks.' Stephen dropped into a chair and lit a cigarette. 'Freddie, you don't seem awfully upset about Cicely Vernon.'

'The lady with the disappearing act? Ah, well,' said Freddie tolerantly, 'girls will be girls.'

'Now what the deuce, Freddie,' Stephen inquired with care, 'do you mean by that?'

Freddie looked a trifle nonplussed. 'Well, to tell you the truth, old boy,' he admitted, 'I don't quite know. After all, is it necessary to mean something every time one speaks?'

'It's usual. But look here, Freddie, aren't you at all perturbed about it?'

'Perturbed, old man? No. Why should I be? I know old Cicely all right. Known her ever since we were kids, in fact.'

'Freddie, you're being remarkably cryptic tonight. Why should that be a reason for your not being perturbed? I should have thought it would have meant the opposite.'

Freddie slipped on his dressing-gown and began to brush his hair with elaborate care. 'Not a bit of it,' he said, somewhat absently. 'Cicely's always been fond of her little joke. I admit she's overdoing it a trifle this time, but that's all there is to it, you can take it from me.'

'You seem very sure,' Stephen observed mildly. 'Where do you imagine she is all this time, then?'

'Goodness knows! I don't. Probably she intercepted a wire or something that her yachting trip was on again, and simply popped off, leaving us standing. Just the sort of thing Cicely'd do.'

'Humph!' said Stephen. 'When did you first think of the idea of playing witches that night, Freddie?'

Freddie glanced at him over his shoulder. 'Me? Goodness knows, old lad. At dinner, as far as I remember. Why?'

'Oh, I was only wondering. But you were talking about that sort of thing in the library, weren't you?'

'Were we? Oh, you mean the old Colonel boy, Starcross and me? Yes, I believe we were. Starcross was making our flesh creep with some of the things he said he'd seen in that line, and the Colonel was trying to tell some ghastly story about Bengal. Yes, the idea might have been started then; can't say, I'm afraid.'

'By the Colonel or Starcross, do you mean?' Stephen asked eagerly.

'Great Scott, no! Can you imagine that mossy old boy suggesting anything so stimulating as a Witches' Sabbath? Come, come, Stephen, old lad, pull yourself together. As for Starcross, he was against it from the first. I remember him saying in the library that spiritualism and all that sort of thing is a pretty dreadful mistake, or some rot like that; playing with fire, and all that sort of thing. Bit of a wet blanket, I thought.'

'You had a book about witchcraft in your hand, didn't you? Where did you get that from?'

'Goodness knows, old boy! Why this cross-examination? May have pulled it down from the shelves, or may have seen it lying about. Can't remember, I'm afraid.'

'I see,' said Stephen.

The talk turned on to other topics.

Soon afterwards Stephen returned to his own room. He wanted as much of the household as possible to be safely asleep before he crept down to the drawing-room.

He waited for half an hour, till a quarter-past twelve, then kicked off his shoes and made his way cautiously downstairs.

The drawing-room door yielded easily enough to his push. He opened it and slipped from the black darkness of the hall into the scarcely less opaque obscurity within the room, relieved only by the tenuous pencils of moonlight which shone between the drawn curtains. Closing the door softly behind him, he stood for a moment listening. In the very moment of passing through the doorway he had experienced an uncanny sensation of not being alone in the room.

He strained his ears. There was no sound of breathing or indeed of any other description, but he was convinced that his instinct had been right. Somewhere, and that within a few feet of him, was another living presence—waiting intently to discover what he would do.

Suddenly Stephen made up his mind. With a couple of swift strides he was half-way towards the electric-light switch. But the other person was quicker. Before he could reach it there was a click and the room blazed with light. By the switch, rather white but thoroughly determined, stood Pauline. For a moment they gazed at each other in silence. Then, as if realizing the joke in the same instant of time, each broke into subdued laughter.

'What an anti-climax!' Pauline exclaimed in guarded tones. 'I really thought I had got him that time.'

Stephen shook his head and the smile died out of his face. 'You shouldn't have come down alone, Pauline dear. You don't know what sort of danger you might have been running your head into.'

Pauline did not look particularly impressed. 'You needn't think you're going to have all the exciting bits to yourself, Stephen,' she said lightly. 'By the way, I thought you weren't coming down here tonight?'

'I decided to leave nothing to chance, after all,' Stephen parried. 'Why did you come down?'

'Oh, I shouldn't have had a wink of sleep all night if I hadn't. Besides, it seemed such a good opportunity to have a quiet look round that little room for the other way out. Have you got your torch with you?'

'Yes.'

'Well, as we are here now, what about a little exploration?'

'Yes, that's a good idea,' Stephen agreed.

He switched out the light, crossed over to the fireplace and set the machinery in motion, preceding Pauline up the narrow stairs into the priest-hole. It was empty.

'All clear,' he called softly down to her, and a moment later she was at his side. They began to carry out a careful examination of the uncompromisingly solid, rough wooden walls.

Suddenly Pauline sniffed. 'Stephen,' she said, 'I'm sure I can smell that scent of Cicely's—Reine des Fleurs. It's faint, but I'm certain that's what it is.'

'Probably the remains from that handkerchief,' Stephen remarked, running his fingers along the edge of a huge beam.

'Oh no; that would have disappeared long ago. Stephen, I'm convinced that Cicely's been in this room quite recently—within the last twenty-four hours!'

'Humph!' Stephen said. 'You realize that would confirm my theory of her being a free agent, don't you? I say, Pauline, does it seem to you that the crack between these two beams here—'

Pauline caught his arm. 'Hush! Listen—someone's coming!'

Stephen held his breath. Undoubtedly light footsteps were approaching on the other side of the wooden wall. He swept his light hastily round the little bare room, and drew Pauline into a corner. 'We'll wait for him here,' he whispered, as they crouched against the wall, and extinguished his torch.

The footsteps drew nearer. There was the sound of creaking wood, and Stephen knew that the hidden door had been opened. The footsteps continued within a couple of feet of them.

Stephen directed the torch towards them and switched it suddenly on. In the little circle of light stood Millicent Carey.

She uttered a faint scream as the light illuminated her, and halted abruptly, turning a face drawn with terror towards the unseen holder of the torch. 'Who—who is it?' she asked in strangled tones, standing as if petrified in her attitude with fear.

'It's all right, Millicent,' Pauline replied reassuringly. 'Only me and Stephen. We were expecting somebody rather different.' As if to confirm her words, Stephen passed the light of the torch over their two faces.

'Oh!' said Millicent faintly, swaying on her feet. 'I thought for the moment it was—it was—'

'Look out, Stephen!' Pauline cried. 'She's going to faint again.'

Stephen sprang forward and supported the half-swooning lady. 'It's the shock,' he said. 'Run down and turn on the drawing-room lights, will you, Pauline? I'll help her down.' He passed his torch to her, and she hurried down the little stairway.

Two minutes later Millicent, a little recovered, was lying on a couch in the drawing-room, her face still very white and her whole body trembling slightly from head to foot. 'I thought,' she kept repeating, 'I thought it was—it was—'

'Yes?' Pauline said gently. 'Who did you think it was?'

'That—that dreadful man!' Millicent said with a violent shudder.

'What dreadful man?' Stephen asked eagerly.

'The one who—who came through my bedroom last night.'

Stephen exchanged a glance of triumph with Pauline. 'Then the other way out of that secret room opens into your bedroom?'

'Yes. Oh, yes.'

'What idiots we were, Stephen!' Pauline observed. 'Fancy wasting all that time looking for it, when all we had to do was to ask Millicent. Why didn't you tell us there were two entrances, Millicent?'

'I don't know,' Millicent replied vaguely. 'I suppose I never thought of it. And I knew Aunt Susan would be very annoyed if she knew I had told you anything at all.'

'Did somebody—a man—go through your room last night, then, Miss Carey?' Stephen asked, bringing the conversation back to the point of main importance.

'Yes,' quavered Millicent with another shudder.

'Did you recognize him?' Stephen asked anxiously.

'No. Oh, no! It was nobody I knew.'

'Nobody you knew?' Pauline echoed disappointedly.

'What did he look like?' Stephen put in.

Millicent looked from one face to the other, her own working convulsively. Without warning she dissolved into tears. 'Oh, there are dreadful things going on here!' she sobbed. 'I know there are. I told Aunt Susan so long ago, but she only laughed at me. Oh dear, oh dear! And now poor Martin! Oh, what is happening to everybody?'

Stephen looked significantly at Pauline. 'But Martin was killed by an accident,' he said quietly.

'Oh, yes, I know. But that doesn't make it any less dreadful, does it? Oh dear, I don't know what to do!'

Pauline dropped on her knees by the couch and began to soothe the distracted lady, while Stephen looked on sympathetically. It was evident that Millicent must have arrived long ago at the same conclusion as themselves regarding the probability of foul play; but whereas they were only guests in the house and could take a detached view, Millicent must have looked upon it as largely her own responsibility. Moreover, they had had each other for the exchange of confidences and suspicions, whereas Millicent had been utterly alone. No wonder the unhappy lady's nerves had been frayed almost to breaking-point.

'Now let's go into this sensibly,' he remarked in matter-of-fact tones, when Millicent had been somewhat restored. 'Pauline and I have been carrying out a few investigations on our own account, Miss Carey, having made up our minds, just as you have done, that something very suspicious indeed appeared to be going on.'

'Have you—have you found anything out?' Millicent asked, with pathetic eagerness.

'Very little,' Stephen confessed. 'Certainly nothing definite. But if we add what you know to what we do, we may be able to see a little daylight. So the best thing is for you to tell us exactly what happened last night, when this strange man came bursting into your bedroom. Will you do that?'

'Oh, yes. There's really very little to tell. I'd been lying awake, worrying about Cicely, and I was trying to read. And suddenly the man rushed out of the cupboard—that's where the other stairs come out; it used to be a powder-closet—and threatened me with a revolver if I screamed.'

'Ah!' Stephen observed. 'So he had a revolver, then. But what did he look like, Miss Carey? Would you know him again?'

'Oh, yes,' said Millicent, shivering. 'Of course I couldn't see him very well, as I only had a candle by my bed, but he was a big, rough-looking man. A—a sort of gardener. And he spoke like that, too. Oh! I wonder if it could have been the new under-gardener here!'

'What, Bridger?' Stephen said incredulously.

'But you'd have recognized him if it had been, wouldn't you?' Pauline put in.

'Yes,' Millicent said, though a little doubtfully. 'I suppose I should have. But I've only seen him once or twice.'

'And you haven't told anyone about this today, Miss Carey?'

'No,' Millicent admitted with a slight blush. 'I—I ought to have, I suppose, but—' She laughed nervously. 'Well, I'm afraid I was too frightened. It was silly of me, but I had the feeling that he'd find out if I did, and then—' She laughed again.

'Of course,' Pauline said understandingly.

Stephen was stroking his hair with his left hand. 'What beats me,' he said thoughtfully, 'is how the fellow knew of the secret room at all, let alone the other way out of it. Have you told anybody about it beside ourselves, Miss Carey?'

'Oh, no,' Millicent responded readily. 'Nobody. But of course he might have seen me using it, mightn't he?'

'Do you often use it, then?' Stephen asked quickly.

'Yes, quite often. You see, it's the quickest way downstairs from my bedroom. If I want to slip down at night for a book or anything like that, as I was doing just now, it saves going all round by the main staircase.'

'I see,' said Stephen.

'Millicent,' Pauline remarked suddenly, 'do you know that Cicely was in that room the night she disappeared, and that she's been there certainly within the last twenty-four hours?'

Millicent looked considerably startled. 'N-no,' she stammered. 'I didn't know that. How could she have been?'

Pauline told her about the handkerchief and scent, and Millicent's face cleared.

'Oh, but that was my handkerchief,' she said. 'I'd always liked that scent of Cicely's, and she very kindly brought me a bottle when she came to stay here. It must have been mine that you smelt.'

'Oh!' said Pauline, not without considerable disappointment. 'I really did think I'd been so clever over that.'

There was a short silence.

'Well,' said Stephen, 'I expert you'll be wanting to get to bed, Miss

Carey; and there doesn't seem anything further to keep you up for at the moment. If Pauline and I find out anything else, we'll let you know, and you do the same for us.'

'Shall I go upstairs with you, Millicent?' Pauline inquired as she helped her to rise.

'Oh, no, Pauline, don't trouble, please. I'm quite all right now. It was silly of me to give way like that. I'll go back the short way.'

They watched her disappear, with steps that were still not very steady. Then Stephen turned to Pauline.

'And I suppose we'd better follow suit. On the whole, we seem to have had rather a fruitless evening.'

'Yes, all right; come along then,' Pauline replied carelessly, and moved towards the door. Outside the room, in the darkness of the hall, she slipped her arm through his and pressed it gently. 'So you think we've had a fruitless evening, do you, my Stephen?' she whispered.

'Pauline, you know that isn't fair,' Stephen expostulated, his thoughts on a little summer-house in a secluded corner of the grounds. 'You know I wasn't meaning—'

'Nor was I, you conceited man!' Pauline laughed softly. 'I was just thinking of our recent interview. I didn't want to say anything in the drawing-room because, as we know, things said there have a habit of being overheard; but seriously, Stephen, do you mean to say that a rather unpleasant conviction hasn't formed in your mind during the last twenty minutes?'

'What are you talking about, Pauline?' Stephen asked in astonishment.

They had reached the bottom of the broad, shallow stairs and began slowly to mount.

'Why,' Pauline said gravely, 'that Millicent knows very much more about this business than she pretends.'

'Good Lord! How do you make that out?'

'Well, I'm quite certain that she suspects, if she doesn't actually know, that Martin's death was not an accident. I'm still more certain that the story she told about this mysterious midnight visitor, with the rough speech and the gardener-like appearance, was absolutely untrue. Millicent's a rotten liar, and to a woman's eye she gives herself away with every word and look. Stephen, she knows who that man was, and for some reason, whether she's been terrorized or whether she's acting by prefer-ence, she's determined to keep it a secret. And I'm not at all sure that what she said about Cicely giving her that bottle of scent wasn't another fib.'

'Good heavens!' said Stephen blankly. They had reached the top of the stairs and paused there for a final word before separating to go to their respective rooms. 'Then what you mean,' he went on slowly, 'is that Mil-licent must not only know the truth about Cicely's disappearance, what happened to her, and probably where she is now, but she also knows the identity of the villain of the piece?'

'I do,' Pauline agreed. 'It's rather an awful thing to say, I know, but I'm convinced that it is so. We'll talk it over tomorrow, Stephen; it's too late now. And there's another thing I want to talk over with you tomorrow,' she added carelessly.

'What's that?' Stephen asked.

'How soon we can be married,' Pauline replied calmly. 'Good night, Stephen.'

XVIII KEEPING WATCH

STEPHEN spent a restless night. Undecided though he was whether to believe or not in Pauline's suspicions of Millicent, he realized that a woman's intuition is often worth all the male reasoning and logic in the world; had Pauline arrived at the truth (or at any rate, a part of the truth) by an intuitive short cut, or was the track which her words had suggested once again a false one? Only one thing was certain; if she happened to be right things looked like becoming even more complicated than before.

But this mystery and its by-paths were not the only thing to worry Stephen that night and cause him to toss restlessly from one side of his bed to the other. When a girl whom it is manifestly impossible for you to marry, asks you how soon you are prepared to marry her, what on earth is to be done? Obviously the situation must be cleared up somehow, and that could only be effected by telling her as gently as possible that the marriage, which had not been arranged, could not take place. Stephen foresaw an extremely awkward quarter of an hour in store for him while he endeavoured to make this plain.

He went downstairs to breakfast the next morning feeling as if he had hardly had a wink of sleep all night.

As he reached the hall he heard his name called and, looking round, saw Lady Susan beckoning to him from the door of her morning-room. He hurried to join her, and she motioned him inside and shut the door behind them.

'Good morning, Stephen,' she said with a grim smile. 'It may interest you to hear that I've had an anonymous letter this morning—from the gentleman you described yesterday as the villain of the piece, I take it.' She held out a piece of cheap paper towards him. 'Here—read the thing!'

Stephen took the paper and read through its contents. They ran as follows:

'If you wish no harm to befall Miss Vernon, place the sum of five hundred pounds (in notes, no cheque) in an envelope and pin it before ten o'clock this morning on the back of the trunk of the same tree under which Martin was killed. If you do not do this, or if you show this letter to anyone else, or if you cause a watch to be kept on the tree, neither you nor anyone else will see Miss Vernon again.'

'Humph!' said Stephen, turning the paper over in his hands. 'Cheap paper, might have come from anywhere; the writing carefully printed; not much of a clue here. Where was it, Lady Susan?'

'Brought up with my other letters. I asked Farrar, and she said it had been in the letter-box. So you see, Cicely was kidnapped after all.'

'So the writer of this letter evidently wants us to think,' Stephen said caustically. 'What are you going to do about it?'

'What do you advise me to do?'

Stephen considered. 'Play for time. I should write a reply, saying that you haven't got as much money as that in notes but you will get it as quickly as possible; and I think you ought to take it there yourself.'

'That I certainly won't, said Lady Susan with decision. 'Millicent can do that for me.'

'I shouldn't send Millicent,' Stephen said slowly, his thoughts upon the events of the previous night, 'Isn't there somebody rather more non-committal? What about—what about Miss Rivers?'

'Yes, she'd do. And she'll be able to hold her tongue, at any rate.'

'And in the meantime, I can keep a watch on the wood. Is there any way of getting there not overlooked either by the house side or the other?'

'Well, the ground dips away a little to the east, and there are a good many trees to shelter you. You might be able to manage it.'

'I must try. By the way, you don't mind if I tell Pauline about this, do you?'

Lady Susan smiled slightly. 'The reverse would be too much to expect. Tell your Pauline by all means. Go along and have your breakfast now,' she added, her smile deepening at sight of Stephen's vivid blush. 'Miss Rivers will leave the house at ten minutes to ten. You make your own arrangements.'

Stephen glanced at the clock on the mantelpiece. The time was just a quarter-past nine. He hurried along to the dining-room.

The usual clatter of the breakfast-table was in full progress. Everybody was already down except Freddie and Henry Kentisbeare, and Annette was trying to get up a hasty sweepstake on which of them would be the last. Stephen, helping himself to bacon and eggs, took a shilling ticket and was promptly informed that he had drawn a blank. Under cover of the noise attending the draw, he slipped into a vacant seat by Pauline's side.

'As soon as possible, on the terrace—urgent!' he said in a low voice.

Pauline nodded slightly and immediately began to discuss the prospects of the day's weather.

Henry Kentisbeare put in an appearance, with Freddie only a second behind him.

'Lost by a short head!' wailed Annette, who had drawn Freddie. 'Mr Starcross, you scoop the pool. Eight bob. Catch!'

Freddie and Henry took their places, and the confusion grew a little less pronounced. Stephen took advantage of the lull to make an announcement for which he had been awaiting a favourable opportunity.

'Oh, I think it's going to keep fine,' he said in a sufficiently loud voice to Pauline. 'Anyhow, what about risking it and trying a walk somewhere? Are you game?'

Pauline evidently recognized her cue. 'Oh, yes, rather,' she said instantly.

'I thought we might explore a little towards Gorsham way,' Stephen remarked casually. Gorsham, it may be noticed, lay in the opposite direction to Thornton.

'Talking of expeditions,' Henry Kentisbeare observed, 'I've got to run up to London for the day, Millicent.'

'So have I,' put in Starcross. 'We might go together, Kentisbeare.'

'With all my heart,' Henry rejoined politely. 'Is there a train some time between ten and eleven, Millicent?'

'Yes, there's one at ten-twenty-seven. It only stops twice before Victoria.'

'Then that,' said Henry with satisfaction, 'is the train for us.'

'What's calling you up to town in such a hurry, Henry?' Annette asked pertly.

Henry glanced towards Pauline and Stephen. 'Business, infant,' he said gently. 'Matters of high finance. Matters of bulling and bearing and other things far too complicated for infants to understand.'

Miss Cullompton broke into a tinkly laugh, and she also looked towards Pauline and Stephen. It did not require very great deductive powers to gather that Henry had acquainted his partner with the gist of his interesting interview of the previous evening.

Nobody made any reference to the absent Sir Julius.

Pauline finished her breakfast first and slipped unostentatiously out of the room. Stephen gulped down his coffee and followed her a minute or two later. She was waiting for him on the terrace, her elbows on the stone balustrade. Stephen took up a similar position at her side, and they gazed with apparent interest over the distant landscape, cloudy with the first mists of early autumn. In a low voice he began to tell her of the new development and the plan he had formed with Lady Susan to meet it. That he had already arrived at the tentative conclusion that it was Cicely herself who had written the letter, he did not think necessary to mention.

'I'm coming too,' Pauline announced, when Stephen had mentioned his intention of watching the wood.

'But, Pauline, you'll be frightfully bored. I shall have to stay there the whole morning at least. I thought we might set out together, and then you could come back saying that you'd felt tired and left me to go on alone.'

Pauline touched his hand lightly with her own. 'My poor Stephen,' she smiled, 'I don't think you're being quite as bright over this business as you were at first. Doesn't it occur to you that the wood has two ends, and that you cannot possibly watch both of them at once?'

'But if the chap comes from the house—'

'How on earth do you know he's going to? You must reckon with the possibility of an accomplice outside. Now what I suggest is that you watch one end and I watch the other.'

'Yes, that is a better plan,' Stephen admitted. 'Much better. And you don't mind crouching under a damp bush for two or three hours all alone?'

'What you don't seem to understand, Stephen,' Pauline retorted, 'is that I'm just as keen on solving this mystery as you are. I admit that the damp bush would be a little more inviting if it were a bush for two instead of one, but we higher detectives are really quite above that sort of thing.'

'Pauline,' said Stephen earnestly, 'if you go on looking as adorable as that I'll kiss you here and now, under the eyes behind all those windows!' Which was perhaps not a very tactful thing for a young man to say to a young woman whom he is determined that in no circumstances whatever can he possibly, possibly marry.

'And that, of course, would never do,' Pauline mocked. 'Anyhow, I'll remove temptation from you, Stephen, by going to put on my hat. We ought to be starting almost at once, I suppose.'

'You'll find me in the hall,' Stephen smiled.

Pauline kept him longer than he had expected. It was nearly ten minutes to ten when she ran down the stairs and joined him in the hall.

'I was called to the telephone directly I got inside,' she explained breathlessly as soon as they got outside the front door. 'Daddy rang me up to say that Julius went there to see him last night. That must be why he left here at such an unearthly hour. He wanted Daddy to hand those shares over to him at once, and brought the papers with him for Daddy to sign and everything.'

'I say! I was only just in time, then.'

'Yes. And Daddy can't say enough in your praise.'

'Hum!' said Stephen uncomfortably. 'What did your father do with Sir Julius?'

'Oh, he's awfully pleased with himself. He listened to everything Julius had to say, and then told him exactly what he thought of him. He says he hasn't enjoyed himself so much since he laid a trap and made the dean of his college fall into a bath full of cold water at Oxford in the year dot. Now then, Stephen, to business! Where are we making for, and how are we going to get round to that wood?'

Stephen explained the plan he had in mind, and they walked on briskly. Safely out of sight of the house, they veered round to the right and then to the right again, till the little wood lay directly in front of them over the brow of a small rise. Here the greatest caution was necessary. At the foot of the rise they separated, Pauline to make for the end of the wood farther from the house and Stephen for the near one. Sheltered behind a huge oak, he watched her move forward to take up her position, hurrying from tree to tree and taking advantage, as he had told her, of every bush and fold of ground. When she finally disappeared into the undergrowth at the top, he was satisfied that she could hardly have been seen by anyone but himself. He proceeded up the hill to his own position.

Stephen had decided, in view of the express injunction in the anonymous letter, that to keep watch on the tree itself would be far too risky. It was imperative to avoid rousing any suspicion that Lady Susan had communicated the contents of the letter to anybody else, still more so that she was not properly impressed by its terms. It was therefore only possible to keep under observation the path which led to and from the wood; but as anybody desirous of reaching the tree would almost necessarily have to make use of the path, the undergrowth a few yards back on either side being composed almost entirely of brambles and very nearly impenetrable, this really amounted to much the same thing. He therefore settled himself in a spot where he could see anybody approaching along the path and could not possibly be himself seen.

For twenty minutes nothing happened. Miss Rivers had presumably been and gone before he arrived, for he saw nothing of her. The first person to appear was Henry Kentisbeare, strolling nonchalantly along evidently bound for Thornton station and the ten-twenty-seven. Stephen noted with surprise that he was alone. Three or four minutes later John Starcross came into sight, walking rapidly. A few yards from Stephen's hiding-place he broke into a run.

Again there was a longish interval, and the next arrival, a tall woman, dressed in black garments of plain and severe style, Stephen had some difficulty in recognizing. It was not until she came abreast of him that he realized that she was the new parlourmaid. The fact surprised him.

Bridger was the next to put in an appearance. He carried an axe over one shoulder and a saw over the other, and his business was obvious. Five minutes later a succession of dull thuds showed that he was engaged upon it.

Stephen was sorry. The presence of Bridger might warn off the scene the person for whom he was waiting. It was hardly likely that the envelope could be taken from right under Bridger's nose. This was an unexpected contretemps.

Whether it were through this cause or not, the rest of the morning passed without incident. Only at a quarter to one did Freddie and Baby Cullompton come into sight, walking towards the house and engaged in deep and inaudible conversation. Stephen waited till they had gone, then emerged from his lair and, working along the outskirts of the undergrowth, made his way to where Pauline was concealed.

A low whistle brought her to his side, and they compared notes. With the exception of Bridger, her list was the same as his. They turned on to the path and began to walk back.

'Well,' said Stephen, 'one thing's certain at any rate; if that envelope's gone, it must have been one of those people who took it. But it's a big if.'

When they reached the fallen bough, still straggling across the path, Bridger had packed up and gone; they had the field to themselves. With rising excitement they hurried forward and passed behind the huge trunk of the tree.

It was bare. The envelope had disappeared.

XIX COLLECTING EVIDENCE

A S soon as possible after lunch Pauline and Stephen slipped unostenta-tiously into the morning-room to make their report to Lady Susan, who was waiting for them there. Stephen had already found an oppor-tunity of informing her that the letter had been taken; now he proposed to go through each person on his list of suspects and examine his or her ostensible reasons for being in the wood during the morning.

'Kentisbeare and Starcross, we know,' he said, 'were going to the station to catch the ten-twenty-seven. They've both got a perfectly good reason.'

'I wonder why they didn't go together, though,' Pauline mused. 'I thought they arranged to at breakfast.'

'I can tell you that,' Lady Susan put in. 'Mr Kentisbeare started off first, without waiting for Mr Starcross. I heard Mr Starcross asking later if anybody had seen Mr Kentisbeare, as he really couldn't wait for him any longer.'

'Humph!' said Stephen thoughtfully. 'That's a black mark against friend Kentisbeare, I think.'

'I still think Henry is the most likely person, in spite of the neat way he turned the tables on us last night,' said Pauline.

'Bridger I think we can wash out at once,' Stephen went on. 'The next one appears to be the new parlourmaid. Do you happen to know where she was going, Lady Susan, and why?'

'Yes. She was going to the station too, to inquire about her luggage. She arrived at a minute's notice, you may remember, Stephen, after I had unfortunately found it necessary to get rid of my footman, and her lug-gage is being sent on after her.'

'I do seem to remember something of the sort, Lady Susan,' Stephen grinned. 'Did she ask to go in, or was she sent?'

'That you must ask Millicent. She's supposed to look after the details of my household; though whether she'll be able to tell you anything is quite doubtful. In any case, I think we might pass on to the next on your list.'

'Well,' Stephen said, a little uncomfortably, 'that appears to be Freddie and Miss Cullompton.'

'Freddie again?' commented Lady Susan equably. 'Dear me, Freddie's name seems to be cropping up rather a lot in connection with this affair. I shall begin to think very soon that he's your villain, Stephen.'

'I'm quite sure, Lady Susan,' Pauline smiled, 'that whatever Freddie may be, he isn't a villain. But I'm not at all so sure about Baby. I wonder whether there's any way of finding out whether either of them, both or neither, went round the trunk of that tree when they came to it.'

'Bridger!' Stephen cried. 'He was on the spot. He ought to be able to tell us.'

'We ought to find that out at once.'

'Yes, I think so too. In fact, if you'll excuse me, Lady Susan, it wouldn't be a bad plan for me to run up there now and see whether Bridger's back at work It won't take me many minutes.'

'I'll excuse you by all means, Stephen,' Lady Susan said kindly.

Stephen hurried away.

In less than twenty minutes he, was back again, somewhat breathless and not a little warm. 'This is what Bridger says,' he remarked, dropping into his chair. 'Freddie and Miss Cullompton came along, and Freddie began to ask Bridger a few questions about Martin. Miss Cullompton was by his side at first, but apparently the details which Bridger saw fit to impart were rather too much for her; she drew a little away. Bridger wasn't taking much notice of her, and the next thing he realized was that she was on the farther side of the branch. How she got there, he doesn't know. Freddie followed her, going round the trunk, and they went on down the path.'

'So they both went round the trunk, no doubt?' said Lady Susan.

'Probably,' Stephen agreed.

'And separately. Well, well; that appears to increase our number of suspicious characters to three, including that unpleasant Mr Kentisbeare.'

'Oh, come, Lady Susan,' Stephen protested. 'I refuse to count Freddie as a suspicious character.'

'Well, perhaps you're right. I must say that I doubt very much whether Freddie has the brains requisite for a suspicious character.'

'It lies between Henry and Baby,' Pauline interposed with confidence. 'Probably they're both in it together. If not, I'm quite certain that it's Henry.'

'I agree,' said Stephen. 'So all we've got to do now is to collect enough evidence to prove it.'

'What a thing it is to be young!' Lady Susan remarked with heavy irony.

A few minutes later the conference broke up.

Annette was lying in wait for them in the hall. 'Well?' she asked with subdued excitement. 'What's going on now? I know all sorts of frightfully exciting things are in the wind, and I don't see why I should be left out of them.'

'Careful!' said Stephen, glancing round anxiously.

'Oh, there's nobody within earshot.'

'No, but it isn't safe to say anything at all inside the house.'

'Stephen, if you don't tell me what you've been talking about to Cousin Susan, I'll stand on the table and shriek out everything I know at the top of my voice!'

'Carry on, then,' Stephen grinned. 'Pauline and I are going to make polite conversation in the drawing-room.'

'That's right,' Pauline nodded. 'Colonel Uffculme's got a story he promised to tell me about pig-shooting or tiger-sticking in Bengal. I'm simply dying to hear it.'

'Oh, do tell me!' Annette wailed. 'Do let me take a hand! I'd make a wonderful sleuth. Can't I disguise myself as a grasshopper or something, and rub my legs together under the suspected party's window? Or is that a cricket? I was never any good at botany. Anyhow, do let me do something!'

'All right,' said Stephen suddenly. 'I tell you what you can do. Go to Thornton station and find out whether two gentlemen took tickets for London this morning, and if not, where.'

'Right-ho! Meaning Henry and J.S., I suppose?'

'Never mind who,' said Stephen sternly. 'Just say "two gentlemen".'

'Curse you! Anything else?'

'Yes. Ask whether—whether the woman who was inquiring about her luggage this morning made any arrangements for it to be sent up here.'

'Who on earth is that?'

'Never mind! Just say "the woman who was inquiring about her luggage this morning".'

'Curse you again! All right, Sherlock. I'll find it out for you, or be bitten to death by mad porters in the attempt.' She fled up the stairs.

'What on earth do you want to know that for, Stephen?' Pauline asked in bewilderment.

'I don't,' Stephen grinned. 'Not in the least. But I do want Miss Agnew out of the way. Now I suppose we'd better go and talk pretty nothings to our junior hostess for a bit.'

The pretty nothings did not take them very long. Colonel Uffculme was not visible, and Freddie, who was teaching Miss Cullompton to play golf, had conveyed his pupil to the links; Millicent was alone in the room. But she stayed there only a very short time. After a hesitating reference or two to the scene of the previous night, and vehement assurances in answer to kind inquiries that she felt ever so much better today quite well again in fact, she made some exceedingly transparent and faltering excuse, and almost fled from the room. As a matter of fact, Lady Susan had told her niece with considerable vigour that impending interesting events between her two guests in question were to be encouraged by every possible means, and if she ever found her said niece playing gooseberry to them and impeding the progress of such events by her wholly undesirable presence, she would cause the niece to be thrown to the wolves. It is a matter of doubt whether Millicent took this statement literally, the absence of any convenient wolves tending to show that the throwing would be metaphorical only; but at any rate one would say that she had the liveliest fears of being thrown to something, if only the chickens, by the precipitancy with which she quitted the room. But of all this the two protagonists were blissfully ignorant.

'The lady doesn't appear to like our society,' said ignorant Stephen, gazing in some surprise at the hastily shut door.

'Doesn't that all go to support what I told you last night?' asked ignorant Pauline triumphantly.

'Upon my soul,' quoth ignorant Stephen, 'I'm beginning to believe you're right!'

Pauline swept him a curtsy. 'Thank you, sir. Well, what would your honour like to do now? Haven't you got any errand to send me on? Wouldn't you like to know the colour of the porter's hair who punched Henry's ticket for him?'

'Apart from all that,' said Stephen, strolling over to the window, 'I was thinking we might be original enough to go for a walk. Short of taking advantage of Henry's absence to search his effects (please note "effects"— the professional touch), I can't think of anything else to do. Oh, bother, it's raining! Well, that appears to indicate Henry's effects.'

'I'll play you a hundred up at billiards,' said Pauline suddenly.

'I am your slave,' returned Stephen—conventionally, but none the less truthfully.

They adjourned to the billiard-room.

'Stephen!'

Stephen turned from the cue rack, from which he was choosing their cues. 'Yes?'

'Put that cue down this instant! You don't imagine we've come in here to play billiards do you, you ridiculous man?' Pauline was smiling, though a little constrainedly, and her colour had deepened.

Stephen's heart sank. He realized that she was determined to get things straightened out between them, and it was a prospect to which he was certainly not looking forward. 'Well, I thought that was the usual thing one went to the billiard-room for,' he said with a lame little laugh.

'Surely there's no need for us to fence with one another?' Pauline said reproachfully. 'We got beyond any necessity for that last night. I know that you care for me, and'—she hesitated, then continued bravely—'and I love you. The question is—what are we going to do about it?'

Stephen looked at her dumbly for a moment. 'I—I don't know, Pauline,' he stammered.

Pauline laughed, and the tension was broken. Both felt suddenly more at ease.

'Stephen, you really are a rotten lover! Do you want me to prompt you every time before you say your bits? The right answer to my question was: "Why, get married, of course! And the sooner the better!" Really, Stephen!'

'Pauline,' Stephen said desperately, 'we've got to have this out. You know perfectly well that I can't ask you to marry me.'

'Why not?' asked Pauline, lightly enough, 'You're not married already, are you?'

'Now it's you who are fencing.'

'No, I'm not. As far as I'm concerned, that would be the only thing that could stop us.'

'Oh, Lord, Pauline!' Stephen groaned. 'Surely it's obvious enough. How can I—?'

Pauline laid her hands on his shoulders and looked up at him with a little smile. 'Now, Stephen!' she said softly. 'Don't be absurdly conventional.'

'Conventional?'

'Yes. I know you're going to say that you can't ask me to marry you because I happen to have a little more money than you. Money!' Pauline exclaimed with fine scorn. 'As if money counted against love! Don't you understand, you dear absurd man, that I'd come to you if neither of us had any money at all, or even any prospect of some? That I want to wash, and scrub, and cook, and darn for you? And the fact that I shall have enough to provide the butter for your bread is neither here nor there. Anyhow, I'm not going to be conventional, if you are. Stephen—please may I be engaged to you?'

Stephen looked longingly down into her upturned face. There was nothing he could imagine anyone wanting in the world more than he wanted at that moment to take Pauline at her word; but how could he? He might have wasted his life so far, but at any rate he had kept his decent feelings unimpaired.

'Pauline, darling,' he said, 'you're making it most devilishly difficult for me.'

'I mean to!' Pauline murmured with conviction.

'But you know that it's impossible. It isn't as if I even had a job in view!'

'Get another job as a footman,' Pauline smiled. 'And I'll get one as housemaid in the same house.'

But Stephen was not to be turned aside by having his troubles treated lightly. 'We couldn't possibly be engaged till I've got something definite to offer you.'

'We could be married,' Pauline whispered. 'And my money would keep us till you got your job.'

'Live on my wife's money? No, thank you, dear. I've got a little pride left still.'

'It's false pride, Stephen. Silly, unnecessary, bad pride.'

'I don't think it is. It's just self-respect. If a man can't support his wife, he doesn't deserve to have one. But look at it from your own point of view as well, dear. You say you wouldn't mind the cooking and the scrubbing and—'

'I'd love it!'

'To begin with, perhaps; I'm not saying you wouldn't. It would be a novelty, you see. But when the novelty wore off and began to turn into drudgery! No, darling; it's out of the question. You must see it is, if you think.'

'I don't want to think!' Pauline cried mutinously. 'I want you!'

'And heaven knows I want you, dearest; but—'

'Well, let's compromise,' Pauline interrupted him. 'I think your attitude is simply too silly for words, especially considering that if it wasn't for you I shouldn't have a single penny to come to me, but of course I love you for it, because it's all part of that dear, big, ridiculous creature called Stephen. Anyhow, let's compromise, as you are so terribly obstinate; besides, I think I've been snubbed quite enough for one afternoon. Let's be engaged till you do get this job, and married as soon as you've got it!'

'But, darling, I don't see that there's the least prospect of my ever—'

'Be quiet, Stephen! I won't have another word. That's settled. Now then—kiss your fiancée, please!'

It was very far from being settled as far as Stephen was concerned. This sort of thing was all very well, but it was not fair to a girl to let her bind herself indefinitely, with no prospect of marriage for, possibly, years to come. Stephen himself was very far from being cold-blooded, but he did realize dimly that Pauline was not only blinded by the glamour of love, but was suffering a severe, though unconscious, reaction from the horrors of her recent engagement. He steeled himself to resist the temptation of her offered lips.

'Kiss me!' Pauline whispered. 'Kiss me!'

There is a limit to every man's powers of resistance to temptation. Stephen discovered suddenly that he had overrated his own. He gathered her closely into his arms and bent his head.

'Struth!' observed a voice from the door a full minute later. 'Now I begin to see why little Annette was sent on a wild-goose chase to Thornton station. Sorry if I'm intruding, by the way.'

'Hullo, Annette,' said Pauline, quite calmly. 'Well, as you are here, you may as well congratulate us. Stephen and I are engaged to be married.'

XX STEPHEN'S INSPIRATION

IT is impossible for anyone with the least pretension to good manners to give a lady the lie direct. By tea-time the news of Stephen's engagement was general property, having been assiduously promulgated by an excited Annette, who had more than forgiven the trick that had been played upon her in her realization of its object. Stephen's appearance in the drawing-room was hailed with loud and embarrassing congratulations. Even Pauline was not there to support him, for she and Annette had retired upstairs to powder their noses and discuss the exciting event in all its bearings.

Lady Susan, sitting behind the tea-table and awaiting the tray, was grimly genial. 'Well, my first house-party has not been held in vain,' she said, with a smile less ironical than usual. 'And when is the wedding to be, Stephen?'

'I don't know, Lady Susan,' Stephen replied uncomfortably. 'It depends rather on—on circumstances.' He was only too well aware that the nature of the circumstances must be glaringly apparent to everybody.

'Well, I should think your ridiculous father-in-law ought to give you a very handsome wedding-present, considering everything,' Lady Susan remarked with devastating candour.

The entrance of the new grenadier-like parlourmaid at that moment with the tea-tray came to Stephen as immense relief.

'Did you get your luggage this morning, Collins?' Lady Susan asked casually.

'No, my lady. It hasn't arrived yet. They told me to come again tomorrow morning. Will that be convenient?'

'As far as I'm concerned, perfectly.'

'Thank you, my lady.' The grenadier moved the table two inches nearer to Lady Susan and retired.

To Stephen's relief the break in the conversation led to the introduction of other topics. He retired as far as possible into the background and encouraged Colonel Uffculme to talk to him about Bengal. The Colonel needed very little encouragement.

In due course Pauline and Annette came downstairs and the congratulatory note was sounded again, mixed this time, as inevitably in the presence of Annette, with an undercurrent of chaff. However, it was now Pauline and not Stephen himself who had to bear the brunt of it; all he found himself required to do was to sit in the background and grin with uneasy politeness. Tea over at last, the rest of the party dispersed and Stephen found himself left alone with Pauline and Lady Susan.

Lady Susan came to the point with her usual directness. 'And what do you two ridiculous young people imagine you're going to marry on?' she inquired disconcertingly.

'Stephen's going to get a job,' Pauline replied quickly, 'and till then we shall live on some of the money he's just been making for us.'

'I see.' Lady Susan considered this. 'And what sort of a job is Stephen going to get, may I ask? A boot-boy's, for instance? You'll have some difficulty in keeping a wife with expensive tastes on a boot-boy's wages, my friend.'

'Stephen's wife won't have expensive tastes, Lady Susan,' Pauline smiled. 'And he won't have to take a job as a boot-boy. It's only a case of waiting till he can find the one he deserves.'

'Humph! Well, I will admit,' said Lady Susan kindly, 'that your young man doesn't seem quite such a fool as most of his generation.'

Stephen, an unwilling sharer in these confidences about himself, continued to grin uncomfortably.

The entrance of Miss Rivers the next moment checked for the time being the flow of Lady Susan's candour. 'The post's just come, Lady Susan,' she murmured, handing her employer three or four letters. 'I thought you'd like to have it at once.'

'Thank you, my dear,' Lady Susan returned, in the almost cordial tone which she reserved for this model of efficient companions. Miss Rivers effaced herself from the room as unobtrusively as she had entered it.

Lady Susan glanced through the envelopes in her hand. 'Ah!' she said suddenly, pouncing upon one of them. 'This looks uncommonly like—' She tore it open and glanced through the contents.

'Not another from your anonymous friend, Lady Susan?' Stephen asked eagerly.

'No less!' Lady Susan replied with a grim smile. 'Here—what does my private detective make of this?'

Stephen took the letter from her and read it through quickly, Pauline leaning on his shoulder. It ran as follows:

'You are given twenty-four hours' respite. If the five hundred pounds is not in place by ten o'clock tomorrow morning, the plans already made for the disposal of Miss Vernon will be carried out. Do not attempt to have a watch kept, or it will be the worse for you and her. This is the last chance.'

'Well, well, well!' said Stephen thoughtfully.

'Of course, mind you,' Lady Susan remarked slowly, 'I don't take any of this nonsense seriously, but on the other hand I don't want to run any risk of anything happening to Cicely. It seems to me the time's come when I must put it in the hands of the police.'

Stephen exchanged a significant glance with Pauline. 'I don't think you need do that, Lady Susan,' he said. 'And I wouldn't think there's the least chance of anything happening to Cicely.'

Lady Susan looked at him sharply. 'Why? Do you know anything that you haven't told me?' Her tone was imperious.

'Yes,' Stephen answered boldly, 'I do, Lady Susan. But please don't ask me what it is, because I'm not going to tell you. It's much better that you shouldn't know—for the present, at any rate.'

For a moment Lady Susan regarded him with regal wrath. Then her sense of humour came to her aid and she laughed. 'I see you've been reading up your part, Stephen. It's quite in accordance with the best models that a detective should preserve a mysterious silence, isn't it? Very well, I won't venture to intrude on your secrets, even though I should have said that they concerned me a good deal more than you. But I shall expect some result from all this mystery, mind you. Well, as you're apparently so determined to manage this affair yourself, would you be so kind as to tell me what you require me to do regarding this letter?'

'Oh,' said Stephen, somewhat uncomfortably, 'I think you could leave that for the time being. I'm sure that it's quite an empty threat. We'll arrange something for tomorrow morning and try and catch the culprit red-handed.'

'Very well. But if things go wrong, I shall hold you entirely responsible.'

'I accept all responsibility,' Stephen smiled, with rather more confidence than he actually felt.

'In the, meantime, you'd better keep the letter. And now perhaps you'll excuse me while you two detectives talk over your case.'

She rose from her chair and Stephen opened the door for her.

'Distinctly ruffled, I'm afraid,' he remarked with a somewhat rueful smile, as he closed it behind her.

'Well, one can't be surprised,' Pauline said judicially. 'After all, it's her house and her responsibility, and I'm quite sure she's worried to death over Cicely; though she'd rather die than admit it, of course. You really don't think we ought to tell her about the yachting trip?'

'No.' Stephen said with decision. 'I'm quite sure we shouldn't. It would only upset her still more. Besides, it wouldn't be fair to Miss Vernon—yet. She may have a reasonable explanation for that ticket to Brighton after all. Though I must say,' he added, 'that I shall be very surprised if she has.'

'I don't agree there, Stephen, as you know. Still, we won't go into that. Does this second letter suggest anything to you?'

Stephen began to pace up and down the room, his hands in his pockets. 'She must have accomplices,' he said thoughtfully. 'One at least. And it must he somebody inside the house.'

'Stephen,' said Pauline softly, 'do you think it's wise—?' She nodded towards the fireplace.

'By Jove, yes, I was forgetting. Come out on to the terrace. Not too cold for you, is it?' The rain had ceased by now, and a somewhat watery sun was doing its best to dry the landscape.

'Not a bit. I should like a little air.'

They opened the French windows and made their way outside. Stephen slipped his arm through Pauline's and they began to pace slowly up and down the length of the terrace.

'Now, where was I?' he said. 'Oh, yes, Cicely's accomplice, if she is the leading spirit herself, and Cicely's kidnapper if she's an innocent victim. Put it like that.'

'That's better,' Pauline approved.

'Well, it must be somebody who—' He stopped suddenly and looked at Pauline. 'Wait a minute! I believe—Just let me think! Yes—yes, it all fits in. And—by Jove!' He stared at his companion with excited eyes. 'Pauline! What a tremendous brain-wave! I've absolutely got it—I've solved the mystery!'

'You've solved it?' Pauline repeated eagerly. 'Stephen! How?'

Stephen paused. 'Half a minute; just let me get it a bit clearer in my head. Yes, that's right. Pauline, I've suddenly had a blinding revelation!' He beamed at her triumphantly.

'What?' Pauline cried. 'If you don't tell me this minute, I shall scream.'

'Well—!' Stephen considered how to put his enlightenment into the most telling words. 'We've been going on the idea all this time that Cicely disappeared, haven't we? Well—she never did anything of the sort.'

'Stephen, what do you mean? Why didn't Cicely disappear?'

'Because she was never there,' Stephen said simply, and continued to beam.

Pauline caught him by the arm and shook it vigorously. 'Explain, you exasperating man!'

'Well, just throw your mind back to the facts of Miss Vernon's return here that evening. I opened the door to her. She was distinctly agitated and trying hard to control herself. I thought she was upset; actually she was nervous. The lights were all extremely dim; her cold was much worse, you remember; she had a scarf round her neck, which she frequently held in front of her mouth; it was she who volunteered to disappear; her voice was almost unrecognizable through hoarseness; she spent only the barest minimum of time talking to Lady Susan—it wasn't Cicely Vernon at all!'

'Then—then who was it?' Pauline asked breathlessly.

'Miss Rivers!' Stephen almost shouted.

They looked at each other for a moment.

'The way I see it is this,' Stephen went on rapidly. 'The two of them were probably in league. Cicely goes off saying she's going to Folkestone and leaving some of her clothes with Miss Rivers. By Jove, yes! They actually went for a walk together that afternoon—to arrange the final details, no doubt. Miss Rivers knows all about the electric light failing, and times her arrival accordingly. She—'

'But Miss Rivers isn't a bit like Cicely, Stephen,' Pauline interrupted.

'She's dark and Cicely's fair. And those spectacles of hers.'

'The whole point, my dear! A disguise! Hair dragged back from the forehead and disfiguring spectacles—there couldn't be a simpler disguise for a girl, or a more effective one. And of course she'd be wearing a fair wig when she came back. Well, what does she do? Gets herself appointed official disappearer, and as soon as the lights go out takes off her disguise, somehow changes the appearance of her dress, tip-toes over to the door and announces she's Miss Rivers. Then, of course—'

'Stephen,' Pauline interrupted gently, 'you're an awfully clever man and I love you terribly; but aren't you forgetting something, dear?'

'What?'

'That Annette says she hid Cicely behind her on the couch, angel,' said Pauline, very, very gently.

Stephen's triumphant expression vanished from his face as if it had been wiped off with a sponge. 'Good Lord!' he exclaimed blankly. 'Yes—I was rather forgetting that.'

'I thought you were,' said Pauline airily, and examined the view with some reflection. Pauline was a tactful girl.

'I don't care!' Stephen said rebelliously, after a little pause for rueful reflection. 'I'm sure I'm on the right tack, even if I've got the details a bit mixed. Look here, Pauline,' he added suddenly, 'I suppose Annette is trustworthy, is she?'

'How do you mean?'

'Well, can we take it as an axiom, so to speak, that she was telling the truth about what happened during the séance?'

Pauline smiled. 'Do you mean, might Annette herself be in league with our mysterious villains?'

'Something like that,' Stephen admitted.

'You'll be suspecting me next.'

'Then you don't think it's very likely?'

'I do not,' said Pauline with the utmost decision. 'In fact I don't think I've ever heard anything quite so unlikely in all my life.'

'That's a pity,' Stephen remarked, and gave himself up to further reflection.

'Well,' he went on a few moments later, 'leaving Annette out of it, just look how everything fits in if only one makes Miss Rivers an accomplice. The letter on the tree this morning, for instance. We couldn't make out who took it, could we? Well, nobody took it—because it was never put there!'

'Never put there?'

'Obviously not. Lady Susan delivered herself straight into Miss Rivers' hands, so to speak. Why, everything points to it. She's only been here three or four months: what more likely than that she came with the express intention of carrying out a coup like this? With an accomplice, either inside or outside, of course. Then it must have been she who took the jewels. After all, who could take them more easily or with less suspicion? It was even she who was supposed to have put them in the safe the night before, you remember. Ten to one those jewels never went into the safe, any more than that letter went on to the tree. Pauline, it's all too good to be untrue.'

'Then you really do think that it was she who came back that night and not Cicely?'

'I'm convinced of it.'

'But how can you account for Annette's story?' objected Pauline, determined to be logical.

'If Annette's story is true, she must have been somehow tricked into thinking that she was hiding Cicely, in order to provide a useful alibi if it were wanted later.'

'It does sound very plausible,' Pauline agreed thoughtfully. 'But I still think you're wrong in making Cicely herself one of the villains, Stephen. After all, it isn't in the least necessary to this startling new theory of yours. The thing might have been done just as well without Cicely's connivance as with it.'

'Well, there's quite an obvious way by which we can test that once and for all. We know what their game is now—they're out to obtain money by working on Lady Susan's affection for Cicely. If Cicely is shown to be hard up and in need of money, that's the final link in the chain; the evidence against her would be simply overwhelming.'

'I suppose it would,' Pauline said, slowly and reluctantly.

Stephen looked at her closely. 'Come on, Pauline!' he admonished with mock severity. 'Out with it! You know something about that particular point, don't you?'

'I hate the idea of Cicely descending to this sort of thing,' Pauline said irrelevantly. 'I thought I knew her pretty well, and it really does seem almost incredible.'

'What do you know about her hard-uppishness?' Stephen insisted.

'Well, if I must tell you,' Pauline said, even more reluctantly, 'Millicent mentioned something about it to me. In fact she was saying that she was afraid Cicely had got into a bad set. Gambling and racing and goodness knows what. Millicent's lent her a hundred and fifty pounds during the last two months.'

'Well, that appears to clinch it as far as Cicely's concerned,' Stephen said grimly.

For a few moments they walked in silence.

'Stephen,' Pauline remarked, 'if this idea of yours about Miss Rivers coming back as Cicely has anything in it, doesn't it go to prove what I told you last night—that Millicent knows much more about this business than she'll admit?'

'You mean, that she couldn't have failed to recognize Miss Rivers, however well disguised, and therefore she must have been in the secret?' Stephen said thoughtfully. 'Well, it's possible, I suppose. But on the other hand, I'm just as convinced of Millicent's innocence as you are of Cicely's. With all due respect to Miss Carey, I really can't see that she's got the brains for a successful conspirator. And this, by the way, not only looks like a successful conspiracy, but a remarkably cunning and well-worked out one as well.'

'Do you still think that Martin was murdered?' Pauline asked abruptly.

'I'm certain of it. In fact I don't see that there can be any question about it; the saw-marks prove it quite conclusively. And that can't have been done by a girl. There's at least one man in it too, of course; we've known that all along. There may be two; quite probably. The question is, who's the moving male spirit? Is it somebody in the house, or another accomplice outside it? I'm inclined to think the former, you know.'

'So am I,' Pauline agreed.

'But of course the idea of an accomplice outside fits in with Millicent's story about her midnight visitor, doesn't it?'

'Very conveniently,' Pauline remarked dryly.

Stephen smiled at her. 'But you don't believe that story?'

'I'm afraid I don't. I believe that she had a visitor, but not that he was the uncouth person she described to us. In fact, Stephen, if you want a short cut to the truth, I should advise you to tackle Millicent herself and frighten it out of her. She knows it.'

'Well, I'm not going to argue with you about that, or even repeat myself,' Stephen grinned. 'Over both Millicent and Cicely we must agree to differ. So let's get back to the question of our villain-in-chief. You know, Pauline, I do wish we could find out who that ex-convict of Martin's is. It might be Kentisbeare himself, and Martin mentioned it just to show that Henry needn't think he could play any tricks with him; but somehow I'm doubtful. It's far more likely to have been Sir Julius. And there isn't anyone else, except Freddie and Starcross. Freddie we can wash out at once, and Starcross—!' He broke off and looked at Pauline intently. 'And Starcross!' he repeated softly.

'Mr Starcross?' Pauline said in surprise. 'Surely, Stephen, you don't think he could have anything to do with it?'

'Half a minute!' Stephen said slowly. 'Pauline, I believe I'm on the verge of another brain-wave. Starcross! Wait—certain interesting facts begin to occur to me.' He whistled gently. 'Oho!' he observed significantly, and was silent again.

'What, Stephen?'

'Well, just consider these points. Who was outside in the garden the night we heard the screams? Starcross. Who did all he could to egg on the first séance by telling Freddie he was playing with fire and so making him all the more keen? Starcross. Who tried to egg on a second séance by the same tactics? Starcross. Who is a complete mystery, about whom nobody seems to know anything except that he disappears for long periods and comes back saying he's been away exploring? Starcross. Who stuck to us like a leech the morning Martin was murdered and so established an unimpeachable alibi? Starcross!' Stephen smote his fist into an open palm. 'Pauline, it seems to me that Master Starcross will bear a little examination.'

'Stephen,' Pauline demurred, 'this is a little rapid, isn't it?'

'Thoroughly,' Stephen agreed. 'But that's the way of all inspirations. And I must say I do feel that I've got a distinct hunch about friend Starcross.'

'What?'

'That he's our mysterious ex-convict!'

'But—but how can you possibly find out?'

'Ask him,' Stephen replied simply. 'Ask him, and watch his reactions. I've an idea they ought to be distinctly interesting.'

XXI A FRONTAL ATTACK

FOR all Stephen's assurance to Pauline he did not proceed to put his plan into operation immediately. It is an awkward thing to walk up to a man and say casually: 'Well, how did you like prison the last time you were there?' If one has after all made a mistake, the man may resent the question quite actively, and then explanations become a trifle difficult. Stephen therefore spent most of the evening checking over his suspicions of Starcross and searching for further ones, and to assist the concentration of his thoughts he escaped from the drawing-room and retired to the seclusion of the library.

Morally certain though he was of being on the right tack at last, he wished to make still more sure before forcing the issue; for action, when it did come, must be decisive. There must be no half-hearted measures, just enough to give the man sufficient warning to enable him to make his escape in safety: it must be all or nothing. Not that Starcross (if it was Starcross) could fail to know that Stephen was on his track, for it must have been he who flashed his electric light and kicked Stephen so neatly in the chest a couple of nights ago.

And the more Stephen thought of it, the more inclined he was to give credence to the theory that it had been his own death which was intended under that elm tree and not Martin's. If that were the case, Starcross must be getting almost desperate—always assuming that it was Starcross. Something must have gone wrong with his plans, and certainly nothing had yet resulted from them; except the anonymous letters, of course, and they looked uncommonly like an afterthought.

Was Cicely in it herself? Pauline was still convinced that she wasn't, but how could she fail to be? That suspicious behaviour before anything happened at all, her own voice on the telephone, her urgent need of money—! The case looked too black against her. Pauline was allowing her loyalty to swamp her reason.

And Miss Rivers? Stephen felt that he had proved an uncommonly satisfactory case against her too. But for Annette's statement Miss Rivers' complicity seemed, by all the rules of probability, quite definitely proved.

And was Annette so utterly trustworthy as Pauline thought? Was it quite impossible that she should be in league with Cicely? On the face of it Stephen would have set her down as the most candid and truthful person imaginable, but really, things were getting so involved and such unexpected people were being drawn into the net of suspicion that nothing seemed impossible now. The contingency might certainly be kept in mind.

Then what about this matter of the male accomplice outside the house? Whether Starcross were the villain of the piece or not, there could hardly be room for any further doubt as to the certainty of the former's existence. The manner of Martin's death proved that clearly enough. And the more Stephen considered this particular point, the more plainly did it appear to indicate Starcross's own complicity.

But it was no good laying one by the heels without the other. Perhaps after all the secondary character would be the best point of departure. Find the accomplice first, and then work back from him to the principal. Yes, he could see Bridger and ask whether any suspicious person had been seen prowling about the grounds recently. In fact he might almost—

At that moment Starcross entered the library, and Stephen's plans underwent a swift revolution. Here was an opportunity ready to his hand; not to grasp it would be simply foolish.

Starcross glanced at him. It seemed to Stephen's suspicious eyes that he wore a somewhat preoccupied air, but his smile was ready enough.

'Hullo, Munro!' he observed pleasantly. 'All alone?'

Stephen had no plan ready; he had to trust to the inspiration of the moment. All he knew was that his surprise, if it were to be effective, must be sprung abruptly.

This he proceeded to do. 'Ah, Starcross,' he said curtly. jumping to his feet, 'I was wanting a word with you. I think you ought to know that there are some very ugly rumours about. Have you ever been in prison?'

As a frontal attack this was about as blunt as could well be imagined. Nor did it fail to meet with success, but hardly in the way Stephen had expected. Starcross did not flush up, nor did he begin to bluster: the veins did not even stand out like cords upon his forehead. Instead his smile, without quite disappearing, took on a tinge of sadness and he nodded his head slowly.

'Yes,' he said quietly, 'I was afraid this would happen. Martin, of course?'

Stephen began to feel slightly uncomfortable. Things did not seem to be going quite right.

'Yes,' he said, not without awkwardness. 'But—well, I don't think anyone except myself knows. When I said "rumours" I was exaggerating.'

Starcross brightened. 'Thank heaven for that!' he said simply, and paused. 'You mean, you'd like an explanation?'

'Well—' Stephen was beginning, already more than doubtful of the conclusions which had seemed so obvious before and wondering how he was going to explain his breach of decent manners if the man really was as innocent as he made one feel. 'Well, thinking that in the circumstances you might like—'

'I understand perfectly,' Starcross interrupted with a faint smile. 'What you're feeling, though you're too decent to put it into words, is that if there's been dirty work going on here (which there certainly has), the suspicious character must be the first to be called on to explain himself. You're perfectly right, and I should be feeling exactly the same myself. I'll tell you; and of course I needn't add that I should prefer you to regard the matter as confidential and only to be brought out if you think it quite necessary.'

In some embarrassment Stephen agreed, and without further preamble Starcross embarked upon his story.

Stephen, leaning with his back on the mantelpiece, listened with growing discomfort. Before Starcross began at all he was morally certain that he had been making a mistake; as the tale proceeded his conviction was strengthened beyond all shadow of doubt. It was not so much what Starcross said, for the most convincing tale may fail to impress if the narrator has not sufficient faith in it himself; it was the way he said it. If ever there was a transparently honest man, Stephen assured himself, telling a simple, unvarnished, transparently truthful story, it was the one sitting on the arm of a chair and speaking in such a plain, unemotional manner before him.

The story was simple enough.

Starcross had been in his youth, according to his own admission, a somewhat wild young man and the close friend of a still wilder one. The friend had got entangled with a girl and was anxious to marry her; to which his family, in the pleasant way of such families, retorted that in such an event not only would his allowance be summarily ended but that it would have nothing more to do with him on any terms whatever. In the usual manner of somewhat wild young men, neither the friend nor Starcross himself took the family and its intentions in the least degree seriously and proceeded to lay their heads together and consult as to what must be done.

Unfortunately for himself, Starcross (that was not his real name in those days) had a pretty turn for imitating the handwriting of other people and had often exercised it when humorously inclined. The friend suggested that he should use his talent to counterfeit the signature of a wealthy relative of his own on the back of a bill, by flourishing which he would be able to raise the necessary wind. Regarding the whole thing as a joke, Starcross promptly agreed, never dreaming for a moment that the bill would ever be presented for actual payment. The friend, however, had other ideas—and the wealthy relative failed signally to see the joke. The friend, having earlier information, got away in safety to America; Starcross was arrested and in due course sentenced to two years' imprisonment.

On his release from prison he changed his name and, his parents being already dead, made haste to leave the country. A desire to escape as far as possible from the scenes of civilization, combined with a natural bent for out-of-the-way things, sent him exploring in a desultory fashion some of the hitherto unpenetrated hinterland of South America, and a subsequent series of papers in one of the scientific journals brought him a certain recognition if not actual kudos. He had the wit to recognize his function in life and, possessed now as he was of a comfortable private income, at once planned another expedition. This had been followed in turn by others, and now his assumed name was already something of a household word.

This was the story he told Stephen, baldly and straightforwardly, mentioning freely names, dates and places by which Stephen could, if he wished to do so, check its truth a hundred times over. Only one thing he concealed, and that was the name of the friend who had run away and left him to face alone the consequences of the 'joke'.

Martin had been a young footman at the friend's house at the time of the disaster, and Starcross had recognized him almost immediately on his arrival at Wintringham Hall. Martin had said no word, but Starcross had felt sure that he too had been recognized in his turn. The news that Martin had been intending to levy a little mild blackmail did not surprise him in the least.

'Well, all I can say is that I'm most awfully sorry to have butted in like this on your past history,' Stephen was beginning to stammer, when Starcross waved his words aside with a smile.

'Not a bit, Munro. As I said before, it was obviously the right thing for you to do. And now let me ask you a question or two. I gathered that you and Miss Mainwaring have been trying to get to the bottom of this extraordinary business: have you had any luck?'

'A certain amount,' Stephen said cautiously. 'But nothing that throws any real light on the solution. We're still just as much in the dark as ever. Have you any theories?'

'I'm quite convinced that Miss Vernon was forcibly carried off,' Starcross returned gravely. 'Don't ask me how she was, because I haven't the least idea. But I'm sure she was. What do you think?'

Stephen considered rapidly for a moment. It was on the tip of his tongue to tell the other at the very least Annette's story, if nothing more, by way of some compensation for the unfounded suspicions he had been holding; but something was whispering to him to hold back. It was not that he distrusted Starcross any longer, or anything like that; simply that the secret was, after all, not his to tell, and he was quite certain that Lady Susan would not wish him to part with a single item of the information he had to one who was, when all was said and done, more or less a complete stranger.

He hedged. 'Yes, I think you're right. But what I can't discover is not only the means by which she was carried off, but the reason for doing so. That's what continues to puzzle me.'

Starcross looked at him quizzically. 'Surely that's obvious enough? To use her, and the affection Lady Susan has for her, as a lever for the extraction from the latter of money. I shouldn't be a bit surprised if Lady Susan doesn't get a message soon saying that if such-and-such a sum isn't deposited in some out-of-the-way place by a certain time, something pretty dreadful is going to happen to Miss Vernon.'

'Really?' said Stephen, considerably startled; Starcross's surmise was a good deal nearer the truth than its author knew. 'And if that did happen,' he went on with sudden inspiration, 'what would you advise Lady Susan to do, supposing your advice was asked?'

'I should tell her to pay it immediately,' Starcross replied without hesitation.

'Good Lord! Give in to the blighters? Why?'

'Because it's quite clear, to my mind, that they're a remarkably clever and desperate lot,' Starcross explained seriously; 'and if that's the case, Lady Susan would have everything to lose and nothing to gain by standing out against them. At least, that's assuming that they're working on the lines of the American kidnappers, who are very tough nuts indeed. You'll remember from the newspapers no doubt that ransoms over there are paid without the least hesitation.'

'That's true,' Stephen muttered, balancing on his heels on the low fender.

There was a little pause.

'What I can't understand,' Starcross resumed a few moments later in a meditative tone, 'is why Lady Susan doesn't inform the police about it all and let them take a hand.' He reflected. 'Perhaps she has, though?' he added suddenly, glancing up at Stephen.

Stephen shook his head. 'No. I advised that, naturally; but she won't. Or at any rate, not yet a while. She hates the idea of the scandal, you see.'

'But it's quite impossible to keep dark the plain fact that Miss Vernon has disappeared!'

'She's trying her best to do so.' Stephen smiled.

Starcross did not seem at all satisfied. 'We haven't got to the end of the trouble yet,' he said gravely. 'I'm quite convinced of that. Still, if Lady Susan doesn't want to call in the police there's certainly no power on earth that can make her. At least, not yet. That's entirely her own affair. But in my opinion she's running a very grave risk by not doing so. Very grave indeed!'

They discussed the business for a short time longer and then, as it was well past midnight, parted to go to bed.

In the quiet of his own room Stephen reviewed the conversation as he slowly undressed and got into bed. He was inclined to think that Starcross exaggerated the danger. He had hit the mark cleverly enough with his prophecy of a demand for ransom, but it had been impossible for Stephen to hint his suspicions that Cicely herself might be on the side of the anonymous note-writers. And he was glad now that he had kept his knowledge and his ideas to himself. In a matter like this it is quite certain that too many cooks spoil the broth; and besides, it did not seem as if Starcross had anything equivalent in value to offer in exchange. Boiled down, all he had to say, apparently, amounted to the quite obvious conclusions that something was very wrong and something else ought to be done about it.

Stephen switched off the light and jumped into bed.

Dismissing Starcross altogether, with a passing regret that he should have failed so signally to step into the role which Stephen had allotted him, his thoughts reverted to the matter of the outside accomplice. Obviously that must now be the main line of attack. He must see Bridger directly after breakfast tomorrow morning and have a talk with him. In fact he had better take Bridger a little into his confidence. He might well have done so before. Bridger had his head screwed on the right way, and there was no question of whether he could hold his tongue or not. Yes, he would have a talk with Bridger the next morning.

Once again the goddess of Chance, in the curious way she often has, proceeded to anticipate his human intention. A handful of gravel, pinging on his window, brought Stephen out of bed with a jump. He leaned over the sill, to discern a shadowy black figure on the ground below. 'Hullo?' he called softly. 'What is it?'

'That you, sir?' came the voice of Bridger, cautiously pitched. 'Could you come down a minute?'

'Yes. What's the matter?'

'I found a chap dodging round the house a few minutes ago, sir, very suspicious like. I'd an idea you might like a word with him before I tell anyone else.'

'Good man!' Stephen exclaimed softly. 'Yes, I should think I would. Where is he?'

'In a tool-shed, round at the back, sir,' Bridger replied grimly. 'He won't get away in a hurry.'

'Right! I'll be down in two ticks.'

Hurriedly slipping on the barest minimum of garments required by decency and the chilly night air, Stephen sped downstairs and let himself cautiously out of the front door. Bridger was waiting for him outside, and they walked swiftly across the grass.

'How did you know I should like a word with anyone you found prowling suspiciously round the grounds, Bridger?' Stephen asked curiously.

'Well, sir, I knew you were wondering about that Miss Vernon, you and Miss Mainwaring,' Bridger replied woodenly, 'so I thought to myself that you'd be interested in anyone I found 'iding about the place at night.'

'I see. And what were you doing, out at this time?'

'Me, sir? Oh, I was 'aving a bit of a look round myself. There's funny things been going on here, sir. No 'arm in looking round for oneself a bit.'

'We ought to have taken you into partnership before this, Bridger,' Stephen said with conviction. 'And what's your theory about Miss Vernon's disappearance?'

'You mean, what do I think about it, sir? Well, what I think is, the sooner we find her the better, poor young lady.'

'Oh! Then you don't imagine she went off by herself?'

Bridger looked at his companion queerly. 'No, sir, I don't. And nor do you.'

'Well, I'm dashed!' Stephen exclaimed in astonishment. 'Do you know, Bridger, I believe you're right—I don't! And only ten minutes ago I was quite sure that I did.'

'Things often 'appen like that, sir,' Bridger observed dryly. 'This is the shed. I've got 'im well tied up inside.'

Stephen had taken the precaution of bringing with him the electric torch he had borrowed from Freddie. As Bridger opened the door, he flashed it into the interior of the little shed. Sitting on the beaten earth floor, his back against a wheelbarrow, and trussed securely hand and foot, was a dark young man, perhaps four- or five-and-twenty, scowling angrily. Stephen contemplated him with pleasure. He had anticipated a good deal of trouble in getting hold of this young man, and lo! here he was, delivered into his hands.

'So we've got you, my friend, have we?' he said gently.

The young man blinked in the beam of light. 'Who the devil are you?' he growled. 'What's the meaning of all this? Why was I—?'

'Steady, steady,' Stephen interrupted, not without admiration. 'It's no good trying to bluff. We know all about you.' He sat down on an upturned box, his light turned on his captive.

To tell the truth Stephen was not nearly so sure of his ground as he sounded—or hoped he sounded. He was, in fact, perilously near bluffing himself. This swarthy young man, who spoke with a cultured accent and was so evidently consumed with wrath (which might or might not be righteous), was a very different person from the one he had expected to find. For some reason he had got it into his head that the mysterious outside accomplice would prove to be a rough, villainous kind of man; and here was one who might almost as well have been a guest in the house as Starcross himself. Except for a certain shininess about his blue serge suit and a suggestion of frayedness at the edges of his collar he was as correctly turned out as anybody inside the house, always excepting Henry Kentisbeare. Stephen found himself wondering whether after all this really was his man or not.

He decided to surprise the truth out of him with a direct attack. Leaning forward till his lamp was only a couple of feet from the man's face, he said suddenly in a stern voice: 'What have you done with Miss Vernon?'

His shaft went home. There was no doubt about that. The young man started violently, an expression of alarm flitted momentarily across his face and all traces of anger abruptly disappeared. The next instant he recovered himself, but it was too late; he had in that short second given himself away.

'I don't understand,' he said with sulky uneasiness. 'Who's Miss Vernon?'

'You don't know?' Stephen queried blandly, his triumph mounting rapidly. 'Dear, dear! Then is it permitted to ask what you're doing here? Don't tell me you came to pick daisies by moonlight, because I warn you that I shan't believe it.'

The young man withdrew further into his armour of sulkiness. 'What the devil has it got to do with you, in any case?' he demanded. 'If you must know, I came to speak with a man on a private matter. What right have you to—?'

'Who did you come to speak with?' Stephen interjected.

But the young man was not to be drawn so easily. 'That's my business,' he said shortly. 'I insist on your releasing me from this ridiculous situation. Are you trying to kidnap me, or what?'

'Just that,' Stephen agreed silkily. 'After all, it's your turn, isn't it? But I was forgetting: you don't know Miss Vernon. Well, I'll think over what I'm going to do with you and let you know in the morning; and by that time I hope you'll be a little more—shall we say?—reasonable. I shall have a few questions to put to you, and I think you'll find it advisable to answer them.' He turned on his heel and left the shed, not a little pleased; a dull flush had covered the young man's features at this second reference to Cicely Vernon.

'Shall I keep him there for the night, then, sir?' Bridger asked, following Stephen into the open.

'Yes. I don't altogether like it, but it's the only thing to do. He knows what's happened to Miss Vernon all right, and it looks as if he's our only chance of getting at the truth. We'll leave him to meditate for the night, and perhaps he'll be feeling a little more reasonable in the morning. But see if you can make him a bit more comfortable, Bridger, without making him any less secure; you seem to have trussed him up rather tightly. By the way, is he likely to remain undiscovered there?'

'Oh, yes, sir, I think so. But I could shove a bit of a gag in his mouth to stop him shouting out if you like, sir.'

'I don't think you need bother about that. I'm quite sure the gentleman is just as anxious not to be discovered as we are. Well, I'll be out after breakfast, Bridger, and we'll decide what to do with the lad. And many thanks for collaring him; I've an idea that you've done something more important than I should have ever dared to hope. Good night.'

Stephen went back to bed and slept excellently.

In the excitement attendant on his new theories and on Bridger's capture, Stephen had temporarily forgotten that arrangements would have to be made early the following morning for dealing with the second anonymous note. As he lay in bed for that precious last half-minute before getting up it recurred to his memory.

He pondered the problem as he shared. It was too valuable a clue to be disregarded; properly handled, the situation could be turned to immense advantage. The anonymous letters and the capture of the swarthy young man were two lines of approach: if they would be made to converge on any one person, the whole puzzle was solved beyond doubt.

Stephen hurried over his dressing and went downstairs to seek Lady Susan, his plan formed.

She was waiting for him already in her morning-room, and greeted him with a slightly sarcastic smile. 'Well, has my private detective decided what I am to do?' she asked.

Stephen grinned. 'Yes, my lady. As I said last night, I don't think Miss Vernon is in any real danger, but on the other hand there's nothing like taking precautions. So I think it would be best on the whole if you were to write a distinctly frightened answer to the note, calculated to delay any remotely possible action for another twenty-four hours. By that time I hope to have the whole thing cleared up.'

'You do, do you? Very well: I'll do that. And Miss Rivers can take it as before.'

'No!' said Stephen very decidedly. 'Not Miss Rivers.'

Lady Susan's eyebrows rose. 'Indeed? Why not?'

'It isn't advisable, I think,' hedged Stephen, who had no intention of acquainting the old lady with his suspicions regarding her paragon; Lady Susan might prove more than difficult if her actions were required openly to controvert her extremely firm views. 'I've given the point a good deal of consideration, and I really think you ought to take it yourself, Lady Susan.'

He held his breath, but Lady Susan proved unexpectedly amenable. 'I agree,' she said shortly.

Stephen glanced at her sympathetically. It was obvious to him that, however heroically she might strive to conceal it, she was acutely anxious for her protégée, and firmly believed her to be in real danger. In the circumstances Stephen could not but feel flattered by the extent to which she was leaning on himself.

'Good!' he said, with an air of brisk efficiency. 'You see, the person who sent the note may well be watching to see who brings the answer, and nothing could show more convincingly that you mean to treat with the opposition than for you to appear with it yourself. Now, if you'll time yourself in the same way as yesterday, Pauline and I will be in place before you get there and we'll keep watch as before. And this time I think we can promise you some result.'

'I shall certainly expect it,' Lady Susan concurred.

They went on to settle one or two trivial details, and then Stephen made his way in to breakfast.

All the party, with the exception of Freddie and Henry, were again in place, and once more Annette was busily engaged in getting up a sweepstake on the last comer. The scene might almost have been a repetition of that of the previous morning, except that this time Pauline signalled to Stephen that she wished to speak to him instead of he to her.

He made a hasty breakfast and followed her out on to the terrace as usual.

'What are we going to do about that anonymous note, Stephen?' she asked at once. 'Time's getting short.'

'I've arranged that with Lady Susan,' Stephen told her, and explained what had been settled. He went on to give a hasty outline of the event of the night before.

'Oh, Stephen!' Pauline exclaimed excitedly. 'A bit of luck at last. Hooray! And when are you going to tackle him?'

'After we've got back from the wood, I suppose. I meant to do it first thing this morning, but I'd forgotten for the moment that we had an appointment with an anonymous note-writer. Anyhow, it won't hurt him to wait a little longer. All the better, in fact. He's going to be a tough nut to crack in any case.'

'And you haven't said anything to Mr Starcross yet?'

'Yes; as a matter of fact, I have. And he's managed to clear himself of all suspicion.' He gave Pauline a hasty outline of his interview with Star cross the night before. 'It's a pity, because that sets us back again to where we were before, you see; though I still think I'm right about Miss Rivers. Still, I feel that this morning is going to clear up most of the trouble for us. Hadn't you better run up and put your hat on? Time's getting short, as you said, and we were late yesterday. That is, of course, if you want to come along.'

'If I want to!' Pauline repeated. 'Stephen, darling, are you trying to insult me?'

When she had gone Stephen leaned his elbows on the stone balustrade and looked out over the garden, misty in the early autumn sunlight. The problem of Cicely was not the only one that was worrying him just then; indeed for the moment it had retired abruptly into the background of his mind. The puzzle of what he was to do about Pauline was, for the instant, infinitely more disturbing.

One thing was quite certain: this impossible engagement could not be allowed to continue. It wasn't fair to Pauline. Since tea-time on the previous day he had scrupulously refrained from all endearments, and Pauline must know perfectly well, although she never showed it for an instant, that he was determined sooner or later to put an end to the false position in which he felt himself to be.

Stephen heaved a heart-felt sigh. He would rather contemplate a dozen interviews with dangerous suspects than this one inevitable one with Pauline.

She rejoined him, and they made their way, by the same circuitous route as yesterday, to their lurking-places. As far as Stephen was concerned, their walk was a silent one. He hardly responded even to Pauline's gentle rallying of his melancholy. The shadow of that coming interview with her lay heavy upon him.

Arrived at the foot of the little hill, they separated as before and crept cautiously up to their respective lairs. This time they were punctual. Stephen had been in position a full five minutes before Lady Susan came into sight, walking slowly along the path. She went into the wood, reappeared a couple of minutes later and vanished in the direction of the house. Time dragged on.

By twelve o'clock only one person had passed Stephen's covering bush. This was the new parlourmaid, bound presumably for Thornton station and her missing boxes. She went by at half-past ten and again, on her return journey, an hour later.

Stephen decided that he would not make a good sleuth. By twelve o'clock he had worked himself up, what with one thing and another, into such a state of nervous recklessness that action of some sort was imperative. Shamelessly abandoning his post, he began to worm his way as carefully as possible through the undergrowth in the direction of the fatal elm-tree.

Arrived at the edge of the path just before the tree, he gazed cautiously up and down its length, then rose boldly to his feet and walked out. Scarcely willing to believe his eyes, he scrutinized the huge trunk, walked slowly round it, and stood staring all it in perplexity.

There was no sign of a note on its rough surface.

XXII THE NEXT MOVE

'HE must have been waiting in the wood all the time!' Stephen was affirming, as he and Pauline walked disappointedly back together to the house. 'There's simply no other explanation.'

'None that I can see, certainly,' Pauline agreed.

Stephen ruminated. 'Believe me, Pauline,' he delivered judgment, 'this is an uncommonly downy bird—or a covey of uncommonly downy birds for that matter. Well, there's one of our pointers gone west, I'm afraid.'

'We can try again tomorrow,' Pauline suggested.

'We can, yes. But I don't imagine that we'll have any better luck than today. It's evident that our man isn't to be caught napping so easily.'

Pauline stopped suddenly. 'But if he was in the wood all the time, he may still be there now!' she exclaimed. 'We haven't seen anyone come out of it. What about going back and drawing it, Stephen?'

'I don't think that would be much use; he'd hardly be there now. He must have suspected that the path was being watched, you see, or else he'd never have troubled to hide at all; and that being the case, he'd certainly have edged out at the side while we were watching the ends. No, I'm very much afraid that we must write this little manoeuvre off as a failure.'

'Sickening!' Pauline commented. 'Anyhow, there still remains your friend in the tool-shed.'

'That's true,' said Stephen, brightening slightly. 'And by the way, talking of that fellow, did I ever tell you that I've come round to your belief in Cicely's innocence after all? Because if not, I'll tell you now.'

'No, you didn't; but I'm very glad to hear it. I thought you would in the end, too. What changed your mind?'

'Bridger,' Stephen returned candidly. 'He was so emphatic on the point that I really had to agree with him. Bridger's no fool, you know.'

'Meaning that I am, I suppose?' asked Pauline pleasantly. 'And therefore you didn't agree when it was only poor little me who was emphatic?'

'Pauline,' Stephen said severely, 'if you talk like that I shall be compelled to kiss you.' It appeared that Stephen had overlooked for the moment certain recent vows he had taken regarding his future relations with Pauline.

'Meaning that I am a fool, I suppose, Stephen dear?' Pauline said with an air of innocence. 'And after all,' she added airily, 'we are engaged, aren't we? Though I must say that you seem to have been rather forgetting it lately.'

It occurred to Stephen that it was now or never. 'Pauline,' he said, plunging desperately at this opening, 'we really must be serious. You know perfectly well that I can't possibly—'

'I'll race you to the house, Stephen,' Pauline interrupted happily, and at once set off at top speed along the little path. Stephen's opportunity was abruptly reft from him.

Pauline, he reflected as he pounded along in the wake of her flying figure, was a girl of remarkable resource.

His attention was abruptly deflected. Freddie had come into sight on his right, strolling leisurely towards the house on a course parallel to his own. Stephen slackened speed and allowed Pauline to disappear into the house ahead of him. Freddie seemed to be coming from more or less the same direction as themselves, and it occurred to Stephen that a few questions regarding anybody who might have been seen hanging round the little wood would not be out of place. He slowed down into a walk and left the path, striking across to join the other.

Freddie greeted him with a grin. 'Hullo, Stephen. Training for a race, or something?'

'Just a little gentle exercise,' Stephen grinned back. 'Well, Freddie, what have you been doing all by yourself this morning?'

'Oh, just wandering round, you know,' Freddie replied vaguely. 'Topping day, isn't it?'

'Topping,' Stephen agreed mechanically. 'Pauline and I have just been up to that wood to have a look at the place where Martin was killed,' he went on with airy cunning.

'Oh, yes,' said Freddie politely.

'We heard somebody crashing about in the undergrowth, but couldn't make out who it was. Did you catch sight of anyone?'

'Me, old lad? No, 'fraid I didn't. But what's the particular interest, anyway?'

'Oh, nothing particular,' Stephen said with an air of indifference. 'Just a matter of a small bet. Pauline thought it was Henry, you see, and I thought it was—it was you.'

'Then you've lost your bet, old son,' Freddie returned equably. 'As a matter of fact, I haven't been near the place. That sort of thing gives me the creeps.'

'I see,' said Stephen, concealing his disappointment.

They walked on for a few paces in silence.

'Then you didn't show up at the inquest this morning?' Freddie remarked.

'Good Lord, I'd forgotten all about it. No, I didn't. Did you?'

'No, I wasn't called, thank heaven. Only Aunt Susan and Millicent and the fellow who found the body and one or two of the servants were wanted, I believe. "The proceedings were purely formal," as the newspapers say. Rotten business, wasn't it?'

'Rotten,' Stephen agreed, wondering what the verdict had been, and whether he and Pauline might not have spent their morning to much better purpose after all in attending the proceedings.

The intervention of the luncheon bell caused them to quicken their steps. Millicent was crossing the hall as they entered the house, and Freddie, who had evidently been wondering much the same thing as Stephen, stopped her and asked what the result of the inquest had been.

'Oh, accidental death,' replied Millicent, who still looked somewhat shaken, possibly by her debut in the witness-box. 'The whole thing didn't take longer than a quarter of an hour.'

'Did the jury censure Aunt Susan?' said Freddie with a malicious grin.

Millicent evidently considered the grin out of place when dealing with such a topic. 'Certainly not,' she said coldly, and pursued her interrupted way to the dining-room.

During lunch Stephen had leisure, if leisure was required, to collect his ideas and meditate his next move. Little meditation was necessary. Obviously he must concentrate now, and concentrate hard, on the swarthy young man kicking his bound heels in the tool-shed. On him every hope of solution undoubtedly hung. Stephen felt an insensate alarm that he might have succeeded somehow in making his escape. The meal seemed to drag on interminably, so anxious was he to assure himself that his fears were without foundation.

The talk was mostly of the inquest, at which, it appeared, in spite of Millicent's frigid denial, the jury actually had been impertinent enough to express their surprise that measures had not been taken before it was too late to rid the path of its overhanging danger, and their remarks had gone as near to censure as anything that is technically not censure could well do. Lady Susan appeared quite unperturbed; but what she would have to say to her head gardener on the subject later was another matter.

One item of news cropped up during lunch which Stephen was uncommonly glad to hear. The younger members of the party, it seemed, were going off in one of the cars to pay a surprise visit to a neighbouring country house, and would therefore be safely out of the way for the afternoon. Stephen and Pauline were both invited to accompany the expedition, and both hastily invented improbable excuses for declining.

When at last the meal was over, Stephen hung cautiously about until the car-party had taken their departure. Then, having arranged with Pauline that she should remain somewhere near the terrace in order to be at hand to learn the result of the interview at the first possible moment, he was free to hurry off in search of Bridger.

Bridger was run to earth in a rose-bed, apparently as impassive as ever. It made not the slightest difference to Bridger, one gathered, whether he stood in the middle of a rose-bed or on the brink of a volcano, or whether his captive remained trussed up and without food or drink for nine hours or fifteen.

Together they made their way to the shed.

Their victim greeted them with hearty abuse, rich and unstinted. Stephen noted with regret that captivity had done little to soften his spirit; if anything he seemed even less amenable than the night before. In the twilight of the shed his eyes gleamed furiously.

'Now look here,' Stephen said peremptorily, cutting short the rapid lengthening catalogue of his pseudonyms which was issuing from the swarthy young man's lips. 'Look here, you can stop all that. I warn you, I'm going to stand no nonsense. I told you that I'm going to get the truth out of you, and that's just what I'm going to do. What's more, you'll stay here till you tell it, and if your arms and legs atrophy and drop off in the process that's your look out. The truth, please! What have you done with Cicely Vernon?'

'Nothing, curse you!' spluttered his victim angrily. 'How many more times? I don't even know who she is.'

Stephen sat down once more on the upturned box and regarded the young man more with pity than anger. 'In Africa,' he observed, 'I understand they have an admirable way of making a man speak when he doesn't think he wants to; they light a little fire on his chest, and quite soon he's talking away like winking. You almost force me to wish that we were in Africa.'

'I wish I was in Africa,' remarked the young man with heat, 'as long as you were in England.'

'You'll be wishing it still more very soon, my friend,' Stephen retorted grimly. 'Now kindly stop being childish and speak the truth. I don't mind telling you that I know a great deal of it already. I know how Miss Vernon was spirited away from that séance, for instance. What I want to know is where she is now, and who is in league with you to keep her there.'

The young man's expression changed. The anger died out of his face and he looked at Stephen first blankly and then in a puzzled way. 'What in the name of all that's holy are you talking about?' he asked blankly.

'You know what I'm talking about,' Stephen replied impatiently. 'Your kidnapping of Miss Vernon, of course.'

'You're mad! I never—' The young man paused and a look almost of alarm crossed his features. 'Miss Vernon hasn't—hasn't disappeared, has she? Good heavens, what are you talking about, man? Kidnapped, did you say?'

For the first time a spasm of doubt shook Stephen's confidence. Was it possible that this young man was not, after all, the missing accomplice? If his surprise was not genuine, it was singularly excellent acting.

He hedged. 'Ah, so you do begin to remember something about Miss Vernon now after all, do you?' he said ironically.

'Oh, don't beat about the bush, man. Tell me—has anything serious happened to Miss Vernon? Here, undo these infernal ropes, for heaven's sake! Can't you see we may be wasting time?'

Stephen's doubt grew. The ring of acute anxiety in his victim's voice was unmistakable. 'Look here,' he temporized, 'tell me exactly who you are and what your connection, if any, is with Miss Vernon. Then if I'm satisfied you're genuine, I'll tell you what's happened.'

The young man looked as if he were going to reply with another outburst, but if so he changed his mind and began to speak in a sulky voice.

'Oh, all right, then. You appear to have got me in a cleft stick. But you're butting into private matters, understand, so I shall expect you to have the decency to keep them to yourself. My name's Meredith—Graham Meredith. Miss Vernon and I were engaged, or supposed to be engaged; I'm not quite sure what we are now. Her people are all against her marrying me because I work for my living (I'm an engineer) and don't possess a large private income. We decided to elope. She was going to tell everyone that she was going on a yachting trip with some friends of hers, and meet me in Brighton. She turned up all right, but after a long pow-wow (which there's no need to recount to you) decided that she couldn't go through with it and came back here. I came along yesterday to see if I couldn't get her to change her mind. She's in love with me all right: it's only the financial snobbishness of her people that's holding her back. I suppose you're something to do with them?'

'No,' said Stephen, who had been listening to this recital with a lengthening face. 'I'm not.' He jumped up and began to undo the other's bonds. 'I'm afraid,' he said ruefully, 'that I've been making a bit of a mistake. That comes of jumping to obvious conclusions. Here, Bridger,' he called to that gentleman, who was hovering helpfully just outside the shed, 'we've made a bloomer. This gentleman leaves the shed without a stain on his character.'

'Very good, sir,' replied Bridger impassively, and, shouldering a spade, walked away. It took a great deal to upset Bridger.

Meredith rose somewhat stiffly to his feet and began to massage his wrists and ankles. 'Well, thank goodness you seem to have come to your senses,' he grumbled. 'Now then, it's your turn. Who are you? Why was I collared like that? And what's all this about Miss Vernon?'

'I'm afraid I've got a bit of a shock for you,' said Stephen sympathetically, and began to tell him the whole story.

Meredith took it badly. His remarks upon Stephen's colossal ineptitude, not so much in capturing himself as in not having by this time discovered his Cicely's whereabouts, were both lurid and pithy. Stephen, realizing that he was consumed with anxiety and fear on Cicely's account, submitted meekly to the storm. Incidentally he was not feeling any too pleased with himself; this was the second bad blunder he had made in one day, if not the third.

'You must take me to Lady Susan at once,' Meredith fumed. 'We must waste no more time. The thing must be taken in hand properly, the police called in. Good heavens, to think that—! Take me to Lady Susan at once, please. I shall tell her everything. I shall—'

Stephen took him.

Lady Susan was in the drawing-room. Stephen asked her if she could spare a minute and led her into the morning-room where Meredith was waiting. He introduced them, and Meredith plunged headlong into his story and his demands. Stephen left them together and went in search of Pauline; it seemed that the least he could do was to acquaint her with this new development.

Pauline was still on the terrace. She listened with interest not unmixed with satisfaction to what he had to tell her, and at the end nodded wisely.

'I knew there must be some simple explanation for that ticket to Brighton and the yachting trip,' she said. 'I hate to have to say "I told you so", Stephen, but after all, you would not listen to me, would you? And— Hullo, here's your friend Bridger. What does he want?'

Bridger was walking rapidly towards the terrace, signing to Stephen as he came. He looked carefully up and down the length of it as if to assure himself that there was no possibility of being overheard, then spoke up towards them.

'Could you come along with me, sir?' said Bridger. 'I believe I know where the young lady may be.'

'You've found her?' Stephen exclaimed. 'Miss Vernon?'

'I couldn't be sure, sir,' Bridger replied cautiously. 'But I think I know where she might be. I shall want your help.'

'You shall have it,' Stephen cried, vaulting over the balustrade to where Bridger was standing eight feet below. 'Where's the place?'

'Wait for me!' Pauline put in, running along to descend in more orthodox manner by the steps.

'Round here, miss,' Bridger remarked, and led the way.

He took them to the back of the house, a few yards up the little path that led to the wood, and then bore round to the right, along a barely discernible track which led into the heart of a dense shrubbery, perhaps a hundred and fifty yards away from the house. In the centre of the shrubbery, hardly visible among the dense undergrowth which completely covered it, was a low, square erection, apparently of solid stone, not more than four feet high above the ground. Bridger pulled aside a thick bush and disclosed a flight of moss-grown stone steps leading down into the earth towards it.

'What on earth is this?' asked Stephen.

'It's the ice-house, sir,' Bridger explained.

'The ice-house! Good heavens, yes.' Stephen had seen specimens before of those curious half-underground structures in which the owners of country mansions used to preserve great blocks of winter ice into, sometimes, the middle of the summer, before the days of refrigerators and artificial freezing mixtures.

'I've been having a look round myself this last day or two, you see, sir,' Bridger was continuing quite chattily, 'and I wondered if there mightn't be an ice-house somewhere about. Nice 'andy things to hide anyone in, ice-houses. So when I found there was, along I come to 'ave a look at it and found the door locked. Now what do they want to lock the door of a place that 'asn't bin used for per'aps fifty years? I said to myself. Better fetch Mr Munro along an' see if we can bust the door in between us and 'ave a look inside. So along I come, sir.' And with these words Bridger signified his triumph by breaking all previous long-speech records.

Stephen had run down the shallow steps and was examining the door. 'Good for you. Bridger!' he exclaimed excitedly. 'And did you notice this? A new lock, my boy! Come along and see what we can do to it. It's a hefty piece of wood, but I think we ought to be able to make matchboard of it between us.'

Bridger joined him on the bottom step and the two men began to charge the stout oak door with their shoulders, while Pauline looked on in breathless excitement. Half a dozen heaves brought no perceptible result. Then there was a loud crack.

'She's coming!' Stephen cried exultantly. Never mind bruising your shoulder, Bridger. Let her have it!'

Bridger grinned, and the two of them redoubled their efforts. The door heaved, groaned, and finally fell in with a crash.

At once the two men were over it and inside the dank, moss-grown interior, Pauline close on their heels. At first they could see nothing in the murky gloom through which the light from the shaded doorway scarcely penetrated. A faint sound in front of them set their hearts beating rapidly, and Stephen struck a match.

By its flickering light they saw Cicely Vernon lying, bound and gagged, on a rough mattress on the floor by the opposite wall.

XXIII CICELY APPEARS

IT was some time before Cicely was sufficiently recovered to tell her story. As they were untying her bonds in the ice-house she had fainted, and Stephen carried her to the house, laying her on a sofa in the morning-room, where Lady Susan and Meredith were still talking. Meredith had gone nearly off his head with relief at seeing her safe and wrath at the treatment she had undergone, but he had been unceremoniously bundled out of the room with Stephen while Pauline and Lady Susan fussed round the now just conscious Cicely with restoratives and stimulants. For over an hour Stephen had been compelled to listen to the swarthy young man's vows of terrible vengeance upon a certain person or persons unknown.

At last Pauline appeared on the terrace to summon them in. Freddie and the others were still away, so that only Colonel Uffculme and John Starcross were in the house; and beyond expressing their satisfaction at Cicely's return, these kept tactfully in the background.

When Meredith and Stephen returned to the morning-room, Cicely was still lying on the couch, but her colour had come back and she looked as nearly fit as a person who has spent several days in a damp cellar might well be expected to appear.

Lady Susan cut short without ceremony her attempts to thank Stephen for rescuing her.

'Thank my under-gardener, my dear,' she said brusquely. 'He's the person who deserves it. Stephen and Pauline have just been thoroughly enjoying themselves, playing boy-scouts in the wood and locking your young man up in the tool-shed. Now then, let's hear all about it, if you're feeling up to it.'

From Lady Susan's words Stephen gathered that Cicely had already been told what had happened outside her prison. He settled himself into a chair to listen eagerly to her own story, and Meredith sat down too, his eyes never leaving Cicely's face.

'Oh, I'm feeling up to it all right,' Cicely began, 'but really I've absurdly little to tell you. In fact I don't see that my side of it is going to clear up the mystery in the least.'

'We'll leave that to my private detective,' observed Lady Susan, with an ironical glance at Stephen. 'That's his job, not ours. You just tell us exactly what happened after Annette left you alone in the drawing-room.'

'Yes. Well, I got out from the couch as soon as Annette switched the lights off, and then I waited in the dark for a minute or two just to make sure that the coast was clear. I meant to slip out into the garden, you see, and keep up the joke a little longer. I was looking out through the open French windows when suddenly a sort of bag was whipped over my head from behind and pulled tight round my neck, so that I couldn't cry out or anything, and the next instant my wrists were pulled behind my back and handcuffed together.'

'Handcuffed?' exclaimed Pauline.

'Yes; I knew they were handcuffs because I saw them later. Then the same person tied my ankles tightly together, and I was hustled into that cupboard by the piano and the door locked.'

'Good Lord!' It was Stephen's turn to exclaim. 'Then you were never in the secret room at all?'

'Secret room? What secret room?'

'Stephen,' Pauline cried, 'she was in the cupboard all the time, then— when we came back from the garden, you remember, and had a last look round the drawing-room. I thought I heard a funny sort of bumping going on. I said so at the time.'

'That was my little heels on the floor,' Cicely smiled.

'Yes, I was an idiot,' Stephen agreed. 'I remember noticing that the key wasn't in the cupboard door then, but it never occurred to me that there was any significance in it; I just thought Miss Carey had taken it away when she shut it before. Ass!'

'Perhaps it's a good thing you're not applying for a job at Scotland Yard after all, Stephen,' remarked Lady Susan maliciously.

'Go on, Cicely,' Meredith interposed, sweeping aside these trivialities.

'Well, I can tell you, I didn't lie there for a couple of hours without making any plan. I hadn't the least idea what was going to happen, but it seemed to me that the best thing I could do when anybody came was to sham dead. Then the man would think I'd been suffocated, you see, and take that wretched bag off to find out how I was; whereupon I should have an opportunity to scream, and scream convincingly.'

'Which you did,' observed Stephen.

'Which I did, twice. But he was too quick for me. He had some chloroform with him this time and held a handkerchief-full to my face while he got the bag back into place. Then he picked me up as if I'd been a bag of buns, slung me over his shoulder and marched off with me. For all the use my frantic struggles were I might have saved myself the trouble.'

'Um!' Lady Susan looked thoughtful. 'And you haven't the least idea who it was, my dear?'

'Not the faintest! All I can tell you is that he's diabolically strong and extraordinarily light on his feet. I never heard a single sound the first time he came up behind me. And I never saw his face at all, from beginning to end.'

'Not even later on?'

'Not even later on.'

'What did happen later on, Cicely?' asked Pauline.

'Well—nothing! I was dumped in that ice-house, or whatever it is, still wearing my nose-bag, and simply left there. I never set eyes on the man again.'

'Then there was an accomplice!' Stephen put in.

'Had you and Pauline arrived at that conclusion? How clever of you. Yes, there was an accomplice. But it wasn't a man. It was a woman.'

'A woman!' exclaimed Lady Susan, Pauline and Stephen in unison.

'Anyone you knew?' asked Pauline.

'You did see her, though?' asked Lady Susan.

'Can you describe her?' asked Stephen.

'Oh, dear!' Cicely laughed. 'One at a time, please. No, Pauline; nobody

I knew. Yes, Lady Susan; I did see her. Yes, Mr Munro; I can describe her. She was a tall woman, well-dressed, rather a lot of scent, and probably handsome; but unfortunately I never saw her face at all. She used to bring me food about twice a day and that sort of thing, but she always wore a mask.'

'Curse the woman!' said Stephen heartily.

'That's what I've been doing,' Cicely agreed.

Meredith said nothing. But he looked volumes.

'But what about that telephone message, Cicely?' Pauline wanted to know. 'And the letter in your writing? We simply could not make those out. They didn't seem to fit in anyhow.'

Cicely blushed slightly. 'Well, I may as well confess at once that over those I was an arrant coward. The fact of the matter is that the woman stood over me with a revolver and made me write the letter, and she stood by me while I was speaking into the telephone with the muzzle of the revolver screwed into my neck. I was terrified to death and simply did what she told me.'

'I don't wonder,' said Pauline sympathetically.

'Then you telephoned from the ice-house?' asked Stephen, and Cicely nodded. 'Humph! Tapped into the line, I suppose. Could that be done?' he added to Meredith. 'You're an engineer.'

'Oh, yes. Quite easily.'

'Well, it evidently was done,' remarked Cicely, 'because I did it. And that's all. This morning, for some reason, the abominable woman put the handcuffs on me again (they'd been taken off before) and tied my ankles as well; why, I can't imagine.'

'I can,' said Stephen grimly. 'That was in case they'd got the money, no doubt,' he added to Lady Susan. 'They'd have just cut off and left her.'

'Oh, Stephen, how horrible!' Pauline shuddered. 'Supposing they had—and we hadn't found her!'

Cicely shivered, and Meredith ground his teeth.

'Well,' Lady Susan interposed briskly, 'can my detective make anything of all this?'

'It seems to complicate matters rather more than simplify them, doesn't it?' Stephen confessed.

Lady Susan snorted sarcastically.

'This woman,' Stephen meditated. 'You never saw her face, Miss Vernon, you say. That seems rather significant. And she was tall, too. Was she strong?'

'She was,' said Cicely, with a ruefully reminiscent little smile.

'She was. And had she a deep voice?'

'Yes, I think she had. Yes, decidedly.'

'Ah!' Stephen looked wise.

'You're not pretending you know who she is, are you?' queried Lady Susan.

'Oh, no. I was just wondering what she was, let's say.'

'I suppose you mean whether she was a man in disguise?'

'It had crossed my mind,' Stephen admitted.

'And everybody else's too, no doubt,' observed Lady Susan crushingly.

'Do you still think that one of them was somebody in the house, Stephen?' Pauline came to his rescue.

'I don't know!' Stephen groaned. 'This has upset my calculations altogether. And I thought I was getting on so nicely this morning. No, on the whole it's beginning to look more now as if they were both outside the house, isn't it? I wonder—I wonder whether they could have been one and the same person! Do you think that's possible, Miss Vernon?'

'I suppose it is.' Cicely said, somewhat doubtfully. 'It never occurred to me before, but—yes, I suppose it's possible. Of course I never saw anything of the man at all (it was quite dark when he took the bag off me in the drawing-room) and I haven't the least idea even of his general shape or build.'

Stephen relapsed into silence. He was wondering whether the time had not come to tell Lady Susan what he knew of the circumstances of Martin's death. On the whole he thought he ought, though it was impossible to do so in front of the others.

'Lady Susan,' he said, 'could you come into the library with Pauline and me for a moment? There's something I want to speak to you about, and I'm sure we ought not to worry Miss Vernon any more just now.'

'Oh, I'm all right,' Cicely protested. But she did not look at all averse to being left alone with Meredith.

Lady Susan rose and preceded them out of the room.

Stephen had chosen an unfortunate moment. While the door was still open, Annette passed in front of it and looked inside.

'Cicely!' she exclaimed.

Stephen caught her arm. 'Hush! She's back, and safe, but we don't want anyone to know for the moment. Not a soul, Annette. Understand?'

Annette grinned at him impishly. 'All right; I won't tell. But it's a pity in one way, isn't it, Stephen? You won't be able to send me off on any more convenient wild-goose chases about tickets to London and mythical people inquiring after mythical luggage. Can I go in and ask her all about it?'

'I don't think you'll be welcome,' Stephen grinned back, following Lady Susan across the hull. 'She's got her young man in there with her. The others are back too, I suppose? Not a word, mind, there's a good little girl.' He hurried on to the library.

Lady Susan took the story Stephen had to tell her with remarkable calmness. 'I'm not the least surprised,' she said. 'I always thought Martin would come to a bad end. He was a good butler, but a rotten human being. I suppose I ought to tell the police?'

'Is it essential?' asked Stephen, who had not thought it necessary to say anything about his other theory regarding Martin's death—that Martin was an accidental victim and not the one intended. 'I think we might defer that for a little, in any case, just to see if we can't uncover a little more daylight of our own first.'

To this Lady Susan agreed, and she and Pauline went on to discuss the whole affair and particularly Cicely's story. Stephen allowed himself to drop out of the conversation and relapsed promptly into a brown study. He had an idea—a fascinating, enlightening idea, and he wanted to test it by the facts of the case.

For perhaps half an hour he sat silent, consuming cigarette after cigarette and oblivious of the amused glances which Pauline and Lady Susan flung at him from time to time. Then he jumped suddenly to his feet.

'I think I really have solved it this time,' he said abruptly. 'You haven't got a revolver, have you? Oh, well, it doesn't matter. Wait here for me; I'll be back soon.' And he was gone from the room.

XXIV THE TRUTH AT LAST

IT was at least an hour before Stephen made his re-appearance. Tea-time came and Pauline and Lady Susan adjourned to the drawing-room, the former scarcely able to conceal her anxiety, even the latter hardly less perturbed. Starcross too, as Pauline noticed, did not put in an appearance. On Lady Susan's whispered instructions Pauline carried a tray for two into the morning-room, where she found Annette, indifferent to the rules governing what is company and what is not, eagerly drinking in Cicely's experiences. On Stephen's earnest request, nothing regarding her return had been mentioned to the others who had been on the expedition. Even Millicent herself remained in ignorance.

After tea Pauline and Lady Susan returned to the library, politely ejecting Colonel Uffculme who had gone there in search of The Morning Post and a nap. Lady Susan settled down patiently enough, but Pauline, whom an uneasy restlessness had invaded, could do nothing but wander aimlessly about. At last, well after five o'clock, Stephen entered the room.

'Oh, thank goodness!' Pauline exclaimed, running over to him. 'I was beginning to feel sure something dreadful had happened to you, Stephen.'

'Because I mentioned the word "revolver"?' Stephen smiled, drawing her arm for an instant through his. 'I know; it was silly of me. I only wanted one for purposes rather of terrorizing than defence.'

'Stephen!' Lady Susan interjected. 'Stop squeezing Pauline's arm and pay some attention to me. Have you got to the bottom of this wretched business, or have you not?'

'Yes, Lady Susan,' Stephen beamed, not ceasing for a moment to squeeze Pauline's arm. 'I have.'

'Then for goodness sake tell me what you've been doing, and all about it!'

'Who is the villain of the piece, then, Stephen?' Pauline demanded almost simultaneously.

'I'll begin at the beginning of the end,' Stephen replied. 'Sit down, Pauline, and I'll stand up to show my male superiority. Well, something that Annette said just now gave me the first real pointer, and I'm afraid I must confess that, once I'd guessed the significance of it, the rest simply fell together. I worked it all out in that ten minutes after I'd told Lady Susan about Martin's death.'

'Ten minutes!' repeated the old lady indignantly. 'Half an hour, you mean! Don't try to make yourself out cleverer than you are.'

'That would be difficult, Lady Susan,' returned Stephen modestly. 'Was it really half an hour, though? It didn't seem as much as ten minutes.'

'What did Annette say, Stephen?' Pauline asked patiently. 'What did

Annette say? What did—'

'She said something about mythical people inquiring about mythical luggage,' Stephen replied hastily. 'That was the clue, you see. I worked the whole thing out from that, and so could you if you wanted to.'

Pauline frowned. 'Oh! Yes, I see. Nobody inquiring for luggage, but somebody going off to inquire about luggage. Somebody going through a wood on two mornings running and not to inquire about luggage. Somebody passing without suspicion a certain tree in that wood, where—'

'That's it!' Stephen exclaimed delightedly. 'You've got it, Pauline.'

'One minute,' Lady Susan said in frankly puzzled tones. 'Do I understand that you're accusing my new parlourmaid—Collins, or whatever her name is—of being at the bottom of the whole business, Stephen? Is that what you're driving at?'

'Something like that, Lady Susan, though not quite so important. By the way, here's something of yours.' He put his hand into his pocket and dropped a stream of necklaces, rings, pendants and bracelets into Lady Susan's lap. 'You ought to check these over some time,' he added paternally, and winked at Pauline.

For once in her life Lady Susan was unable to hide her astonishment. 'Stephen!' she gasped. And then: 'Come over here this minute. I'm going to do something I should never have dreamed possible two hours ago. I'm going to kiss you!'

'What, in front of Pauline, Lady Susan?' grinned Stephen, and bent to kiss the withered old cheek held up towards him. 'She's got an awfully jealous nature, I ought to warn you.' Stephen can hardly be blamed for feeling rather pleased with himself. It was a satisfaction to have arrived, alone and unaided, at the solution of the mystery at last; it was a still greater satisfaction to be able to repay the kindness of the old lady, for whom he had conceived a genuine and strong affection, with so tangible a return as the restoration of her jewellery.

'And what's more I take back all the nasty things I've been saying to you, Stephen,' Lady Susan went on. 'You're the best private detective I know, and you'd be wasted at Scotland Yard. Now that, let's hear all about it.'

Stephen collected his thoughts. 'Well, having established the identity of Miss Vernon's mysterious feminine gaoler, and with her one of those responsible for, if not the prime instigator of, the anonymous notes, I looked round to see what pointers that gave me. I was taking it for granted then, as we've been doing all the time, that the object of the whole business was to play on your affection for Miss Vernon to the extent of forcing you to pay the ransom of five hundred pounds for her to be set at liberty.'

'And wasn't it?' Pauline cried.

Stephen smiled. 'Wait! Well, as to pointers there were, of course, two very definite ones. I was trying to get at the identity of the man who actually made the attack on Miss Vernon and never appeared again, you see. And what man's name crops up at once in connection with the introduction of the new parlourmaid into the house?' We had that ages ago, from Miss Carey herself, though I never took any notice of it at the time.'

'Martin, of course,' Lady Susan remarked uncomfortably.

'Martin, yes. And from now onwards Martin bulks very large indeed.'

'Then is Martin the villain of the piece?' Pauline asked.

'You've hit the coconut again. He is. And a thoroughly outsize, all-wool, thorough-paced villain too.'

Pauline looked puzzled. 'But—but I thought Martin had been murdered?'

'So did I. And I was wrong. Martin wasn't murdered at all—unless a man can be said to murder himself by mistake. But I'm getting on too fast.'

'Wait a minute, Stephen,' Lady Susan put in. 'Who took my jewels?'

'Martin. I'm coming to that. Well, having arrived at the person of Martin, I thought hack a little further. Martin of course knew all about your fondness for Cicely; that fitted in. But then several curious things began to crop up which didn't fit in at all. How did Martin arrive in the drawing-room to attack Cicely? He might have come in from the hall, but that didn't seem likely. Much more probable that he came down from the secret room. Did he know of the secret room? Obviously, because he was going up there when I chased him the first night Pauline and I kept watch.

'Then there was that voice at the séance which said "Yes!" That must have been Martin's. And the raps, and the picture falling down: obviously they must have been caused by somebody in the secret room. Very well, then. Martin was in the secret room during the whole of the séance, working as hard as he knew how. Why?'

'Ask me another,' said Pauline helplessly.

'I will,' Stephen replied equably. 'Why did Miss Carey say that it was a stranger who came through her room that night, when we know now that it must have been Martin?'

'Ah!' said Lady Susan. 'Now we come to Millicent, do we? I suspected more than once that she had a hand in it.'

'She did: but let me say at once that it was a perfectly innocent hand. She knew all the time who the chief villain was, but she didn't know he was a villain; she hadn't the slightest idea what he was up to. This is really the clue to the whole secret, and I can't think now how I can have been so dense never to have spotted it before—this connection between Miss Carey and Martin. It had been staring me in the face. I knew there was, at the very least, an understanding of some sort between them; I saw it that first afternoon when Martin took me into the drawing-room to be shown to you. I knew that she was, for some reason, afraid of him, because I'd seen her shrivel up with sheer fright when he made his presence known unexpectedly—in the hall, when we got back from our first walk,' he added to Pauline.

Pauline nodded. 'Yes, I remember.'

'And lastly I knew that there must have been a very much closer bond between them than usually between mistress and servant, because she fainted out of hand when she heard of his death. I knew all these things, but I'd never realized them, so to speak. Now I realized them as well, and the conclusion was obvious.'

'Not to me,' Lady Susan confessed. 'No doubt I'm extraordinarily dense, but what is this obvious conclusion?'

'That they were married,' said Stephen simply.

'Married!' exclaimed Pauline, while Lady Susan gasped.

'Yes: how otherwise should Martin know about the secret room, with its convenient second exit in Miss Carey's bedroom? Of course—he used it to visit her. Don't be too stern with her, Lady Susan. I think it was a case of the snake and the rabbit, as it were. Martin exercised a horrible fascination over your niece; you might say loosely that he probably hypnotized her into marriage. I don't know whether she's ever had any affairs before, but—'

'Never!' Lady Susan ejaculated.

'Exactly. Well, you can guess what it means to a woman who's never been loved to meet with it (or what she mistakes for it) at last. It wouldn't matter to her whether it was a duke or a dustman; the point is that it's a male who finds her attractive. And as for Martin, doubtless he found her, in his turn, extremely attractive. She was not only your niece, you see; she was your heiress as well. Now do you see what was the mainspring of the whole thing?'

'I'm completely bewildered, I'm afraid, Stephen.'

'Even when I remind you that Martin's whole efforts at first were concentrated on getting another séance? That was the object both of the letter from Miss Vernon and the telephone message, you remember; the matter of ransom only cropped up afterwards.'

'Oh!' said Pauline suddenly. 'Yes, I think I see. How horrible! You mean—well, Lady Susan's heart?'

'Yes,' Stephen agreed in grave tones. 'I'm afraid it was all a good deal more serious than we ever imagined, Lady Susan. Martin had murder in mind, no less. You see, after had comfortably secured your heiress, you—didn't die! I don't know how long Martin waited patiently, but he lost his patience in the end. Then he heard the forthcoming séance being discussed at dinner and saw his opportunity.

'He knew all about your weak heart: it might seem an easy matter to frighten you to death. Any sudden shock or fright, you see. Well, it didn't come off. Possibly Annette saved you by putting you on your guard. The kidnapping of Miss Vernon was a pure after-thought. Martin, watching everything from the secret room, saw another opportunity, and took that, too.

'I think his only idea at the time was to use her as another means of frightening you—by the telephone, for instance; and, of course, of inducing you to hold another séance, when he no doubt intended to try again and more drastically than ever.'

'I never did like Martin,' observed Lady Susan, apparently quite unmoved.

'Well, he didn't succeed. And before he could try another plan, he had met the death he had been planning—for me.'

'For you?' repeated both his listeners.

'Yes. I mentioned the possibility to Pauline at the time that the trap might have been laid for me and not Martin, and I was right. Martin saw me that night I chased him up into the secret room, and evidently I gave him a bad fright. He knew then that I was hard on his heels. And when a man is trying to carry out one murder already, the thought of a second isn't going to worry him overmuch. It was a cunning little plan, too. The parlourmaid would have reported to him that I was going to pass along that path at a certain time, you see; he knew he'd got just about two hours to lay his trap. Unfortunately he miscalculated, and sawed just half an inch too much. As he was arranging his prop in position the bough began to give. He tried to jump clear, but didn't jump far enough. That's how I see it—and a more deliberate case of poetic justice you'd have to go far to find.'

'Good gracious!' said Lady Susan.

'And that's very nearly all. Martin out of the way, his accomplice (she's his sister, by the way) didn't see why she should have all her trouble for nothing, so turns the scheme round a bit and makes it a case of ransom. Hence the anonymous letters. I've been having a long heart-to-heart talk with the lady and verified most of the facts from her. She's upstairs now in her room, with Starcross on guard, waiting your pleasure; you'll have to decide what to do with her. I've said she'll be handed over to the police, of course, but I'm not altogether sure that that is advisable; it would mean a lot of nasty scandal inevitably coming out. You may think it better to let me frighten her into silence and compound half a dozen felonies by letting her go. And that really is all, I think.

'Oh, about the jewels. Martin didn't actually take them himself. He made Miss Carey do that; terrorized her into it, no doubt. As you refused to die, you see, he thought he might as well have a little on account, so to speak. The sister had them with her each time she went to collect the answer to her note, ready to fly off with them at once if the five hundred pounds was forthcoming. She told me she would have gone tomorrow morning in any case, sending a wire about Cicely from Dover—which I take leave to doubt.'

'Stephen, you're a marvel,' said Lady Susan.

'Isn't he?' Pauline exclaimed with proprietary pride.

They went on to tell Stephen how clever he was and discuss what was to be done with the ex-parlourmaid. In the end it was decided to let Stephen frighten her within an inch of her life and then let her go, and to leave everything else (including Millicent's marriage) exactly as if it had never been discovered at all. Each of them was agreed that only in this way could unnecessary heartburnings be saved, unnecessary dirty linen be spared from public washing and unnecessary fuss be avoided; besides, there was really no object in doing anything else. Beyond the three of them, the mysterious doings at Wintringham Hall were to remain a mystery for ever.

'And now,' said Lady Susan an hour or so later, when they had discussed and discussed the thing until there was really no more to discuss. 'Now, Stephen, I want to ask you a personal question. When are you two foolish young people thinking of getting married? I do feel I owe you a wedding-present.'

Stephen returned to earth with a heavy bump. 'Well, as a matter of fact, Lady Susan—' he was beginning unhappily, when Pauline chipped in.

'As soon as Stephen's got a job, Lady Susan,' she said.

'I see. Well, in that case, I wonder, Pauline, if he'd listen to me when I tell him that I was rather looking out for an energetic young man to take on the job of agent, bailiff and general overseer of this unwieldy estate of mine. Do you think he would? My present man is getting old, and quite ready to retire on a pension. Of course the salary is almost an insult to such a brilliant person as your young man, a beggarly six hundred a year; but if you think you could persuade him to do me the inestimable favour of—'

But Pauline had risen and flung herself upon her hostess. 'Lady Susan,' she cried rapturously, 'you're a dear and an angel and a darling!'

'I'm nothing of the sort, my dear. I'm a cross old woman, with a weakness for private detectives. Now let me go, because I've got to go into my morning-room and cultivate a weakness for engineers too, apparently— and that means talking round Cicely's ridiculous mother, I'm afraid: and I know what that means.'

The door closed behind her.

'And now, Miss Mainwaring,' said Stephen happily, 'I'm going to propose to you. I was done out of it before but I'm not going to be this time. Do you think you could marry an estate-agent?'

'It's always been the ambition of my life, Mr Munro,' Pauline affirmed fervently, as she moved into his arms.

THE END

www.ingramcontent.com/pod-product-compliance
Lightning Source LLC
Chambersburg PA
CBHW071250130626
46556CB00003B/1243